DARK LIGHT

Titles by Jayne Ann Krentz writing as Jayne Castle

DARK LIGHT
SILVER MASTER
GHOST HUNTER
AFTER GLOW
HARMONY
AFTER DARK
AMARYLLIS
ZINNIA
ORCHID

Titles by Jayne Ann Krentz writing as Amanda Quick

THE THIRD CIRCLE
THE RIVER KNOWS
SECOND SIGHT
LIE BY MOONLIGHT
THE PAID COMPANION
WAIT UNTIL MIDNIGHT
LATE FOR THE WEDDING
DON'T LOOK BACK
SLIGHTLY SHADY
WICKED WIDOW
I THEE WED
WITH THIS RING
AFFAIR
MISCHIEF
MYSTIQUE
MISTRESS
DECEPTION
DESIRE
DANGEROUS
RECKLESS
RAVISHED
RENDEZVOUS
SCANDAL
SURRENDER
SEDUCTION

Other titles by Jayne Ann Krentz

SIZZLE AND BURN
WHITE LIES
ALL NIGHT LONG
FALLING AWAKE
TRUTH OR DARE
LIGHT IN SHADOW
SUMMER IN ECLIPSE BAY
TOGETHER IN ECLIPSE BAY
SMOKE IN MIRRORS
LOST & FOUND
DAWN IN ECLIPSE BAY
SOFT FOCUS
ECLIPSE BAY
EYE OF THE BEHOLDER
FLASH
SHARP EDGES
DEEP WATERS
ABSOLUTELY, POSITIVELY
TRUST ME
GRAND PASSION
HIDDEN TALENTS
WILDEST HEARTS
FAMILY MAN
PERFECT PARTNERS
SWEET FORTUNE
SILVER LININGS
THE GOLDEN CHANCE

Anthologies

CHARMED
(with Julie Beard, Lori Foster, and Eileen Wilks)

Titles written by Jayne Ann Krentz and Jayne Castle

NO GOING BACK

DARK LIGHT

JAYNE CASTLE

THE BERKLEY PUBLISHING GROUP
Published by the Penguin Group
Penguin Group (USA) Inc.
375 Hudson Street, New York, New York 10014, USA
Penguin Group (Canada), 90 Eglinton Avenue East, Suite 700, Toronto, Ontario M4P 2Y3, Canada
(a division of Pearson Penguin Canada Inc.)
Penguin Books Ltd., 80 Strand, London WC2R 0RL, England
Penguin Group Ireland, 25 St. Stephen's Green, Dublin 2, Ireland (a division of Penguin Books Ltd.)
Penguin Group (Australia), 250 Camberwell Road, Camberwell, Victoria 3124, Australia
(a division of Pearson Australia Group Pty. Ltd.)
Penguin Books India Pvt. Ltd., 11 Community Centre, Panchsheel Park, New Delhi—110 017, India
Penguin Group (NZ), 67 Apollo Drive, Rosedale, North Shore 0632, New Zealand
(a division of Pearson New Zealand Ltd.)
Penguin Books (South Africa) (Pty.) Ltd., 24 Sturdee Avenue, Rosebank, Johannesburg 2196,
South Africa

Penguin Books Ltd., Registered Offices: 80 Strand, London WC2R 0RL, England

DARK LIGHT

A Jove Book / published by arrangement with the author

PRINTING HISTORY
Jove mass-market edition / September 2008

Cover hand lettering by Ron Zinn.
Cover design by George Long.

For information, address: The Berkley Publishing Group,
a division of Penguin Group (USA) Inc.,
375 Hudson Street, New York, New York 10014.

ISBN-13: 978-0-7394-9865-1

JOVE®
Jove Books are published by The Berkley Publishing Group,
a division of Penguin Group (USA) Inc.,
375 Hudson Street, New York, New York 10014.
JOVE® is a registered trademark of Penguin Group (USA) Inc.
The "J" design is a trademark belonging to Penguin Group (USA) Inc.

PRINTED IN THE UNITED STATES OF AMERICA

This one is for Elvis.
Good to know he made it through the Curtain.

A Note from Jayne

Welcome back to my other world, Harmony.

Two hundred years ago a vast energy Curtain opened in the vicinity of Earth, making interstellar travel practical for the first time. In typical human fashion, thousands of eager colonists packed up their stuff and lost no time heading out to create new homes and new societies on the unexplored worlds. Harmony was one of those worlds.

The colonists brought with them all the comforts of home—sophisticated technology, centuries of art and literature, and the latest fashions. Trade through the Curtain flourished and made it possible to stay in touch with families back on Earth. It also allowed the colonists to keep their computers and high-tech gadgets working. Things went swell for a while.

And then one day, without warning, the Curtain closed, disappearing as mysteriously as it had opened. Cut off from Earth, no longer able to obtain the equipment and supplies needed to keep their high-tech lifestyle going, the colonists were abruptly thrown back to a far more primitive existence. Forget the latest Earth fashions; just staying alive suddenly became a major problem.

But on Harmony folks did one of the things humans do best: they survived. It wasn't easy, but two hundred years after the closing of the Curtain, the descendants of the First Generation colonists have managed to fight their way back from the brink to a level of civilization roughly equivalent to the early twenty-first century on Earth.

Here on Harmony, however, things are a little different, especially after dark. You've got those dangerously sexy ghost hunters, the creepy ruins of a long-vanished alien civilization, and a most unusual kind of pet. In addition, an increasingly wide variety of psychic powers are showing up in the population.

Nevertheless, when it comes to love, some things never change. . . .

If, like me, you sometimes relish your romantic suspense with a paranormal twist, Harmony is the place for you.

Love,
Jayne

Chapter 1

ELVIS HAD NEVER LOOKED BETTER. HE WORE HIS NEW cape, the white one with the high, flared collar and the glittering rhinestone trim. The sunglasses gave him a dashing air of mystery.

With a star's unerring instinct for the spotlight, he had managed to find the most dramatically lit position in the room, the center of the Guild boss's vast desk. The light from the nearby lamp struck small sparks off the rhinestones.

"Don't think I've ever seen a dust bunny wearing a cape and sunglasses," Fontana said.

His full name was John Fontana, but as far as Sierra McIntyre had been able to determine, no one called the new chief of the Crystal City Ghost Hunter's Guild anything except Fontana.

She looked up from her notes, distracted, and smiled

in spite of her tension. If you didn't notice the six tiny paws that were just barely visible in the fluffy gray fur and the innocent bright-blue daylight eyes, it would have been easy to mistake Elvis for a large ball of dryer lint; in this case, a ball of lint in a cape and sunglasses.

"Elvis has a sense of style," she said proudly. "He knows what looks good on him."

Fontana leaned back in his chair and steepled his fingers. "I can see that. How did you end up with a dust bunny for a pet?"

The black and amber ring on his powerful hand glinted ominously. The amber gem was engraved with the seal of his office. He had ascended to the highest post in the Crystal Guild only a few days earlier, but he appeared to be very much at home here in the executive suite. Then again, he had no doubt been preparing for the position for years. Becoming a Guild boss required the ability to commit to a long-term strategy. Skill at outmaneuvering your opponents and a ruthless streak were minimum job requirements.

Unlike Elvis's baby blues, Fontana's eyes were anything but innocent. They were the color of the gem in his ring, dark amber. Sierra was as familiar with Guild politics as it was possible for any outsider to be. She was well aware that no man—and to date all of the Guilds were headed by men—got as far as Fontana had with his innocence intact.

Under the force of his disturbingly thoughtful expression, she found herself shifting in her chair. She uncrossed her legs and then crossed them again. The odd, fizzy excitement that she had been experiencing since she walked into the room had not diminished one bit. The hair on the back of her neck was still stirring. Energy hummed through her, both the physical and the paranormal kind. All of her senses were fully rezzed. What was wrong with this picture?

You expected a Guild boss to be intimidating, but somehow you didn't expect one to look thoughtful, at least not the way Fontana did thoughtful. The heads of the organizations were traditionally men of power, both physical and psychical, men who had clawed their way to the top using whatever means were required to achieve their objectives. You expected streetwise cunning in a Guild boss, but not the sort of cool-headed intelligence and the aura of centeredness and control that Fontana exhibited. For some reason the knowledge that he was the kind of man who considered carefully before he acted only made him seem more dangerous.

More dangerous and, for some inexplicable reason, more interesting. She was here to do the most important interview of her very short career as a journalist, and she could not concentrate. She just wanted to sit there and stare at Fontana—maybe forever.

Maybe she was coming down with the flu or something. Now that she thought about it, she definitely felt a little feverish.

The day had not started out well in spite of the promise of the exclusive with Fontana. For starters, she'd endured a sleepless night, unable to escape the creepy feeling that someone, somewhere, was *watching*. She knew it was a totally irrational sensation, but that didn't make any difference. Her intuition did not respond to logical argument.

Elvis had seemed restless as well, although that was probably because he had picked up on her unease. He was very sensitive to her moods. Countless times she had risen from the rumpled bed and gone to the window. Elvis had followed every time, hopping up onto the sill.

Together they had surveyed the narrow street two floors below, but there had been very little to see. That was hardly surprising, of course. It was early fall, and the fog was thick in the Quarter. The locals referred to the season as the Big Gray for a very good reason. The seemingly endless mist that blanketed the city at this time of year was legendary. On the rare occasions when the fog lightened temporarily, rain moved in to take its place.

The lack of sleep had definitely affected her edge this morning, but the real disaster had occurred en route from her office to Guild headquarters. She had taken a taxi because parking spaces were notoriously hard to find in the Quarter in the vicinity of the Guild offices. The driver had let her out on the side of the street opposite the entrance of the Colonial-era building.

She never saw the big Oscillator 600 bearing down on her in the heavy fog. It was only her intuition and Elvis's anxious chortling that had caused her to leap back onto the curb in the nick of time. The close call had left her already sleep-deprived senses badly jangled.

The last straw had been walking into Fontana's office a short time later and discovering that the subject of her interview had the power to raise the hair on the nape of her neck.

"Elvis isn't a pet," she said, pulling herself together with an effort. "He's a companion. Now, if you don't mind, I have another question regarding your plans for the Crystal City Guild."

Fontana looked amused. "You seem to be obsessed with the future of this organization."

"The Guilds wield enormous power in all of the city-states. That was especially true here in Crystal under your predecessor's administration. Naturally my readers are anxious to know what to expect now that there is a new chief."

Fontana shrugged. "The Guilds are respected, well-established institutions. They have always played active roles in the political and social affairs of their communities. I see no reason for that to change."

In Sierra's opinion, the Guilds were all about power, and there was certainly a lot of it here in Fontana's office—not just the political and social kind but also the sort produced by raw psi energy. Some of that was coming from Fontana himself. But the room also shimmered faintly with energy. In fact, there was so much psi swirling in the atmosphere she knew there had to be a secret entrance to the ancient underground tunnels somewhere nearby. Here in the Old Quarter there were reputed to be hundreds of old holes-in-the-wall, as they were called.

She straightened a little in her chair. She had come here for answers, and she intended to get them.

"I'll allow that the Guilds are well-established institutions," she said briskly, "but don't you think it's going a bit too far to say that they are respected? I'm sure you're well aware that all of the organizations have serious problems when it comes to public relations."

Elvis chose that moment to leave the spotlight. He drifted across the desk, cape fluttering behind him, and came to a halt in front of Fontana's coffee cup.

"Any large corporation has a few public relations issues," Fontana said. He watched Elvis with a mildly wary expression. "Is the bunny housebroken?"

"Dust bunnies are naturally very clean, and the Guilds are not normal business entities," Sierra shot back. "The best that can be said about them is that they are uneasy crosses between emergency militias and closely held, highly secretive private corporations."

Fontana's dark brows rose slightly. "Would that be the dust bunnies or the Guilds?"

She flushed. *He's trying to push your buttons. Don't let him do it.* "I'm talking about the Guilds, of course."

"Corporations run like military organizations," Fontana repeated in that maddeningly thoughtful way. He inclined his head. "That's a fairly accurate description. You have to admit that the Guilds are unique."

"Many people feel that it would be more accurate to say that they are little better than legalized mobs of gangsters. Guild chiefs have traditionally considered themselves to be above the law."

"No one is above the law, Miss McIntyre," Fontana said gently.

"The former chief, Brock Jenner, took a different view. Some would say a more traditional view. He ran the Crystal City Guild as if it were his own private fiefdom. There were persistent rumors to the effect that under his watch the organization dabbled heavily in a variety of illicit activities."

"You ought to know, Miss McIntyre. Your stories in the *Curtain* were responsible for a lot of those rumors."

"Naturally my readers want to know if they can expect more of the same now that you're in charge."

"I think that is what is known as a loaded question."

"Are you going to answer it?"

"Are you certain that your readers care about my plans for the Guild? I was under the impression that the readers of the *Curtain* were more interested in insightful investigative reporting about people who have the misfortune to get kidnapped by aliens and dragged down into the catacombs for strange sexual experiments."

Sierra bit back her frustration. She had done some good work at the *Curtain*. The problem was that when you ran a piece with a headline like "Guild Conceals Discovery of Secret Alien Lab" next to a story entitled "Woman Pregnant with Alien Baby," credibility became an issue. Few people seemed to notice or care that the gutsy tabloid was the only paper in town that had dared to print negative stories about the local Guild organization.

"If you have such a low opinion of me, my paper, and its readers, why did you agree to do this interview?" she asked.

Elvis chose that moment to go up on his hind legs. He hooked his front paws over the rim of the coffee mug and dipped his head inside.

"Oh, dear." Mortified, Sierra leaped to her feet, pen and notepad clutched in one hand. She leaned over the wide desk, scooped up Elvis, and sat down quickly. "Sorry about that. He's a little caffeine junkie."

"Not a problem." Fontana got to his feet with a lithe uncoiling motion and crossed the room to a handsome serving cart. He picked up the coffeepot and filled a mug. "Does he take cream and sugar?"

"Uh, no." Sierra clutched the wriggling Elvis. "He likes his coffee straight. But this really isn't necessary."

Fontana carried the mug back across the room and set it down on the corner of the desk.

"Help yourself, big guy," he said.

Elvis did not need a second invitation. He bounced from Sierra's knee up onto the desk and ducked his head into the mug. Tiny slurping sounds followed.

Sierra watched him uneasily. Elvis usually had excellent instincts when it came to people. If he didn't like someone, he made his feelings clear. But he had taken to

Fontana right from the start. She wasn't sure what to make of that. Or course, it was possible that dust-bunny intuition, like her own, wasn't infallible.

Fontana looked at Sierra. "Another cup for you, Miss McIntyre?"

"No, I'm fine, thank you." She glanced at her notes, determined to take charge. "Are you aware of the growing problem of the illegal drug called ghost juice?"

"I've read your stories about it, yes."

"Then you know that, for some reason, the majority of the addicts are former Guild men who are now living on the streets of the Quarter?"

Fontana lounged against the edge of the desk and crossed his arms. "I believe I read that in your last piece on the subject, yes."

"It's the truth. The experts think that for some reason, ghost hunters might be more susceptible to the drug because of their particular parapsych profiles. There's an old saying that the Guild takes care of its own. Don't you think that the Crystal organization should be actively working to get the drug off the streets?"

"You know, my public relations people advised me not to grant this interview."

"I'll bet they did. I'm sure they would prefer that you not talk to the press at all."

"It isn't the press, in general, they're worried about." Fontana smiled. "It's you, Miss McIntyre. You have something of a reputation."

"Your public relations people don't like me very much, if that's what you mean."

"That's what I mean." He uncrossed his arms and reached back across the desk to pick up a copy of the *Curtain*. He held up the front page so that she could read it.

"This is your most recent scoop, I believe," he said. "Oddly enough, my PR people felt that it was a little biased."

She glanced at the paper. Beneath the masthead with its familiar slogan, "Go Behind *The Curtain* for the Truth," was a screaming banner headline: "Mystery Man in Charge of Crystal Guild. What Is He Hiding?"

The headline was accompanied by a photo of Fontana getting out of a sleek, black Raptor sports car. Phil Trager, the *Curtain*'s staff photographer, had grabbed the shot on the fly, but it was a good one. In the picture Fontana looked a lot like he did in person: dangerous. But the impression was not a function of his looks or size. Fontana dominated his environment with his seemingly effortless aura of controlled power.

Brock Jenner had been a big, thick man, both physically and, in Sierra's opinion, intellectually. There was no question that he'd wielded power. Self-control, however, had certainly not been his forte. He'd been a heartless womanizer, and his temper had been explosive. Although he had officially died of natural causes, Sierra suspected that the reason he was no longer around was directly related to his habit of stabbing his fellow associates in the back. She wondered if the last back he had taken aim at had been Fontana's. If so, he had miscalculated badly.

If Jenner had been a bull of a man, Fontana was a specter-cat. You wouldn't know he was hunting you until you saw the fangs, and by then it would be too late.

He was a couple of inches above average height; not so tall as to tower over everyone in the room, yet somehow you would always know that he was the man in charge. No one would ever call him handsome, Sierra thought, but that did not matter; not to her at any rate. What he was, was fascinating. As in, the most intriguing man she had ever met. No wonder the hair on the back of her neck refused to settle down. Her pulse had been skipping along at high speed from the moment she had walked into the room. She was intensely, intimately aware of him in a way she could not explain.

There was nothing nervous or fidgety about Fontana. You got the feeling that it would require, at the very minimum, a volcanic eruption right here in his office to catch him by surprise. Even then, you would probably discover that he had contingency plans for such an event.

Rank-and-file ghost hunters were very big on tradition, right down to their wardrobes. They favored a lot of khaki and leather, probably because it went with the swagger. But those who made it to the top of the Guild preferred to dress like the CEOs they pretended to be. Today Fontana wore black, a lot of it. His black trousers, black shirt, black tie, and black jacket would have looked perfectly appropriate in her father's boardroom or any of her brothers' clubs. Each item screamed expensive fabric and brilliant tailoring; discreetly, of course.

The sartorial difference lay in the details. Unlike the silver or gold accessories that her male relatives favored, Fontana wore amber. Even the buttons of his shirt and his cuff links were set with amber. So was his belt buckle, the face of his watch, and, of course, the seal ring.

She was sure that every bit of the amber she could see was tuned. What's more, she suspected that he had amber elsewhere on his person, perhaps embedded in a shoe or on a key chain. Guild men carried backup amber in the same spirit that cops carried concealed guns. They knew that someday their lives might depend on the extra firepower.

But ghost hunters worked underground in the catacombs and the mysterious alien rain forest where the unpredictable currents of psi energy made high-tech weaponry and most machinery useless. Down below in the tunnels and in the jungle, survival depended on the ability to work tuned amber.

The paranormal ability to psychically resonate with amber and use it to focus the brain's natural energy had begun to appear among the colonists shortly after they had settled on Harmony. At first it had been viewed as a kind of biological quirk or curiosity. Scientists had concluded that something in the planet's environment stimulated the latent power in the human mind.

But the true value of the para-resonating talent had

soon become evident. Now, two hundred years after the energy Curtain had closed, isolating the colonies, amber was the chief source of energy. It was used to power everything from washing machines to computers.

For most people, the ability to generate and direct currents of psychic energy was a low-level, generalized talent. There were those, however, who exhibited much higher levels of para-resonating ability. In such cases the talent always took a highly specialized form and was directly linked to objects and artifacts left behind by the first colonists on Harmony, the long-vanished alien empire. All of the relics of the lost civilization radiated heavy psi energy.

The aliens had disappeared eons before the arrival of the settlers from Earth, but they had left behind a vast network of catacombs that crisscrossed the planet beneath its surface. Recently a massive underground rain forest had also been discovered. Like the tunnels, the jungle was filled with strong currents of psi. Some of it took dangerous forms. That was where ghost hunters came in.

Hunters were prime examples of para-resonators with strong but extremely limited talents. Their psychic abilities, while admittedly impressive, were not exactly multifunctional skill sets. As far as anyone had been able to discover, the only use for a hunter's talent was to manipulate and control the highly volatile, potentially lethal balls of fiery, acid-green alien energy known technically as unstable dissonance energy manifestations—UDEMs.

Everyone called the miniature storms *ghosts*, because they seemed to drift like lost specters through the underground world, creating major hazards for those who ventured beneath the surface.

Getting singed by a ghost was no small disaster. A close encounter with the wild energy fields could destroy a person's psychic senses. It could also put the unlucky victim into a coma from which he might never recover. The only people who could control the ghosts were those who could resonate with the chaotic dissonance energy that fueled them: ghost hunters.

Exploration and excavation of the mysterious tunnels and, more recently, the rain forest was big business. Corporations, university research teams, and private individuals all competed to discover and recover the secrets that the aliens had left behind. Only hunters could offer protection underground in the heavy psi environment. If you wanted to hire a few as security for your research or exploration team, you had to go through the Guilds.

The result was that the Guilds exerted enormous control over who got to conduct business underground. The law of supply and demand being what it was, the organizations had become extremely powerful over the years. Their tentacles reached down into the underworld and throughout society as well. A man in Fontana's position could exert enormous pressure on politicians, CEOs, and influential people at every level.

In Sierra's opinion, the situation had gotten considerably worse in the past year with the opening up of the rain forest to explorers, researchers, and old-fashioned treasure hunters. The Guilds, never slow to recognize a business opportunity when they saw it, had moved swiftly to exert their authority over the eerie buried jungle, just as they did over the catacombs.

There was no question but that jungle exploration was hazardous. In addition to a host of strange new plant and animal species, treacherous currents of energy flowed through the rain forest. It turned out that certain types of hunters could navigate the so-called ghost rivers. The Guilds had found a new and extremely profitable market niche.

Power was power, and whether he admitted it or not, Fontana wielded a lot of the stuff.

He looked up from the piece she had written on him, his expression politely neutral. "You seem to think that, on their good days, ghost hunters are just a bunch of overpaid bodyguards. On our off days we're flat-out criminals."

"I never wrote that you were all criminals," she said quickly. Ivor Runtley, publisher and editor of the *Curtain*, had made it clear that, while he was willing to allow her a lot of leeway, he definitely did not want her bringing the full wrath of the new Guild boss down on his beloved paper.

Fontana tossed the paper aside. "Okay, I'll concede that you did not actually use the word *criminal*. But it's obvious that you don't think highly of those in my profession."

"I believe that the Guilds have far too much power

when it comes to what goes on underground. A great deal of power in the hands of any one organization is always dangerous."

"Do you really think it would be a good idea to strip the Guilds of their authority underground?" he asked.

"I'm not saying that some control and organization isn't necessary. Everyone knows that people with your sort of talents are necessary for safe exploration."

"My sort of talents?" he asked softly. "What do you know about my talents?"

"You're obviously a hunter, a powerful one, I'm sure. You wouldn't have made it to the top of the Guild unless you were a very strong dissonance energy para-rez talent." She paused. "Of some kind."

She tacked on that last line very deliberately. Historically, the Guilds had always maintained that there was only one sort of hunter talent: the ability to work green ghost light. But in the course of her new career as an investigative reporter, she had picked up some very interesting rumors hinting that some hunters could work other kinds of alien psi, specifically silver and blue light. If it was true that there were some exotic hunter talents, it was yet another secret that the Guilds were keeping. She doubted very much that she could trick Fontana into admitting it, but it had been worth a shot.

"Let's assume for the moment that you know all you think you need to know about me," he said, ignoring the subtle dig about unpublicized talents. "What about you?"

She froze. Elvis, sensing her distress, left his coffee

and skittered across the desk. He jumped down onto her knee and then bounded up her arm to sit on her shoulder. She reached up and touched him in a reassuring manner.

Fontana could not possibly know about her own talent, she told herself. He was fishing in the dark, trying to provoke her the same way she had tried to prod him. They were after each other's secrets.

"I'm a reporter, Mr. Fontana," she said coldly. "Whatever talents I have are in the realm of journalism."

He gave her a slow, knowing, shatteringly intimate smile. "I'm not buying that, not for a minute. I know power when I sense it, Miss McIntyre."

"I did not come here to talk about myself. This was supposed to be an interview with you." She closed her notebook and slipped it into her purse. "But it appears that isn't going to happen, so I might as well be on my way."

"You surprise me. I didn't think you'd give up so easily."

She got to her feet. "I don't mind wasting your time, but I'm not real keen on wasting my own."

"Sit down, Miss McIntyre."

"Why?"

"Because I am, as the old saying goes, about to make you an offer you can't refuse."

"Are you threatening me?"

"I hope you won't take it that way."

"And if I refuse?"

He smiled. "You won't."

"Why won't I?"

"Because I'm going to give you a shot at a real exclusive, the biggest story of your career."

"Sure."

"You don't trust me, do you?"

"No farther than I could throw you."

He watched her with a steady, unwavering look. "I'm dead serious."

It was the word *dead* that aroused all her new journalistic instincts. Okay, maybe he was serious.

"This would be a Guild story?" she asked warily.

"Yes."

"What, exactly, do I have to do to get this hot exclusive?"

"Marry me."

Chapter 2

SHE SAT DOWN AGAIN. HARD. SO HARD THAT THE DUST bunny on her shoulder bounced a little and had to scramble to hang on to his perch.

The stunned, vaguely horrified expression on Sierra's face would have been a lot more satisfying if it had not been elicited by the prospect of marrying him, Fontana thought. So what if they had only met forty-five—he glanced at his watch—make that forty-seven minutes ago? So what if she had made it crystal clear that she considered Guild bosses, as a class, to be legalized mobsters? The fact that she was literally shocked speechless by the notion of marrying him was proving a little hard on the ego, probably because when she had walked through his door forty-seven minutes ago, he'd been nearly floored by the rush.

It had taken a great deal of willpower just to make

normal conversation. He'd experienced his share of fast-acting attractions in the past. Hell, he liked women. But this all-consuming fascination with Sierra McIntyre was startlingly, disturbingly, intriguingly different.

The effect had struck full force on both the normal and the paranormal plane, shaking him to the core. His psychic senses were as dazzled as his physical senses, and that was nothing short of unique in his experience. Always, *always*, he had been able to separate the two realms when it came to his relationships with women. But this time it was as if something deep inside him had instantly recognized and responded to Sierra McIntyre, as if he'd been waiting for her without having been consciously aware of it.

It wasn't just her looks. He'd seen any number of more beautiful women in his life. Which wasn't to say that Sierra was not attractive, he thought. The appeal, however, was unconventional and wholly unexpected, at least for him. He usually went for the polished, sleek, sophisticated type, the kind of women who knew how to play the sexual game. He liked them tall. Sierra McIntyre was on the short side, even in her high-heeled pumps. He liked them willowy. Sierra had a definite tendency toward roundness. He liked blondes who wore their long hair in dramatic upswept styles.

Sierra's hair was the color of fall leaves. Wildly curly, it looked as if she had lost control somewhere along the line and had simply given up trying to tame it. Her face was intelligent. Her eyes were the alluring blue green of a tropical lagoon, very big and very knowing. They were framed by a pair of serious-looking glasses.

Although this was the first time they had met in person, he knew a lot about Sierra McIntyre. As was his custom, he'd done his research before he'd plotted his strategy.

It was Sierra's gutsy determination that had first drawn his attention. There weren't many people in Crystal, male or female, who were willing to criticize the Guild and its policies, let alone go after Brock Jenner. Two possible explanations had come to mind. Either Sierra's obsession with exposing Guild secrets was driven by a personal vendetta or else she was one of those irritating, naive do-gooders bent on righting wrongs and speaking out for those who had no voice.

Now that he had met her, he knew for certain that the latter was the answer. No wonder Jenner had been so annoyed with her. It was hard to crush do-gooders. You couldn't buy them off, and overt threats were risky, especially for a man in Jenner's position. It would not have looked good for a Guild boss to send a couple of goons to a lady journalist's door, especially when it was a given that the journalist in question would go straight to the cops and then splash the story across the front page of a tabloid.

Sierra finally got her mouth closed. "What did you say about marriage?" she asked very carefully.

"This is going to take a little explaining," he said.

Her dark brows scrunched together above the frames of her serious glasses. "I think so, yes."

He went to stand at the window and looked out at the towering green wall that enclosed the ancient alien ruins of the Dead City. Traces of ambient energy whispered everywhere throughout the Old Quarter. He could feel them here in his office, and he knew that Sierra sensed them, too.

Not that you had to be a high-level para-rez to respond to the stuff. Even those with average sensitivity picked up on the currents that leaked from the ruins and the tunnels below. Almost everyone got a little buzz from alien psi. For that reason the seedy Old Quarters in all of the city-states were popular with tourists and the nightclub crowd.

Two hundred years earlier the colonists from Earth had established their first towns in the shadows of the ruins of the four Dead Cities that had been discovered on Harmony. Crystal was no exception. The two-hundred-year-old structures built by the humans appeared stolid and grimly functional compared to the ethereal spires and the fantastical domes that the aliens had left behind.

But unlike the aliens, the colonists from Earth had been at home on Harmony right from the start. Even after the energy Curtain that had made travel between Earth and Harmony possible mysteriously closed, the settlers had not only survived but thrived.

Things had evidently been much different for the aliens. The experts had come to the conclusion that something about the very atmosphere of the planet had been poisonous to the ancients. The long-vanished people had been forced to enclose their cities within towering green quartz walls that gave off the psi they must have needed to survive. Eventually they had retreated underground. In the end they had either abandoned the planet altogether or simply died out. No one knew for certain what had become of the Others. It was one of the many mysteries that surrounded them.

"I'm waiting for your explanation, Mr. Fontana," Sierra said.

He could tell from the cool tone of her voice that she had herself back under control. He also sensed that her reporter's curiosity had surfaced. That was good. His entire plan hinged on it.

"What I'm going to tell you stays between us and is strictly off the record until I say otherwise," he said. "Is that understood?"

"I'm making no promises until I know what I'm getting into."

He turned around to face her. "You really don't trust anyone connected to the Guild, do you?"

"Nope."

"Because you are convinced that there is some conspiracy going on inside the organization."

"Yep."

He went back to the desk and picked up the copy of the *Curtain*. "A conspiracy to conceal the discovery of an alien lab somewhere in the rain forest."

"Uh-huh."

"Care to tell me why you're so sure there's been a

discovery of such potentially monumental significance and why the Guild would want to conceal it?"

"Gee, no, I don't think so."

"Because it would mean revealing your sources?"

She hesitated for a couple of beats before she answered. "That's right."

Why the slight pause before what should have been a predictable professional response? he wondered. Maybe she didn't have any solid sources, after all. If that was the case, his scheme was doomed.

But that didn't make sense. She had not merely reported vague rumors of the alien lab. She had linked it to the dealing of the illegal drug known as ghost juice, and she had documented the disappearance of a number of homeless men who had become addicts. She knew more about the damn conspiracy than he did. He needed her.

He angled himself onto a corner of the desk, one foot on the floor.

"You know," he said, "this conversation probably isn't going to go far unless one of us takes a flier and decides to trust the other person."

She raised her brows. And waited.

"Guess that would be me," he said finally. "Okay, here goes. I happen to agree with you, Miss McIntyre. There is a conspiracy going on. What's more, my predecessor was involved in the cover-up."

Her eyes widened. "You're admitting it?"

"Yes."

"Hang on." She unzipped her purse and started to delve inside for her pen and notepad.

He reached down and captured her hand. The bones of her wrist felt delicate and graceful.

"No notes," he said.

Her mouth tightened. She looked pointedly at his fingers encircling her wrist.

He realized that he did not want to let her go. Reluctantly, he released her.

There was a moment of tense silence. Elvis, having evidently concluded that they weren't leaving, after all, fluttered off Sierra's shoulder and returned to the coffee mug on the desk.

Reluctantly, Sierra sat back in her chair, drumming her fingers on the arms.

"All right," she said. "No notes. Tell me about the cover-up."

"Unfortunately, I don't know much more than you do. Maybe less."

She acknowledged that with a small, disdainful sniff. "Try again, Mr. Fontana."

"A few months ago some of the other members of the Crystal Council and I began to suspect that Jenner was involved in the ghost juice business."

"The police think that the juice is being distributed by the Night Riders, a motorcycle gang," she pointed out.

"It is, but that doesn't mean that Jenner wasn't involved. He covered his tracks very well, but there were rumors. We hired an outside investigator to go undercover."

"You brought in a private investigator?" She was clearly intrigued.

"A former hunter."

"What happened?"

"Three weeks into the job, he turned up dead."

"Nathan Harder." Sierra was suddenly very focused. "I wondered about that. The official story was that he got caught in a ghost river whirlpool, and when they finally pulled him out, he was brain-dead."

"Following Harder's death, my associates and I decided that whatever was going on was more widespread and more dangerous than we had realized. We figured it was time for Jenner to retire."

"According to the press release, Jenner suffered a stroke and died. Is that the Guild's idea of a golden parachute?"

"We believe Jenner was murdered."

She sat very still in her chair. "By you?"

He smiled his faint, dangerous smile. "I know this will come as a great disappointment to you, Miss McIntyre, but the answer to your question is no. I didn't kill Jenner. I think someone put something lethal into his IV line."

"I see." Well, you couldn't expect the man to confess to a reporter.

"The strategy the other Council members and I put together did not call for Jenner's death," Fontana added patiently. "We just wanted him out of this office. We thought that would be sufficient."

"What was your so-called strategy for getting rid of him?"

"An old-fashioned one. I challenged him to a duel. He lost."

"Good grief. The Guilds still conduct ghost energy duels to determine the next chief?" Disgust dripped in every word. "I've heard rumors, but I assumed that sort of archaic approach to running the organizations had been halted long ago."

"Occasionally there's something to be said for the old ways."

She raised her eyes to the ceiling. "Talk about primitive, testosterone-driven behavior."

"Within the Guild we prefer to call it tradition."

"Right. Tradition."

"Jenner wasn't married. That made things easier."

"He was between Marriages of Convenience," she said sharply. "Everyone said that he was shopping for his fifth wife."

"Like I said, that situation made things simpler."

"Why is that?" she asked, baffled.

"Theoretically, anyone in the Guild can challenge the chief to a ghost light duel. If the Council approves, the duel takes place."

"Sounds like a Guild version of a vote of no confidence in the CEO."

He smiled humorlessly. "It is. But a Guild boss's wife has certain privileges. She can go before the Council and demand that the challenger be denied. No one can override her. It's another old tradition designed to stabilize the power structure of the Guilds and protect the chief from dealing with the distraction that would be caused by constant challenges."

Sierra whistled softly. "Well, that certainly explains why Guild bosses are almost always married."

"The tradition does tend to reinforce family values."

"Some family values. Jenner went through a lot of wives, but he never got involved in a Covenant Marriage. His relationships were always Marriages of Convenience."

Her disapproval amused him. Marriages of Convenience were legal, if short-term contracts, but a lot of well-bred, conservative-minded people tended to view them as nothing more than socially sanctioned affairs. There were major differences, however, and he was intimately aware of the high cost of those differences.

When the First Generation colonists had found themselves cut off forever from Earth, they had understood that the survival of their small society depended on stability. Given that the basic building blocks of any civilization are families, the Founders had done everything in their power to make the ties that bind as strong as possible.

They had set up two forms of marriage. Covenant Marriages were formal and intended to be permanent. Getting out of a CM was a legal and financial nightmare. If there were children involved, it was impossible to dissolve the contract until all of the offspring were eighteen years of age.

The second form of marriage, the kind Jenner had favored, was known as a Marriage of Convenience. They were arrangements that, while offering all the legal protections of marriage, could be dissolved in a heartbeat by either party, *unless there were offspring*. The birth of a child immediately transformed an MC into a formal Covenant Marriage.

The Founders had done their best, but all the legal and social engineering in the world could not prevent the occasional birth of someone like himself, Fontana thought. A bastard.

"We believe that Jenner terminated his last marriage because he didn't think he could count on his wife to defend him if there was a challenge," Fontana said.

Sierra's eyes narrowed faintly. "There was gossip to the effect that he had abused her."

"As I recall, that gossip appeared only in the *Curtain*. One of your pieces, I believe."

She shrugged. "It was no secret."

"Actually, it was. No one on the Council was aware of the abuse until the story ran in your paper."

"Talk about willful ignorance. The former Mrs. Jenner spent several days recovering in a private hospital after her husband lost his temper and beat her up the last time. Evidently it was the final straw for her. She wanted to warn other women about him. That's why she agreed to talk to me."

He shook his head, straightened away from the desk, and went back to the window. "You're amazing, Miss

McIntyre. How the devil did you find Alison in that private clinic? We all believed that she'd gone off to spend a week at a spa in Resonance City. The next thing anyone knew, she had filed for divorce and disappeared."

"As a matter of fact, she contacted me."

"Probably because she knew you would be willing to print the story. I doubt if any other paper in town would have touched it."

"Probably. Why were you the one chosen to go against Jenner in a ghost duel?"

He deliberated a few seconds, deciding how much to say. In the end he compromised. "Jenner was no ordinary hunter. He was extremely powerful. Everyone knew that there was no one else on the Council who stood a chance against him."

"Except you."

"Except me," he agreed quietly.

"What makes you so special?"

"It's complicated."

"In other words, you're not going to tell me."

"No," he said.

"Just another Guild secret?"

"Yes."

"You know, one of these days, someone really ought to introduce the concept of democracy to you guys. It's this really cool way of running things. You get to elect your leaders."

He smiled. "Sounds inefficient."

"It's messy, but it works, and it sure beats dueling with

ghost light. Never mind, let's get back to Jenner. You said you didn't kill him?"

"I won the duel, but Jenner didn't die because of his injuries. He was temporarily brain-fried, but he would have recovered." He paused. "Although his para-rez talents would never have been as strong as they were before the duel." In fact, they would have been nonexistent, but he saw no reason to elaborate.

"In other words, you really burned him."

He said nothing. The duel had been a hellish business that had almost cost him his life. Jenner had not only been a strong para-resonator, he'd worked deadly blue light, not regular green ghost energy. But there was no way to explain that to Sierra. The very existence of psi energy from the blue end of the spectrum was, like so many other things, a deep Guild secret.

There was a small scurrying motion at his feet. He looked down and saw Elvis. The dust bunny hopped up onto the windowsill, cape flying.

"Who got to Jenner?" Sierra demanded.

He looked at her over his shoulder. "We don't know. But the fact that someone took the risk of murdering a former Guild boss told us that the conspiracy was a bigger problem than we had assumed."

"How much of a risk was there? He was a *former* boss, after all."

"Jenner still had his secrets. I wanted them."

"Wait a second, you think his fellow conspirators murdered him in order to keep him from betraying them?"

"Yes."

"Any idea who those folks might be?" she asked quickly.

"I have a hunch about one of them, but there may be more. At the moment I can't prove a damn thing."

"What about you?" she asked. "Is your position as the new Guild boss somewhat, uh, untenable, too?"

"I think it's unlikely that I'll get hit by a truck this afternoon, if that's what you mean."

"Why not?"

He turned to face her. "This isn't the first time there's been a problem deep inside one of the Guilds."

"Imagine that."

The sarcasm was starting to irritate him, but he told himself he was big enough to overlook it, at least for the moment.

"There are procedures in place to deal with this kind of thing," he said. "Given the power a Guild commander wields, the potential for misuse of that power is always present. The leaders of the organizations recognized that fact from the beginning. That's why the Chamber was established."

Chamber was short for the far more unwieldy Chamber of the Joint Council of Dissonance Energy Para-resonator Guilds, the overarching governing organization of the Guilds.

"I'm well aware of the existence of the Chamber, but everyone knows that the Guilds function autonomously,"

Sierra said. "Individual chiefs respect each other's territory."

"That's true unless a problem arises that might impact the safety and well-being of the city for which a particular Guild is responsible. I know you don't appreciate the role of the Guilds in society, Miss McIntyre, but the truth is, their main job is to protect you and everyone else, not only from the natural hazards underground but from would-be tyrants like Vincent Lee Vance."

She blew that off with a wave of her hand. "I did my time in fourth grade, just like everyone else. Trust me, I know that decades ago ghost hunters saved the city-states from Vance and his followers. The Guilds aren't likely to ever let us forget it. I'm also aware of the old saying that the Guilds police their own. But I certainly didn't know that the Chamber sometimes gets involved when there's trouble in one of the organizations."

"For the most part, individual Guilds are expected to take care of their own problems. But when that doesn't work, the Chamber steps in."

"How?" She sounded skeptical.

"The Chamber maintains an investigative office." He clasped his hands behind his back. "Officially it's called the Bureau of Internal Affairs, but unofficially it's just known as the Bureau."

"Why haven't I ever heard of this Bureau?"

"Probably because the Chamber prefers to keep quiet about it."

"Right. Yet another Guild secret. So why are you telling me this?"

"Because I think I can trust you, Miss McIntyre. And because I need your help. Forty-eight hours ago I met with the other Guild chiefs in a secret emergency session of the Chamber. I explained what was going on here in Crystal and how I planned to clean up the mess. They offered backup and assistance if I need it, but everyone would prefer that I take care of the problem on my own as quietly as possible."

She looked startled. "The other Guild bosses know that you've got a situation on your hands?"

"They do now. Trust me, they all want answers, not only about the drug operation but more critically about the possibility that something very important has been discovered in the rain forest and that the find has been concealed."

She thought about that for a moment and then nodded. "Okay, I can see where the other Guilds might want you to fix your own problems here in Crystal as fast and as quietly as possible. Does having the other bosses involved buy you some protection from whoever took out Jenner?"

"You're the one I'm worried about."

She started so violently that she almost knocked over Elvis's coffee mug.

"Me?" she gasped.

"Ever been underground, Miss McIntyre?"

"Once on a school field trip." She shuddered. "I hated

it. I'm claustrophobic. And the way the catacombs branch out in a thousand different directions like a maze, it's downright weird."

"It's not for everyone," he agreed. "But aside from the alien nature of the design and the fact that it's easy to get lost underground, there are two basic kinds of hazards: the energy ghosts and illusion traps."

"Everyone knows that."

"When you started your series of investigations into the workings of the local Guild, you began playing with a very nasty illusion trap," he said. He put a lot of quiet emphasis on the last two words. "There's a good chance you might trigger it."

Her eyes widened behind the lenses of her glasses. He knew she got the metaphor. When one of the ancient traps was accidentally triggered, the victim was instantly plunged into an alien nightmare. The feverish images were too bizarre for the human mind to copc with. Thc experience did not last long because unconsciousness and, in extreme cases, coma and death, soon followed.

She swallowed hard and clutched the arms of her chair. "Do you really think that someone inside the Guild might try to kill me?"

"I'm not going to try to sweeten this, Miss McIntyre. The answer is maybe."

"Nothing like a solid *maybe* to reassure a person."

"You could try packing your bags and leaving town—"

"*No*. I can't leave now. I've got to find out what happened to those missing men."

"I thought you'd say that. I'm not sure leaving Crystal would keep you safe anyway. You've gone too far. I'm the only one who can offer you some protection."

"Is that right?" she asked coolly.

"Believe it or not, people usually think twice about murdering a Guild boss's wife."

"Because it would attract the attention of the other bosses?"

"The Chamber tends to frown on that sort of thing," he said gently.

"Oh, jeez." She gripped the arms of her chair again. "You're serious, aren't you?"

"Very. In addition to the implied threat, there's another reason why marrying me will buy you some protection."

"What's that?"

"Most people, including everyone in the Crystal Guild, will assume that I married you to shut you up."

She bristled. "You mean they'll assume you're doing what you have to do to keep Guild secrets, is that it?"

"Something like that."

"If you think for one minute that you can keep me quiet once I'm your wife—"

"That's not the objective."

"Really? Then what is the goal?"

"The idea is to join forces, Miss McIntyre. I've got my sources inside the Guild. You've obviously got a few of your own outside the organization. We need each other's help to conduct this investigation, and we need to work together covertly."

She slumped back into her chair, bewildered now, rather than angry.

"I don't understand. Jenner mocked my reports. None of the other mainstream media picked up my stories, so I never got any traction with them. No one's afraid of me."

"Jenner paid more attention than you knew. Now that he's gone, I think we should assume that the others involved in the cover-up may also consider you to be a problem."

Excitement and determination lit her expressive face. "So, there really is something big going on."

"Yes."

She leaned forward a little and lowered her voice, although there was no one around to overhear.

"Is it a conspiracy to conceal the discovery of an alien lab?" she asked.

"To tell you the truth, Miss McIntyre, I don't know what the hell is being covered up beyond the drug running. What I know for sure is that there have been at least a couple of suspicious deaths, including the PI hired by the Council, and Jenner himself. At this point, there are very, very few people I can trust within the higher ranks of the organization."

"What makes you think you can trust me?"

He smiled slowly. "Once you know what someone wants, you know whether you can trust that person. You also know how far you can trust him or her."

She searched his face, intrigued. "You think you know what I want?"

"You want answers. So do I. That means we can work together."

She drew a long, steadying breath. "Okay, in spite of some opinions to the contrary, I'm not an idiot. If you think I'm in danger, I want all the protection I can get. And you're right. I want to find out what happened to those missing men."

He could feel the currents of energy that shimmered invisibly around her. She was definitely a woman of power. The question was, what kind?

She didn't wear amber, so she probably was not a standard para-rez talent. But there had always been stories of other kinds of talents, the sort that had nothing to do with alien psi and did not require amber, talents that occurred naturally in some people. Such psychic abilities were said to have existed since time immemorial, long before humans had gone through the Curtain.

"I made an appointment for us to pick up a Marriage of Convenience license at the registrar's office this afternoon at five o'clock," he said.

She looked as if she might fall off her chair. "You were that sure I'd cooperate?"

"Like I said, I know what you want. My job was to convince you that marrying me was the best way to get it."

She shook her head, amazed. "No wonder you became the new chief of the Guild. You're good."

"Just think, you'll be going back to your office with the scoop of the week. 'New Guild Boss Weds Reporter.' "

She wrinkled her nose. "That's a little tame for the *Curtain*. I'm sure my editor will come up with something more exciting."

"I don't care how the headline reads so long as you don't leave me standing alone at the registrar's office this afternoon."

"My colleagues at the paper and my friends are going to have a lot of questions."

"One thing I should make clear," he said evenly, "this arrangement will work best if we convince people it's for real."

For the first time, she looked amused. "You expect me to imply to everyone I know that you and I have been secretly involved for some time and just now decided to get married?"

"I think that would be the simplest approach, yes."

"Get real."

"No one will think it strange that we kept the relationship secret until now. It's a little awkward for a Council member to admit that he's dating a journalist who specializes in exposés of the Guild."

She blinked and then frowned a little. "Okay, I can see that."

"Given your opinions of the organization, I'm sure your colleagues won't be the least bit amazed that you kept quiet about dating me, as well."

She contemplated that for a moment and then shook her head. "I'll do my best, but I'd better warn you that I doubt very much that I'll be able to fool my editor. Ivor

Runtley has great instincts when it comes to sensing a story."

"If you have to tell Runtley the truth, try to make him see the importance of keeping quiet."

"Okay, I'll give it a shot. He'll do just about anything if the story is worth it." She got to her feet and slung her purse over one shoulder. "I hope you know what we're both doing." She glanced at Elvis. "Time to go, pal."

Elvis hopped down from the windowsill. He drifted across the floor and vaulted up onto the back of the chair. Sierra held out her wrist to him. He leaped aboard and bounded up to perch on her shoulder.

"I'll meet you at the registrar's office at a quarter to five," Fontana said. "Did you drive?"

"No, I took a cab."

He opened the door and looked at the anxious young man seated at the smaller of the two desks. Dray Levine was the new second assistant to the new chief executive assistant, Harlan Ostendorf. A week ago Dray had been a clerk in the records department. He was still adjusting to the rarified atmosphere of the executive suite.

"Dray, please see my fiancée downstairs and into a Guild limo."

Dray stared, clearly dumbfounded. His throat worked. "Fiancée, sir?" he finally managed.

"That's right." Fontana smiled. "Miss McIntyre and I are getting married today."

"Uh, congratulations, sir."

"Thank you," Fontana said.

"A limo isn't necessary, really," Sierra said.

Fontana smiled. "Sure it is. I'm not sending my future bride home in a taxi when there's a fleet of perfectly good limos sitting downstairs in the garage."

Dray's stunned expression finally smoothed out into his more customary anxious-to-please look. He jumped to his feet.

"I'll be happy to escort Miss McIntyre downstairs, sir," he said. "Will there be anything else?"

"Yes." Fontana looked at the empty desk. "When does Harlan get back?"

Dray glanced at the clock. "Mr. Ostendorf took an early lunch. He's due back in about ten minutes."

"Good. When he returns, please tell him I want to see him immediately."

"Yes, sir."

Fontana studied Dray's ill-concealed astonishment. Rumors and gossip flowed rapidly through the Guild. The news of his marriage would be common knowledge within the organization in less than an hour. He smiled, satisfied.

"My work here is done," he said.

He closed the door, went back to his desk, and sat down. Dray wasn't the only one who was still a little stunned.

He had never intended to suggest a marriage contract to Sierra. The original plan had been to offer her a full-time bodyguard and around-the-clock protection until he had cleaned up the mess.

But he had revised the strategy in a heartbeat when she walked through his door. The result was that at five o'clock today, he would have himself a bride.

He'd never had one of those before. There had never been time for anything other than brief affairs. He'd been too busy. Surviving his career at the Bureau and the lightning-fast climb up through the ranks of the Crystal Guild that had followed had required his full attention.

Tonight he would go to bed a married man. True, it was only a Marriage of Convenience, which was, admittedly, barely a step up from having an affair. He also knew that his new bride viewed the move as purely a business arrangement.

Nevertheless, it felt real.

Chapter 3

"WHAT THE HELL IS GOING ON, SIERRA?" IVOR RUNTLEY, better known to his staff, behind his back, as the Runt, flattened his big hands on Sierra's desk and loomed over her. "And don't try to tell me that you've been dating Fontana in secret for months, because I'm not buying it."

Sierra glanced quickly around. Fortunately, it was lunchtime. They had the newsroom to themselves.

Runtley was anything but a runt. Sixty-one years old and as bald as a golf ball, he was built like a two-ton boulder. His sheer mass often caused people to make the mistake of thinking that he was as dumb as a rock. It was a serious misconception.

Once upon a time Runtley had been an investigative journalist. He had worked for a mainstream paper, the *Crystal Herald*. But somewhere along the line he had become obsessed with the mysteries left behind by the aliens. Rumor had it that he had gotten badly fried by a ghost while investigating a story. He had blamed the Guild, claiming it had tried to silence him. Whatever the truth of the matter, the experience had left him with an illogical fixation that had led him to file increasingly bizarre and unsubstantiated stories at the *Herald*. He had eventually been fired.

His response had been to scrape together enough money to buy the *Curtain*, a nearly moribund little weekly that had been about to go out of business altogether. Within months he had transformed it into a sensational, moneymaking tabloid that now published daily. Sierra knew he didn't give a damn about the celebrity gossip or the scandals that were the lifeblood of the paper. All he cared about was having the opportunity to print what he considered the truth about alien and Guild secrets.

Like everyone else at the *Curtain*, Sierra was pretty sure Runtley was crazy when it came to the subject of the long-vanished aliens, but she liked him, anyway. He had given her a job, after all, even though she'd come to him with absolutely no journalism credentials whatsoever. All she'd had six months ago was a growing conviction that something was very wrong on the streets of the city's Old Quarter and that the Guild was involved. Runtley had hired her instantly. When it came to the subject of the Guild, they shared a mutual distrust that some felt bordered on paranoia.

Her boss wasn't the only person she liked here at the paper. After a depressingly checkered career in a variety of jobs, she was finally in a position that felt right; maybe not perfect but, then, what job was perfect? Perhaps she felt at home here because her colleagues in the newsroom, from Runtley on down, were also misfits in their own way. Certainly none of them had started out looking forward to careers as tabloid reporters. They had all landed at the *Curtain* after erratic and eccentric paths.

Together they faced the disdain of their colleagues in the mainstream media and shared stories about their perennially embarrassed families. *Where does your daughter work? Oh, she's a journalist? What newspaper? The* Curtain*? Isn't that one of those sleazy tabloids*?

She sat back in her chair. "I warned Fontana that I wouldn't be able to fool you, sir."

Runtley leaned farther over the desk. Even though there was no one around to hear him, he lowered his usually booming voice to a low rumble. "This sudden decision to sign an MC with Fontana is connected to your investigation of the Guild's cover-up of the alien lab, isn't it?"

"Yes, sir. He wants my help in the investigation. I'm asking you to trust me."

"Not a problem." Runtley's eyes glittered with the familiar feverish excitement that always came over him when the prospect of a real scoop involving the Guilds or alien relics arose. "Are you sure you can trust Fontana?"

She thought about that, checking in again with her intuition. "Not exactly. He's keeping secrets. But he agrees that there is some sort of conspiracy within the Guild and that it is linked to the juice dealing and maybe to the disappearances. I believe him when he says he wants to get to the bottom of whatever is going on."

"Huh." Runtley did not bother to conceal his skepticism.

She looked at Elvis. He was sitting on the corner of her desk, munching on the peanut butter and banana sandwich she had made him. The coffee mug the newsroom staff had presented to him a few weeks ago was nearby. It featured a photo of an ancient Earth singing icon. The name *Elvis* was spelled out in glow-in-the-dark letters.

"Elvis liked Fontana," she said. "He's a pretty good judge of character."

"Forget the bunny. I don't give diddly-squat about what he thinks. What about you? You're the one with the mega-rez intuition. What was your take on Fontana?"

She hesitated. Runtley was one of the very few people who knew about her odd talent and actually believed in it. Like the others in her family who possessed various unusual paranormal abilities that did not depend on amber, she had learned long ago not to confide in others. When she did try to talk about her intuition, she usually got one of two unpleasant reactions. Most people simply didn't believe her and laughed off the claim. Such cases could prove socially awkward but not particularly devastating.

It was those in the second group—the people who actually believed her—whom she had to watch out for. They frequently concluded that she could be useful. What business executive, stockbroker, or gambler couldn't use an assistant or, better yet, a wife endowed with extremely accurate intuitive talents? She had learned her lesson with Jonathan Pemberley. She had no intention of repeating it.

She had never actually told Runtley that her intuitive powers were off the charts or that she didn't need amber to access them, but he had guessed the truth during her interview. She strongly suspected that his own intuition was well above normal.

"I didn't get any bad vibes from Fontana," she said. "I wouldn't have even considered this MC if I had."

"But he's a Guild boss. What's more, judging by what you just told me, he took out Jenner."

"I didn't say Fontana wouldn't be dangerous under some circumstances; I just said I think I'll be safe with him. At least for the moment." She moved one hand in a small gesture. "He needs me."

The door of the newsroom slammed open. Kay Alcantara stood in the opening. Phil Trager and Matt Delaney werc directly behind her.

Kay planted a hand over her heart and gave Sierra an anguished glare.

"Say it isn't so," Kay pleaded. "Say you aren't actually planning to marry the new head of the Crystal Guild and that you forgot to tell your very best friend in the entire world that you had been dating him in secret for lord knows how long."

Kay was Sierra's age, a tall, vivacious woman with a long mane of discreetly enhanced red hair and an Amazonian body.

Sierra felt herself turning pink. "Well, it isn't quite like that."

Kay grinned. "Of course it isn't. As if you would actually marry anyone connected to the Guild. The rumor will make a great scoop for the *Curtain* tomorrow, though."

"Hot damn," Matt said. He rubbed his hands together and looked hopefully at Runtley. "Can I write the story, boss? Please. I'll do you proud, I promise."

"Hey, I've got the perfect headline," Phil announced. " 'Guild Boss Weds Mystery Woman in Secret Ceremony.' "

Sierra glowered. "There's nothing secret about it. We're due at the registrar's office at five this afternoon, and by the way, this is my story."

"You can't write it," Runtley said, unequivocal. "You're the subject."

"Not fair." Sierra shot to her feet. "I'm the one who is sacrificing her, uh, whatever, for this story. I deserve to write it."

"Kay writes up the wedding," Runtley said. "And that's final."

"Thanks, boss," Kay said, face alight with anticipation. "Can't wait to get back to my computer."

"You can't write the story yet," Sierra said. She glanced at her watch. "I'm not going to get married for another two hours."

Kay laughed. "Since when has a little detail like a timeline ever stopped an intrepid reporter for the *Curtain*? After all, I'm going to get the background directly from you, right? Of course, I'll want a detailed account of the wedding night, too, but that can wait until tomorrow, I guess."

It could wait forever, Sierra thought, because there wasn't going to be a wedding night.

"Holy dust bunny," Phil said, patting Elvis. "This is going to be the biggest story since we broke the news that you somehow made it through the Curtain, King."

Elvis chortled happily and ate another bite of his sandwich.

Kay sat down on a corner of Sierra's desk and crossed her long legs. "Tell me everything. How long have you been secretly dating Fontana?"

"Not very long," Sierra said quickly.

"How the hell did you two meet?" Matt demanded.

"In the course of my investigation," Sierra said with what she thought was commendable cool. "He was a powerful member of the Council, as you know, and I wanted some answers from him."

"Well?" Phil wiggled his brows. "Get any?"

Everyone glowered at him.

"Answers, I mean," Phil said hastily.

Sierra folded her hands on the desk. "Let's just say that I am convinced that Fontana is no Brock Jenner. He will run a very different Guild."

There was a short, startled silence. Phil, Matt, and Kay looked at each other. Then they turned to Runtley, who merely shrugged his heavy shoulders.

Kay stared at Sierra with an expression of dawning wonder.

"Damn, you're serious, aren't you?" she said. "This isn't some kind of joke. You're actually going to marry Fontana?"

"Yes," Sierra said.

Matt whistled softly. "Somebody catch me. I think I'm going to swoon."

Kay frowned. "No offense, but why would Fontana marry you, Sierra? You've been a thorn in the side of the Guild for the past six months."

"Maybe he thinks he can keep her quiet," Phil offered, sounding more than a little concerned. "After all, once she's a Guild wife, she'll be expected to keep Guild secrets."

Matt nodded uneasily. "Yeah, I can see why he might want her locked into an MC while he gets control of things. Besides, Guild bosses are almost always married. Something to do with one of their traditions."

Sierra felt her temper flare. "Let's get one thing clear. Fontana is not marrying me because he thinks he can silence me that way."

"Okay, okay." Matt held up both hands, palms out. "Just a working theory."

"Try another hypothesis."

Phil gave her a quick, head-to-toe inspection. "Well, one thing's for sure."

"What?" Sierra snapped.

"Evidently you're going to be on the cover of tomorrow's edition of the *Curtain*. That means you need to go home and change."

She glanced down at her businesslike skirted suit and pumps. “What’s wrong with these clothes?”

“They’re too boring for a secret mistress who is about to become the wife of the new chief of the Guild,” Kay explained.

“She’s right,” Runtley decreed. “Go back to your apartment and put on something sexy. We can sell a lot of copies if we get a good shot.”

“Make sure whatever you wear is real short and low-cut,” Phil said. “We need cleavage.”

“I’ll go home and change,” Sierra said. “But forget the cleavage thing. I love the *Curtain*, but I refuse to humiliate myself on the front cover.”

“Spoilsport,” Kay said.

Chapter 4

"WHAT DO YOU KNOW ABOUT SIERRA MCINTYRE?" COOPER Boone asked on the other end of the phone.

Fontana walked to the window, phone to his ear, and looked out over the ruins while he thought about the question.

Cooper, the head of the Aurora Springs Guild, was one of his few close friends. The bond between them had been established years earlier when, because of their unusual talents, they had found themselves doing some highly unorthodox jobs for the Bureau.

They were both technically hunters, meaning they could manipulate dissonance energy, but neither of them worked traditional green ghost light. The teams that went underground tended to be traditionalists. Hunters who worked light from other places on the spectrum were not welcome on the exploration ventures. Exotic hunters tended to follow one of two career paths. They either became criminals or they got hired by the Bureau. Once in a while, however, like Cooper and himself, they wound up at the top of one of the organizations.

"What do I know about Sierra?" Fontana repeated. "Well, I think it's safe to say that I'm marrying up."

"What does that mean?"

"She's the daughter of Jason McIntyre."

There was a short pause on the other end of the line.

"Any connection to McIntyre Industries in Resonance?" Cooper finally asked.

"She's Jason McIntyre's youngest daughter."

"You're joking."

"I'm getting married in two hours. Trust me, I'm not in a joking mood."

"What the hell is a McIntyre doing working for a low-rent tabloid like the *Curtain*? Women like her sit on the boards of charitable foundations and eat lunch at their clubs."

"I did a little checking. She comes from a long line of women who do things in addition to the usual charitable foundation and luncheon gigs."

"Such as?" Cooper asked.

"Her mother teaches philosophy at Resonance College. One of her grandmothers is a doctor. The other one ran a successful architectural design business for several years before she retired. There's an aunt who paints and another aunt who writes. And then there's the male side of the family tree."

"I know something about them. Father is CEO of McIntyre Industries. Two of her brothers work in the business. The other teaches, I think."

"Mathematics."

Cooper roared with laughter. "Sounds like you're marrying into a family of overachievers. Serves you right, seeing as how you qualify as one yourself. Congratulations."

"You can save the congratulations. I doubt that the marriage will last very long after Sierra's relatives discover that she's married to a Guild chief who also happens to be a genuine bastard."

"Don't jump to conclusions," Cooper advised. "From what I've heard, the McIntyres as a clan resonate to a different frequency."

"I don't care how independent-minded they are. People that rich and that influential don't let their daughters marry outside their social circles, let alone marry bastards."

There was no need for either of them to comment further, Fontana thought. Although the laws theoretically protected children born out of wedlock and were designed to try to ensure that both parents took equal responsibility for their illegitimate offspring, there was no avoiding the fact that being born a bastard still carried a stigma. In a society that placed a massive emphasis on marriage and family ties, there was little room for someone like him.

His story was one of the oldest in the book. His mother had been a cocktail waitress. His father had been a wealthy man in a Covenant Marriage who had been looking for a little fun.

"Sierra agreed to cooperate with your investigation?" Cooper asked.

"Yes."

"So this MC is purely a business arrangement?"

"Right."

"She must be very hungry for the story if she's willing to marry for it," Cooper said thoughtfully. "Any idea what triggered her interest in Jenner and the drug operation in the first place?"

"It started with some negative pieces she did on the Guild. There were a lot of stories about how many retired Guild men were living on the streets of Crystal and how the Guild ignored their plight."

Guild men tended to begin their careers early, usually in their late teens; not surprising since dissonance energy para-rez talent was strongly correlated to testosterone and other male hormones. That basic biological fact also went a long way toward explaining the very small number of female hunters in the ranks, although it was considered politically incorrect to point out the connection.

Pensions and so-called "fry pay"—disability benefits—were of vital importance in the Guild organizations. Hunters not only started out early, they usually ended their careers within twenty years; many quit long before that. It was no secret that frying ghosts for a living provided limited long-term career options. In addition, the work took a psychic toll. Guild men who hung around the catacombs too long lost their edge and got careless. Getting careless underground could not only get you badly burned, it put the clients in jeopardy. That was not good for the organization's image.

The end result was that if a hunter did not move up into management within the Guild, he usually retired before the age of forty. That meant that a lot of used-up hunters found themselves unemployed with no useful work skills. The retirement benefit plans were generous, but ex-hunters had a bad habit of blowing their monthly checks on the same traditional vices they had enjoyed during their working years: women, gambling, and booze. And now, here in Crystal, on juice.

"After the attacks on the Guild's failure to look after their retirees, Sierra started doing pieces on the ghost juice problem," Fontana continued. "She pointed out that most of the addicts were ex-hunters. Then came the stories about the disappearances. The headlines in the *Curtain* claimed that men were being kidnapped off the streets by aliens. Fortunately, the mainstream media ignored the reports."

"You have to admit it's hard to take that kind of tabloid nonsense seriously," Cooper said.

"I did a little checking. Sierra's reporting was accurate, at least up to a point. Nearly a dozen ex-hunters, maybe more, have vanished in the past six months. They were all juice heads living in alleys or in abandoned buildings in the Quarter. Not the kind of upstanding citizens who get noticed when they disappear."

"They sure as hell weren't kidnapped by aliens," Cooper said.

"No, but something happened to them. They're my men now. I'm responsible for them."

"Understood." Cooper was quiet for a moment. "You really think Sierra McIntyre can help you find out what's going on over there in Crystal?"

"She's getting her information from somewhere. I'm pretty sure that she's got contacts on the streets that I don't have. And there's something else."

"What?"

"She's just about the only person besides Ray that I can trust here in Crystal at the moment."

Ray Takashima was one of them, another former Bureau employee. The bonds between all of them had been forged in ghost fire and would never be broken.

"You and Ray always made a good team," Cooper said. "But if I were you, I'd keep a close eye on your new bride. You don't really know that much about her. Sounds like getting the scoop and bashing the Guild are her top priorities, not playing Guild wife."

"If I thought I could convince her to walk away from the story, I would. But she's sunk her teeth into it, and I can tell she's not the type to let go. My only other option is to try to protect her by throwing the mantle of the Chamber around her."

"Sounds like a solid foundation for a marriage, if ever there was one," Cooper said. "Can't wait to see the cover of tomorrow's edition of the *Curtain*. Don't forget the ring."

Chapter 5

THE UNNERVING WHISPER OF ENERGY FEATHERED THE FINE hair on the nape of Sierra's neck the moment she parked her battered little Float at the curb. The fog had lightened somewhat in the afternoon, but the Quarter was still wrapped in a ragged gray blanket. She could see only as far as the intersection.

She got out cautiously, Elvis perched on her shoulder. He muttered a little.

"You sense it, too, don't you?" she asked softly.

Elvis seemed alert but not unduly alarmed. His calm response reassured her. If there had been an imminent threat, he would no longer look like something that had come out of the inside of a vacuum cleaner. He would be sleeked out in full battle-ready mode, his second set of eyes, the ones he used for hunting, wide open.

She stood on the curb for a moment, surveying the

narrow street. There was the usual ambient alien psi that permeated the Quarter, but it was a pleasant, lightly stimulating sensation. That wasn't what was ruffling her intuitive senses. What she was experiencing was the same sensation that had made it impossible to sleep last night; the creepy feeling that she was being observed from the shadows.

She looked around but saw nothing out of the ordinary. By day Jade Street was always imbued with a slightly seedy, down-at-the-heels atmosphere. The impression was magnified this afternoon because of the ominous gloom of the relentless fog. Nevertheless, this was not a dangerous section of the Quarter.

The two-hundred-year-old Colonial-era buildings that loomed on either side housed a mix of what the newspaper ads like to call "affordable" apartments, such as the one she lived in, a number of low-end antiquities shops that specialized in alien and First Generation relics, a convenience store, and a tavern called the Green Gate.

Unlike some of the other streets in the Quarter, there was no obvious drug dealing going on in the doorways, and no hookers lounged or strolled beneath the old-fashioned streetlights. The women of the night preferred the sleazier neighborhoods on the east and west side of the towering green wall that enclosed the ruins.

"Okay, pal," she said to Elvis. "Here we go."

Elvis chortled happily and leaned forward when she stepped off the curb and hurried toward the entrance of her apartment building. He liked to go fast. Actually, he got excited about anything that promised a bit of an adrenaline rush. Probably all the caffeine, Sierra thought. Then again, maybe it was the predator in him. Underneath all that adorable gray fuzz beat the heart of a natural-born hunter. Dust bunnies, she had discovered, were omnivorous, but they were definitely not vegetarians.

She rezzed the security lock, opened the door, and moved into the small, dark hallway. The manager, Sacker, or the Slacker, as he was known to the tenants, still had not replaced the overhead light. The only illumination came from the dim wall sconces on the landings above. She paused again, waiting to see if the sensation of being watched faded now that she was indoors. It didn't.

"You think maybe I'm going over the edge and getting downright paranoid?" she said aloud to Elvis. "I'd hate to think that when I look at the Runt, I'm seeing my future."

Elvis mumbled something. He was either offering reassurance or asking for a treat. It was hard to tell the difference sometimes.

She went quickly up the shadowed stairs to the third-floor landing and rezzed the lock of her own door. The tiny one-bedroom apartment was tranquil and welcoming. Once inside, Elvis bounded down from her shoulder and disappeared into the kitchen. By the time she arrived, he was on the counter in front of his treat jar.

She raised the lid and waited. Elvis liked to make his own choice. He fluttered up to sit on the rim of the jar. Maintaining his grip with his hind legs, he leaned down and selected a chocolate cookie from the little heap inside.

"That's it for now, King." She replaced the cookie jar lid. "I've got to go change. I wonder what a girl's supposed to wear to a tacky MC wedding. That wasn't covered at Miss Pendergast's Academy for Young Ladies. Guess I flunked out before we got to that subject."

Her short term at what her mother had called a "silly finishing school" had been her own idea. It had seemed like a good one at the time. Several girls in her class had spent a year getting "polished" at Miss Pendergast's. As the notoriously unsuccessful, unfocused underachiever in a family of successful, focused overachievers, she had been lured by the promise of instant sophistication. In her seventeen-year-old fantasies she had seen herself emerging from the academy with elegant social skills and a worldly attitude that would instantly catapult her into a successful, *achieving* life.

But boredom had set in after the first week. She had quickly discovered that devising themes for elegant parties and paying exquisite attention to the details of interior design and table settings had an extremely limited appeal. She had been "counseled out," as the saying went, at the end of the first quarter. She suspected that the only reason she hadn't been asked to leave sooner was because of her family name. The director had been very reluctant to offend a McIntyre.

The entire episode had become just another family joke, one of many founded on her inability to find her passion, as her grandmother Larken liked to say. Grandmother Larken, from whom Sierra had inherited her intuitive talents, was the only one who had ever really understood her. When things went wrong, as they inevitably did, Sierra knew she could turn to the older woman for comfort and advice. But there was no point calling her this afternoon. Like everyone else in the family, Grandmother Larken disapproved of MCs.

Sierra made her way into the bedroom, stripping off her jacket and skirt as she went. She opened the door of her closet and surveyed the contents.

Her wardrobe was a mix of a few of the high-end clothes she had brought with her from Resonance and the more moderate apparel that she had bought for her new life here in Crystal. The last thing she wanted to do was cause her colleagues at the *Curtain* to think that she was a wealthy socialite who was merely amusing herself with a short-term career as a reporter. No one at the *Curtain* knew that she was connected to the McIntyres of McIntyre Industries, and she intended to keep things that way.

For some reason the decision of what to wear to the registrar's office was a lot more difficult than it ought to have been, given the circumstances. When Elvis drifted in, cookie in paw, and took up a position on the windowsill, she turned to him for advice.

"This is a business arrangement," she explained. "Does that mean another suit? Then again, it's supposed to look like a real wedding. Maybe I should wear something a little more formal. Lord knows there will be photos. Fontana and I are going to be plastered across the cover of the *Curtain* tomorrow. Hope he realizes what he's in for now that he's decided to go over to the dark side of journalism."

Elvis munched his cookie. She thought he looked like he was trying to be supportive and helpful, but she couldn't be sure.

A glance at the clock told her that time was getting short. She had to make an executive decision, and she had to make it right now. She yanked the simple, long-sleeved, black, all-occasion dress off the hanger and pulled it on over her head. Everything about it was discreet, understated, and elegant; not too dressy for late afternoon but with enough flair to go smoothly into the evening. She knew that because her cousin Tamsyn had helped her select it. Tamsyn had unerring taste in clothes.

"Tamsyn says you can never go wrong with a little black dress," she explained to Elvis.

She found the pair of black pumps on the floor of the closet, slipped some gold hoops into her ears, and rushed into the bathroom to apply lipstick and a little fresh powder. When she looked into the mirror, only one word came to mind.

"Aargh," she said to Elvis, who had drifted in to watch. "My hair."

In desperation she seized one of her array of headbands and slapped it on her head. It was the only way to tame the raging sea of curls.

Hurrying out into the hall, she shrugged into a light overcoat, grabbed her purse, and raced for the door with

Elvis back on her shoulder. Picking up on her sense of urgency, he muttered enthusiastically.

She went back down the stairs and out onto the street. The fog had thickened. That was going to slow traffic even further. There was a good chance now that she might actually be late to the wedding. Somehow she did not think that Fontana would appreciate that. Guild bosses were probably accustomed to punctuality from others.

She stepped out into the empty street. Halfway across, cold dread and icy panic swept through her senses, an invisible gale-force wind that stole her very breath.

Instinctively, she stopped. Elvis went immediately from a ball of fluff to a sleek little predator, all four eyes showing. He growled softly in her ear. She looked around frantically. This was the same feeling she'd experienced this afternoon just before the Oscillator 600 had nearly flattened her. But there were no vehicles in sight, and she heard no engine.

She searched first one end of the street and then the other, turning on her heel. Nothing moved in the gray mist.

What's wrong with me? Maybe I'm losing it. Too much stress. Not enough sleep.

Elvis muttered again, more urgently this time. She realized that all four of his eyes were focused behind her.

She swung around and finally saw him: a dark, shadowy figure moving out of a doorway. He came purposefully toward her. Elvis growled again and whipped around to stare at another doorway on the opposite side of the street. A second man moved out of another vestibule and glided toward her car.

They were close enough now that she could make out the black leather jackets, leather chaps, and the black motorcycle helmets worn by both men. The visors of the helmets were pulled down, obscuring their features.

Night Riders. There had been a flurry of reports about the gang in the mainstream press lately. The police had started special patrols in certain neighborhoods, but not this one. There had been no trouble here.

Obviously, the situation had changed.

She weighed her options. She would never make it to the safety of her car. Retreating back to her apartment building was equally impossible. That left only one alternative.

"Hang on," she said to Elvis.

Clutching her purse, she ran for the door of the Green Gate Tavern. Her high-heeled pumps skittered treacherously on the pavement, but she made it to the sidewalk.

The Riders had not anticipated her choice of destination, but they changed course quickly. Both of them broke into a run. The ominous thuds of their boots echoed in the fog.

Elvis clung fiercely to her shoulder, teeth bared. She sensed that if they were cornered, he would try to attack the Riders. That was the last thing she wanted. He would be no match for the two men or the mag-rez guns they were no doubt carrying. Theoretically, it was illegal for anyone but a duly authorized member of a law enforcement agency to carry a mag-rez, but that had done little to keep them out of the hands of criminals.

One of the men partially raised his helmet.

"Get her," he shouted to his companion.

The other one needed no urging. They moved in on her from two directions. She vaguely realized that no shots had been fired. That was probably a good sign. Evidently they didn't intend to shoot her dead in the street.

But what did they want? According to what she had read, purse snatching wasn't the gang's style. They were into more sophisticated businesses: extortion and drugs.

She was only a few feet away from the front door of the Green Gate when the heel of her left shoe snapped, throwing her violently to the side. She went down hard on the wet pavement. Her coat protected her from a bad case of road rash, but she knew she would have bruises in the morning. Elvis leaped from her shoulder.

She stared at the door of the Green Gate, willing it to open.

"Help." What she had intended as a full-throated shout for assistance came out as a weak yelp.

Adrenaline got her back on her feet in an instant. Miraculously, her glasses were still on her nose. She staggered on the broken heel and almost went down a second time.

The nearest Rider closed in fast. His associate was not far behind.

"Damn bitch," the first Rider growled. He reached for

her with a black-gloved hand. "I'm gonna show you what happens to women who give me trouble."

She was aware of a flash of movement at the corner of her eye. Then she saw Elvis. He dashed up the Rider's leather-clad pant leg, white cape flying. She realized that he was heading for the only portion of the Rider's body that was not encased in leather: the small, vulnerable area at his throat.

An instant later the Rider screamed in pain and astonishment. He shoved up his visor and scrambled back, batting wildly at his neck.

"Something bit me," he yelped. "Get it off me. Shit, I'm *bleeding*."

The other Rider paused. "What in green hell?"

Sierra half staggered, half ran for the Green Gate. "*Elvis*. Come here. Hurry."

He was already on his way back down the Rider's pant leg. He reached the pavement, deftly avoiding a kick from a heavy black leather boot, and scampered toward her.

"I just got bit by a rat," the injured Rider yelled. "I'm gonna need shots."

The other man ignored him. He charged after Sierra.

She shoved open the tavern door and stumbled inside.

Three khaki-and-leather-clad men lounged on stools at the bar. Simon Lugg, the proprietor, looked at her.

"Sierra?" he said. "What's wrong?"

"Night Riders," she got out, whirling to slam the door shut. "Call the cops. Hurry."

It was too late to get the door closed, let alone lock it.

One of the Riders shoved it open with such force that Sierra was thrown back against the nearest booth.

The Riders surged into the room. One had a hand clamped to the side of his neck. Both raised their visors higher in order to see in the eternal gloom that was the Green Gate.

"Nobody moves, nobody gets hurt," the first Rider barked. "We just want the woman."

"Sorry, I've got a real strict dress code here at the Green Gate," Simon said. "No tie, no service."

"Shut up, old man," the second Rider snarled. He reached into the pocket of his black jacket.

"Man, I really hate being called old," Simon said.

"Look out," Sierra shouted. "I think he's got a gun."

"Who doesn't?" Simon asked, producing a mag-rez from under the bar.

There was a moment of profound stillness as both sides contemplated the standoff. The three patrons swiveled on their stools. They studied the newcomers with keen interest.

"Well, well, well," Mitch Crozier said. "What have we got here? Couple of biker wannabes, you think?"

"Nah." Jeff Duvall shook his head. "Looks more like they just came off a movie set."

"Whoever the hell they are," Andy Bunt announced with a toothy grin, "they wandered into the wrong neighborhood."

Mitch chuckled with anticipation. The tiny chunk of crystal set into his front tooth gleamed. "That they did."

The Riders finally began to comprehend that they had blundered badly.

"We don't want any trouble with you guys," the first one said. "Like I told you, we're after the woman."

"Can't have her," Simon announced. "She's a friend. Don't know how it is with you Riders, but hunters look after their friends."

The atmosphere in the gloom-filled bar suddenly shivered with energy. Four wildly flaring balls of green fire materialized directly in front of the two Riders and began drifting toward them.

"Ghost light," the injured Rider said, backing quickly toward the door. He seemed genuinely awed. "Shit."

"Yeah, who would have thought a bunch of washed-up hunters could still pull a lot of green heat aboveground?" Simon said with menacing good cheer.

Even the most powerful hunters could not maneuver a flaring ball of dissonance energy quickly. At best a ghost could only be driven at about the speed of a fast walk. But the erratic, acid-colored psi fire was scary stuff, especially in a confined space. Sierra knew that even the slightest brush with one of the UDEMs would be enough to knock the Riders unconscious.

The intruders understood that, too. Swearing furiously, they nearly trampled each other on their way out of the tavern. A few seconds later they disappeared into the fog.

Inside the Gate, the ghosts winked out.

The muffled thunder of motorcycle engines sounded

out in the street. Two black cycles flashed past the window and vanished.

Simon made the illegal mag-rez go away under the bar. "You okay, Sierra?"

"Yes, I think so." She collapsed onto the nearest vinyl seat, shivering with reaction. Anxiously, she peered around. "Elvis? Where are you?"

He bounced at her feet, fully fluffed once more, only his blue eyes showing. She leaned down, seized him in both hands, picked him up, and kissed him in the vicinity of the top of his furry head.

"My hero," she said. "Oh, dear, you lost your sunglasses."

"Jake can make him another pair," Andy said.

"I hope so. Elvis loves those dark glasses." She plopped him on her shoulder and surveyed the four men. "Actually, you're all my heroes today. On behalf of Elvis and myself, I'd just like to say thank you, thank you very much."

They grinned.

"Just takin' care of business, ma'am," Simon said modestly. "Like the King here expects us to do."

She smiled at the four. Over the course of the past six months, she had come to know the small group of aging, retired hunters very well. They were regulars here at the Green Gate in the afternoons when they gathered to drink beer, play cards, and reminisce about their glory days down in the catacombs.

Mitch and Jeff were life partners who had formalized

their relationship with a Covenant Marriage shortly after leaving the guild. They operated a small antiquities shop at the end of Jade Street. Andy played a lot of cards and went to the races. Simon owned the Green Gate. At night the tavern was a favorite haunt for ex-hunters. One way or another, all of the stories she had done on the Guild were a result of her friends here at the Gate.

"Where in green hell did those guys come from?" Andy asked, reaching for his beer. "We haven't had any problem with the Riders around here before."

"I don't know," she said. She was safe now, but the unease that had been making her restless for the past couple of days was as strong as ever. "It was as if they were waiting for me when I left my apartment."

Simon frowned. "Think it's related to one of your stories in the *Curtain*?"

She shuddered. "I don't see how. I've never done a piece on the Riders. All of my investigative reporting has been focused on the Guild and the disappearances."

"You mentioned the damage that the ghost juice is causing here in the Quarter," Mitch reminded her. "Word is the Riders are behind the dealing. Maybe they wanted to throw a scare into you. Tell you to keep your mouth shut."

"I've done pieces on the victims of juice but not on the Riders themselves," Sierra said. "In fact, I've blamed the Guild for not doing more to take care of the hunters who become addicts."

"Speaking of which," Simon said, "how did your interview with the new boss go today?"

A fresh wave of panic lanced through her. She leaped to her feet and nearly toppled over when she automatically put weight on the shoe with the broken heel. "Good grief, I almost forgot."

Mitch's forehead wrinkled. "Forgot what?"

"I'm supposed to meet Fontana at a quarter to five." She checked her watch. "That's less than fifteen minutes from now. Come on, Elvis, we have to hurry."

She limped toward the door.

"Hold on," Simon said. "Why are you meeting the new Guild boss again this afternoon?"

She opened the door. "I forgot to tell you that I'm marrying him."

There were a few seconds of stunned silence behind her. Then she heard a sudden scrambling and the scrape of bar-stool legs. Boots hit the old amberwood floors.

She paused and looked back. Mitch, Jeff, Andy, and Simon were rushing to follow her out the door, practically tripping over each other in the process.

"What?" she said.

"You'll be needing witnesses," Mitch said.

"And a driver," Simon added, snapping her keys out of her hand. "After that little incident with the Riders, you're way too shaken up to drive."

She frowned. "I am?"

"For sure," Jeff said, nodding wisely. "Simon hasn't

had anything to drink except coffee. He's your designated driver."

"And on the way to the wedding, you can tell us exactly how the hell you wound up getting hitched to Fontana," Simon said.

Chapter 6

THE LITTLE FLOAT CAREENED AROUND THE CORNER, TIRES squealing, and screeched to a halt in front of the office tower that housed the city's various bureaucracies. The building was a gray, uninspired, all-purpose government structure. You could pay your taxes on the second floor, sign a Marriage of Convenience contract on the fourth, and report for your court appearance on the fifth.

From her position in the front seat, Sierra could see a small cluster of people gathered at the entrance. Ivor Runtley, Kay, Matt, and Phil were clustered around Fontana and a second, dark-haired, dark-eyed man she recognized from news photos. Ray Takashima was the newly appointed head of the Crystal City Guild's Security Department. Like Fontana, he had seemingly materialized out of nowhere a couple of years ago and moved up fast within the organization.

"Damn," Simon said. "Fontana's already here. That makes us officially late."

"It's okay," Jeff said. He was in the backseat, squashed between Mitch and Andy. The rear of the Float had not been designed to carry three burly hunters. "We've got the bride. Brides are allowed to be late."

"Way I hear it, nobody is late for an appointment with Fontana," Andy put in ominously. "At least not more than once."

"Oh, for heaven's sake, don't worry about it," Sierra said. "It's just an MC. Besides, we've got a really good excuse."

"Right, the Riders," Andy said, brightening. "Maybe Fontana will buy it."

"It's not as though he has a choice," Sierra said coolly. The hunters' awe of Fontana was starting to become very irritating.

"Everyone out," Simon ordered. "There's no room to park on the street. I'll leave the car in the city garage and join you in a few minutes."

Sierra popped open the passenger door and climbed out cautiously on her broken heel. Elvis perched on her shoulder, still buzzing with excitement after the wild ride from the Quarter.

Phil detached himself from the group at the entrance and rushed toward the Float. He raised his camera into position as he ran.

Fontana followed him very deliberately. He was dressed in the black jacket, shirt, and trousers he'd worn earlier in the day. The expression on his hard face was unreadable, but that didn't stop Sierra's intuitive senses. She was suddenly fully rezzed, just as she had been that morning when she was shown into Fontana's office at Guild headquarters.

Get a grip, woman. There was nothing personal about any of this. Fontana planned to use her just as she planned to use him. This was all about finding out what had happened to those missing men. She had to stay focused.

She stood precariously balanced on her one good heel and waited for Jeff, Mitch, and Andy to squeeze out of the tiny backseat.

"Cool," Phil said, rezzing his camera again and again. "This is like one of those little cars at the circus that are filled with clowns."

Jeff squinted at Phil. "Who are you calling a clown, son?"

"Sorry," Phil said, firing off more shots. "Slip of the tongue. Sierra, turn this way. Chin up, that's right. Now smile. You're supposed to look like you're in love, not like you're going to a funeral."

Fontana arrived. "Let's save the photo ops for later," he said.

It was not a suggestion. Sierra was amazed to see Phil actually lower his camera. Fontana took Sierra's arm.

"Apologies for the delay, sir," Simon said, leaning forward to speak to Fontana through the open door of the Float. "Sierra had a little problem. The guys can explain it."

"Let's hope so." Fontana surveyed Sierra. "Are you all right?"

"Yes," she managed, pleased that she sounded relatively calm in spite of her skittering senses. "How bad do I look?"

It dawned on her that she had not checked a full-length mirror since the fall in the street and the mad dash to safety in the Green Gate. She probably appeared somewhat the worse for wear.

"I don't care how it looks," Fontana said. "I'm asking about the damage."

"Oh." She noticed that her glasses were slightly crooked. She adjusted them and then looked down at her muddied coat. In the process she saw that her stockings were shredded. "A couple of bruises, I think, and my shoe is ruined, but that's about it."

"What happened?" he asked.

"It's a long story," she said. "I'll tell you later."

"I want the story now," he said quietly.

He probably couldn't help that air of command, she thought. Nevertheless, she was not in the mood for it.

"In case you haven't noticed," she said, "everyone's waiting for us."

That information did not seem to register. Fontana made no move to steer her toward the waiting onlookers.

Andy cleared his throat. "Couple of Night Riders tried to grab her purse in front of her apartment building, boss. She took a nasty fall in the street."

"We ran the bastards off with a few ghosts," Mitch explained.

"Don't worry," Jeff said. "They won't be back anytime soon. We explained to them that Jade Street is hunter territory."

Sierra blinked. "Well, what do you know. Guess it was a short story, after all. Could have sworn it would take longer to tell it."

Fontana tightened his grip on her arm. She winced and sucked in a sharp breath.

"What?" he said, loosening his grasp.

"That's the side I fell on when I tripped," she explained. "It's a little sore."

He released her swiftly and took her other arm. This time his hand closed around her with a tenderness that surprised her.

"Are you certain that they were Night Riders?" he asked.

"Or a good imitation thereof," she said dryly. "They were in full costume. Black helmets and lots of black leather."

"And big black Wave bikes," Jeff volunteered. "They're a Rider trademark."

Fontana looked at the four men. "I owe each of you, gentlemen. Anytime. Anywhere."

It was a somber vow. Jeff, Mitch, Simon, and Andy accepted it as such. The new Guild boss had openly declared himself in their debt. Sierra knew enough about

Guild tradition to realize that was a very big deal. The four men had just been given the right to call on the most powerful man in the organization for a favor at any time in the future.

"Glad to be able to help out," Jeff said. "Sierra's a friend of ours."

Fontana nodded. He looked as if he wanted to discuss the matter further and in depth, but to Sierra's surprise, he shot a quick glance at his watch.

"We're due in the registrar's office," he said. "I'll look into this later."

Startled by the hard edge on the words, Sierra pushed her glasses higher on her nose.

"It was just an attempted purse snatching," she said. "The cops almost never pick up those kinds of criminals, not unless they're caught red-handed."

"There are other sources besides the police," Fontana said evenly.

A chill went down her spine, but before she could ask any questions, he steered her toward the entrance where her colleagues were waiting.

Fontana nodded at Ray Takashima, who also wore the Guild exec black.

"Ray, I'd like you to meet my future wife, Sierra McIntyre," Fontana said. "Sierra, this is Ray Takashima. He's a friend of mine."

"How do you do, Mr. Takashima?" She extended her hand. "I've seen you on the evening news a couple of times."

Ray gave her an easy, friendly smile that totally belied the power she knew that he wielded.

"A pleasure, Miss McIntyre, and please call me Ray," he said. He eyed Elvis. "Is that a dust bunny?"

"Yes," she said. "His name is Elvis."

"Didn't know they made good pets."

"They don't. Elvis is a companion, not a pet."

"Got it," Ray said. "I hope you don't mind me attending your wedding. Figured Fontana might need someone to prop him up in case he got a bad case of nerves. His first MC, you know."

"Yes, I know," she said without stopping to think. "I checked out the public records."

Ray laughed. "Watch your step, Fontana, you're marrying a journalist. That means she knows how to do research."

She had been a little amazed that there were no Marriages of Convenience cluttering up Fontana's past. At his age, it would not have been at all out of the ordinary for him to have been involved in a least a couple. As a group, Guild men were known to be somewhat reckless when it came to their love lives. When they did finally settle down into Covenant Marriages, they tended to marry within the Guild. Perhaps Fontana preferred the freedom that came with casual affairs.

That thought gave her a bit of a start. From what she had been able to discover in her hurried background check, Fontana had been unusually discreet in his private life. She had not uncovered any hint of a current mistress, but that didn't mean there wasn't one. If a mystery woman existed, she probably wasn't too excited about the prospect of Fontana entering into an MC with some other woman, even if the arrangement was strictly business.

Ivor Runtley frowned at her. "What the hell happened to you?"

"Long story," Sierra said again. "At least, it seemed like it at the time."

"You look like you got hit by a bus," Matt offered helpfully.

She gave him a dazzling smile. "Gee, thanks, Matt. You really know how to boost a girl's spirits."

"Forget him." Kay grabbed her hand. "Come on, we've got to get you to the ladies' room and perform some running repairs."

"Not now," Fontana said, opening the front door. "We're late enough as it is. Let's get this done. You can clean her up later."

Sierra walked into the lobby, swung around to face him, and dug in her one unbroken heel.

" 'Let's get this done'?" she repeated ominously.

Ray winked at her. "As you can see, Fontana has the soul of a true romantic."

Sierra raised her chin. "I want to stop at the ladies' room first."

"Of course she does," Kay said. She lifted Elvis down from Sierra's shoulder and handed him to Matt. "Here, you take the King. We'll meet you all at the registrar's office on the fourth floor."

She whisked Sierra toward the nearest elevator.

"No, wait," Sierra said quickly.

"Right, sorry," Kay said. "Forgot about your claustrophobia."

She altered course, dragging Sierra toward the stairwell. The last thing Sierra saw before she limped up the stairs was the expression on Fontana's face. He didn't look angry, she thought, or even annoyed. He looked bemused.

"I get the impression that Fontana isn't used to having someone contradict his orders," Kay observed, pausing to catch her breath.

"I get that impression, too," Sierra said.

When they reached the fourth floor, Kay led the way into the room marked Ladies.

"Take off your coat," she said. "Let's see what we've got to work with."

Obediently Sierra slipped off the mud-splattered coat.

Kay's eyes widened with dazed horror. "Sierra McIntyre, tell me you did not wear black to your own wedding."

Baffled, Sierra looked down at the demure, long-sleeved black dress. "What's wrong with it?"

"This is a wedding, not a funeral," Kay wailed.

"The groom is in black," Sierra said, feeling on the defensive.

"So what? It's okay for the groom to wear black. Oh, never mind. Too late now. But just wait until you see what this looks like in tomorrow's edition of the *Curtain*. You are going to be so sorry."

"Why?"

"I can see the headline now. 'New Guild Boss and Mystery Woman Wed in Secret Alien Vampire Ceremony.' "

Sierra narrowed her eyes. "If the word *vampire* appears in that headline, I promise you, there will be vengeance."

"I dunno," Kay said seriously, "sounds like a grabber to me."

Simon was just stepping out of the elevator when they emerged from the ladies' room.

"Great," he said. "You waited for me." He offered Sierra his arm and gave her a surprisingly graceful little bow. "Allow me to escort the bride."

"Thank you," she said.

The staff in the registrar's office was in a state of near-giddy excitement. Guild bosses were always high profile, and Fontana qualified as a celebrity. The fact that the crew of the *Curtain* had shown up to cover the wedding heightened the thrill factor for everyone. Phil took pictures as fast as he could rez his camera.

Elvis also created a small sensation.

"Look at the little dust bunny," a clerk cooed. "Isn't he just the cutest thing?"

"That little cape is absolutely adorable," another staff member said.

Never one to miss a moment in the spotlight, Elvis posed on the counter.

"No offense," Kay muttered to Sierra, "but he looks better than you do."

"Well, sure," Sierra said. "He's Elvis."

There was more paperwork than she had expected, and now that the adrenaline had worn off, she was starting to feel the bruising from her fall. Her left arm and shoulder were going to be very colorful in the morning.

When she had to tear up one of the forms because she'd put down her old address in Resonance instead of her new one in Crystal, she realized she was grinding her teeth.

She could not help but notice that Fontana did not appear to be having any difficulties with his forms. No do-overs for a Guild boss.

Eventually they got to the final stretch. The judge introduced herself as Maryann Partridge and, like the registrar's staff, seemed absolutely delighted to perform the civil ceremony for the new Guild chief.

Using the buzz of conversation as cover, Sierra leaned over to whisper in Kay's ear.

"Why is everyone acting as if this is some kind of major romantic event?" she asked. "These people do Marriages of Convenience day in and day out. They know better than anyone that they're nothing more than short-term affairs dignified by some legal trappings."

Kay looked genuinely shocked. "That's not true. They're real weddings."

Sierra started to argue but stopped when she realized

that a hush had fallen over the room and that everyone was looking at her.

Kay scooped up Elvis and held him as though he were a bridal bouquet while Judge Partridge launched into the ceremony.

"If I may have the rings," Partridge said brightly.

Sierra started violently. She had not given any thought to rings. Traditionally, silver rings were used in Marriages of Convenience. Gold was reserved for Covenant Marriages.

"I don't have a ring," she said.

Fontana seemed briefly amused by her anxiety.

"I have one," he said.

He removed his black and amber seal ring. She watched, a little shocked, as he slipped it onto her finger. It was much too big and far too heavy. Automatically, she closed her hand very tightly so that it wouldn't fall off.

Just a Marriage of Convenience. Don't panic.

The list of vows was shorter, more succinct, and a good deal less binding than those spoken at the more lengthy Covenant Marriage service. They were also a lot more businesslike. Nevertheless, Sierra got a small chill when she listened to herself repeat them to Fontana.

"I promise to remain faithful so long as we both are bound by this agreement . . .

"I promise to honor and respect our commitment to each other so long as we both are bound by this agreement . . .

"I understand that all worldly goods that belong to

me prior to this agreement are my sole possessions and will remain my sole possessions when this agreement is ended . . .

"I understand that if a child is born of this union, that this agreement will immediately become a full and binding Covenant Marriage agreement subject to all the laws and regulations pertaining thereunto . . ."

At last it was over. Sierra took a deep breath. She felt a trifle unsteady and not because of her broken heel. What in the world had she just done for the sake of the story of the decade?

"You may kiss the bride," Judge Partridge announced, beaming at Fontana.

Sierra felt all the air leave her lungs. *Should have seen that coming*.

It was too late to figure out a polite way to finesse the situation. The relentlessly cheerful crowd expected the traditional conclusion to the wedding ceremony. Fontana was already pulling her into his arms.

At his touch, she went still. The exciting whispers of energy that she had been trying to suppress suddenly flared into an intoxicating rush. A shiver of anticipation swept through her. This intense reaction was crazy. It was the result of the aftereffects of all the excitement. There was no other explanation.

Amusement and a shocking, mesmerizing heat gleamed in his eyes.

"Brace yourself, my dear, and think of Earth," he whispered for her ears alone.

The old joke elicited an unexpected burble of laughter from somewhere inside her.

And then he was kissing her, a slow, drugging, claim-staking kiss that slammed all of her senses into overdrive. She forgot that they had an audience. His mouth was the best thing she had ever tasted in her entire life, and she wanted more, a lot more. He responded by tightening his grip on her, crushing her against the broad, solid wall of his chest.

Sparkling thrills chased down her spine. Deliciously hot currents swirled. Liquid warmth pooled deep inside her. Somewhere out on the paranormal plane, energy flashed. Her psychic intuition did the happy dance.

Applause and cheering broke out, shattering the crystalline aura of intimacy into a million fragments. Reality came crashing back.

Dazed, Sierra opened her eyes. She was still pressed tightly against Fontana, but he was no longer kissing her.

"You can let him go now, Sierra," Phil called loudly. "I've got plenty of good shots."

Laughter splashed through the registrar's office.

She was stunned to discover that her arms had somehow wound themselves around Fontana's neck. She was holding on to him as though she were lost in the catacombs and he was her amber compass, as if she dared not let him go for fear of being lost forever.

Mortified, she released him and took a hasty step back, grabbing the edge of the counter to steady herself on her broken pump.

Immediately the hunters moved in on Fontana to shake his hand.

"Congratulations, sir," Simon said. "You're getting a real gutsy lady here. Good choice for a Guild boss's wife."

"And she can cook," Jeff added helpfully. "Wait until you try her chocolate chip cookies."

Fontana winked at Sierra. "I'll look forward to the experience."

He seemed more relaxed now that the business had been concluded. Fontana was not what anyone would call a jubilant bridegroom, Sierra thought, but he was definitely less grim. She groped for the right word and finally found it. He looked *satisfied*, the way a chess player would be after making an important move in a complicated strategy. In spite of the stress and the disorientation produced by the sizzling kiss, her intuition took note.

Coaxing her into this fake marriage had been important to him, perhaps even more important than she had realized. It was enough to make her wonder if maybe he had not told her everything concerning his plan for them to work as a team. The possibility that he considered her a useful pawn, not an equal partner, was disturbing. It was also infuriating.

Kay led the small group out of the registrar's office and down the stairs.

"Listen up, everyone," she announced when they reached the lobby "You're all invited back to the offices of the *Curtain*. It's not every day someone on the staff gets married. We're going to party. We've got cheap bubbly. We've got cheap food. We've got balloons."

"Are you inviting us, too?" Simon asked, angling his chin at Mitch, Jeff, and Andy.

"Of course," Kay said. She spread her arms wide. "You're all invited. Can't let a member of the *Curtain* get married without a major celebration."

Sierra glanced at Fontana, waiting for him to make some excuse to avoid the party. What would it be? she wondered. *Got to get back to the office. Got a late meeting. Got a dinner engagement with the mayor. Got a date with the woman I'm sleeping with.*

For some reason that last possibility robbed the moment of all amusement.

Fontana's mouth curved faintly, as though he knew precisely what she was thinking.

"Sounds like a great idea," he said, his eyes on Sierra. "A man ought to celebrate his own wedding."

Chapter 7

A LONG TIME LATER, SIERRA SAW FONTANA CHECK HIS watch. She had glanced at the clock on the wall a couple of minutes ago and knew that it was going on nine o'clock. Unfortunately, the *Curtain*'s version of a blowout wedding reception was in full swing and showed no signs of abating. In fact, it had taken on a life of its own after Classifieds had sent out for more beer and Marketing ordered in a second round of pizza.

Sierra was sitting behind her desk, elbows propped on the surface, her chin resting on her hands. Fontana lounged against the side, arms folded. He had asked her to dance earlier, but she had demurred on the twin grounds of the broken heel and incipient bruises. He had not pressed her.

The newsroom was draped in paper streamers and balloons. The trash cans beside each desk were crammed with empty bottles of cheap Spectrum Sparkling Wine, used paper plates, and napkins. The remains of a large, square cake sat on Kay's desk. The letters *HAP* from the originally inscribed *Happy Birthday George* were still visible. Kay had explained earlier that due to the extremely short notice, there had been no wedding cakes available at the bakery.

The rez-rock music blasting from the sound system had been cranked up to the point of pain. Desks had been pushed back to make room for the dancers. The lyrics of a current hit song blared forth.

Gonna take my lady underground tonight
We're gonna get rezzed on some hot ghost light

Her four friends from the Green Gate were all happily drunk. Andy was dancing with Liz, the curvy blonde who was Runtley's assistant. Ray Takashima and Kay were talking quietly in the corner. They both appeared completely absorbed in each other. Mitch and Jeff were regaling Phil Trager and the gang from Subscription Services with tales of their old glory days working ghost light down in the catacombs. Matt was finishing off the last bottle of Green Ruin beer. He had long ago abandoned the use of a paper cup.

"Probably not every woman's dream of a wedding reception," Fontana said, studying the scene.

"It was very nice of my friends to throw a party for us," she said, immediately defensive.

Fontana nodded, surprising her. "Yes, it was."

Elvis chose that moment to float past at eye level. Rezzed up on the coffee and cake that he had been sucking down all evening, he was clearly enjoying himself.

"Got a feeling I'm going to be investing heavily in balloons from now on," Sierra said.

"Looks like the bunny was born to fly," Fontana agreed.

Shortly after the second round of cheap wine, Mitch and Phil had hit upon the bright idea of getting Elvis airborne. The plan had involved a light cardboard tray designed to carry paper coffee cups and several of the helium-filled balloons that Kay had brought in to help decorate the newsroom.

The contraption had proved airworthy. Elvis had hopped into the makeshift basket, chortling in delight. With his small weight the miniature airship levitated gently to a height of about six feet off the floor. Delighted with the view from his new vantage point, he had spent most of the evening floating regally among the revelers.

Elvis chortled. Fontana obligingly sent him sailing off in a new direction. Elvis was practically beside himself with glee.

"Something tells me no one is going to miss the bride and groom if we leave," Fontana said.

"I think you're right." Sierra got to her feet. "It's been a long day. To tell you the truth, I'm surprised you hung around as long as you did tonight. It was very nice of you."

His jaw tightened, and his eyes narrowed faintly in response to her polite thanks.

"It's my wedding, too, remember?" he said.

She felt the heat rise in her face. "Well, yes, but since it's not a real wedding, I guess I just assumed you'd leave earlier. This can't be a Guild boss's idea of a good time."

"Shows how much you know about my private life." He straightened from the desk. "I'll get your coat."

"I'll get Elvis."

Elvis allowed himself to be plucked from the balloon's basket and tucked under her arm. When she turned, she saw Fontana waiting at the door with her coat. She thought they might make it out into the hall without anyone noticing, but luck ran out. A shout went up just as Fontana's hand curved around the doorknob.

"They're leaving," Matt announced in a loud voice. "Anyone got rice?"

"No rice," Simon said, "but no worries. We hunters use a different kind of send-off on occasions like this. Isn't that right, guys?"

"Damn right," Jeff declared, the words a little slurred. "This is a Guild wedding. Tradition must be followed."

Andy came to a halt on the dance floor, the blonde cuddled in one arm. "Wouldn't be right if we didn't follow hunter tradition."

Alarm galvanized Sierra. Hunters were very big on tradition, and a lot of those old traditions—dueling, came to mind—were appallingly macho and lamentably archaic. Any hunter tradition dealing with wedding nights could not be good.

"No, that's okay," she said hastily. She raised her free hand in a warding-off gesture. "This is just an MC."

She could have sworn she saw Fontana's jaw twitch.

Jeff leered. "Nobody ever said MCs weren't real weddings." He turned to the crowd. "What do you say, folks? Did the wedding look real to you?"

There was a roar of agreement from the crowd.

"That settles it," Simon announced. "It was a real wedding, all legal and everything. That means we gotta follow tradition. Stand aside, Sierra."

"Why?" she asked, deeply suspicious.

"Just do what the man says," Fontana advised.

Gently he pushed her away from him. She gave ground grudgingly. He took a couple of paces back, putting even more distance between them.

She felt a faint buzz of energy first. A few seconds later there was enough psi swirling in the room to give her goose bumps. Elvis wriggled in the crook of her arm and made excited little sounds.

Four hot balls of ghost fire swirled into existence, each about a foot across. The audience gasped. A low murmur went through the crowd.

"Set fire to my newsroom, and I'll sue the Guild," Runtley warned.

Andy chuckled. "Don't worry, we've got things under control here. This is a test for Fontana."

Deftly manipulated by Jeff, Simon, Andy, and Mitch, the ghosts lined up in a row between Fontana and Sierra.

A fifth ball of energy flared and took its place directly in front of Sierra. Involuntarily, she took another quick step back. She was no expert, but it was obvious that the new ghost was hotter and more tightly wound than the others.

"I'm the best man," Ray said. "Wouldn't be right if I didn't help with the send-off."

"Oh, damn," Sierra said.

Fontana leaned one shoulder against the wall, folded his arms, and contemplated the ghosts as though they were novel inventions he'd never seen before in his life.

"This is for you, Sierra," Jeff explained earnestly. "The boss is going to show that he's worthy of you."

"The only way he gets you is if he gets through our ghosts first," Simon said.

Kay giggled. There was a lot more muffled laughter in the room, mostly from the women.

This was not about proving anything to the bride, Sierra thought. It was about generating a lot of ghost heat. It was common knowledge in certain quarters—hair salons and ladies' restrooms, for instance—that hunters got sexually aroused after working ghost light. It had something to do with the testosterone-heavy, bio-psi hormones that flooded their systems when they used their talents.

The rumors about their sexual prowess when they were in the midst of a post–ghost burn were not unfounded, according to women who had dated Guild men. There was a reason why the taverns and bars that catered to hunters in the Quarter were also popular with college women on spring break and bachelorette parties.

There was an old hunter saying—one of many—to the effect that it took a ghost to kill a ghost. The hunters expected Fontana to destroy their ghosts by rezzing one of his own and using it to neutralize the flaring balls of green fire that stood between him and Sierra.

"No offense," Sierra said, striving to project firm authority, "but you've all had a little too much to drink tonight. I really don't think any of you should be working ghost light in a confined space."

They ignored her, watching Fontana for his reaction.

"What do you say, boss?" Andy asked. "Is Sierra worth working your way through five ghosts?"

Fontana looked at her over the tops of the ghosts that bobbed between them.

"Oh, yes," he said, nerve-shatteringly serious. "She's worth it."

The controlled heat in his eyes was hotter than the UDEMs in front of her. She went still, aware of his desire on both the normal and the paranormal plane. She had sensed some of this masculine energy earlier today in his office, but now it was as if he had just lowered a barrier and let her see the full strength of it.

Once again the hair was stirring on the nape of her neck, but her reaction had nothing to do with the flashing, sparking ghosts that separated them. She was responding to Fontana with every fiber of her being. Heat spilled into her veins. She knew then that, whatever his reasons for the marriage, one thing was clear: her short-term husband wanted her.

Heaven help her, she wanted him, too. That was probably not a good thing. At the very least, it was a very dangerous thing.

Fontana did not move, did not even unfold his arms. He watched her with that dark, unnerving intensity that sent thrill after thrill through her.

More energy swirled in the room; not green ghost light this time; something else, something she had never seen before. She heard several startled gasps and murmurs around her.

A churning river of dark, pulsing shadows appeared. A few inches across and a yard long, it flowed and undulated in a curious wave pattern.

Elvis quivered with excitement. He was still fully fluffed, but his second set of eyes winked open. They glowed like warm amber.

Simon, Jeff, Andy, and Mitch were dumbfounded. Everyone else, with the exception of Ray, who was smiling, seemed speechless.

"I'll be damned," Simon breathed. "That's dark light. The rumors are true."

"Jeez," Jeff whispered. "No wonder he was able to take down Jenner in that duel."

"What the hell is dark light?" Runtley demanded, pushing through the staring onlookers. "Some kind of secret alien technology?"

"No," Ray said calmly. "It's dissonance energy like ghost light. But it comes from the dark end of the spectrum. Very few hunters can pull it."

The river of night flowed around one of the four ghosts, forming a whirlpool. The green ghost was sucked into the spinning darkness and disappeared.

One by one the balls of glaring ghost light were drawn into the whirlpool and extinguished. When the last one disappeared, the dark waves of psi evaporated.

Fontana walked straight to Sierra and swept her up in his arms. Elvis bounded up onto his shoulder.

"We'll be leaving now," Fontana said to the crowd.

The four hunters from the Green Gate sent up a rousing cheer. Everyone else joined in. Someone opened the door.

Fontana carried Sierra out into the hall. The door closed behind them.

Sierra managed to find her voice. "You can put me down now."

"You're not very heavy." He went toward the elevator.

"No, wait," she said. "I don't like elevators. Please."

He set her on her feet. They started down the stairs.

She gave him a sidelong glance. "What's with that dark light thing? Another mysterious Guild secret?"

Fontana put one hand on her arm to help her keep her balance.

"Let's just say that the Guilds have traditionally preferred to play down the fact that some hunters can work energy from different points on the spectrum."

"Right," she said, excitement humming through her. "A red-hot Guild secret. I knew it. You do realize that it will probably show up in the *Curtain* tomorrow?"

"Yes."

He sounded far too unconcerned.

She shot him another searching look. "But?"

He smiled slowly. "But it will be in the *Curtain*. Who, besides your readers, will believe it? None of the mainstream media will take it seriously."

She sighed. "You have a point. Runtley will probably give it a headline like 'Guild Discovers Secret Alien Technology.' "

Fontana's smile widened. "I'm counting on it."

They reached the lobby. Fontana pushed open the glass doors and allowed her to move past him into the damp, foggy night.

"There's a reason the Guilds keep their secrets," he said. "Unusual talents of any kind tend to make people nervous."

She could not argue with that statement.

"I realize that," she admitted.

"When the exotic talents in question belong to hunters, the fear factor is multiplied several times over," he said.

"Okay, I get that. The Guilds have enough public relations problems as it is. I can see why the organizations prefer not to advertise a lot of unusual para-rez talents."

"I'll let you in on another little secret. The Guild researchers have reluctantly concluded that alien psi can theoretically be pulled from any point along the spectrum of paranormal energy."

She stopped beside her car and dug out her key. "Why reluctantly?"

He opened the door for her. "Turns out that each band of psi light has its own distinctive properties. But no one has been able to chart the full range of the spectrum, let alone the various properties of all the individual bands."

"And some are bound to be very dangerous. Is that it?"

"All psi energy is power."

"And all power is potentially dangerous."

His brows rose. "Or useful, depending on your point of view. At this point, there are a lot of unknowns. Until we have more answers, the Guilds intend to keep their secrets."

She slipped into the front seat of the Float. He handed Elvis to her and closed the door. She lowered the window, uncertain what came next. How did you say a casual good night to the man you just married?

"Well, good night," she said politely.

"I'll follow you back to your apartment," he said.

"That won't be necessary."

"Sure it is. You'll want to pack a suitcase."

She stilled. "I beg your pardon?"

"You're spending the night at my house. I assume you'll need a few things."

It was as if all the oxygen had been sucked out of the atmosphere and replaced with pure psi. She felt lightheaded.

She managed to rally. "Look here, Fontana, if you think for one minute that fake wedding ceremony gives you any marital rights or that I'm interested in finding out if the rumors about hunters who are in the grip of an afterburn are true, you've got another thought coming."

He raised his brows slightly. "What rumors would those be?"

"Forget it." She bristled. "I'm not going there. This is supposed to be a business partnership, remember?"

He rested one hand on the roof of the Float.

She started to get nervous. Her sixth sense wasn't picking up any menacing vibes, but there was some serious energy in the atmosphere, and it wasn't alien psi.

"We're supposed to be married," he said calmly. "We've got lots of witnesses, thanks to you, and tomorrow morning we're going to be all over the *Curtain*."

"So? That was the plan."

"The plan isn't going to work very well if you insist on separate quarters," he said patiently.

Why hadn't she considered this aspect of the situation a little more closely? Because she had been rushing around madly all day, that was why. Fontana had given her very little time to think. In hindsight, that had probably not been an accident. He had subtly but deliberately taken charge of their relationship. But, then, that's what Guild bosses did. They took command.

"I don't care how it looks in the media," she said, going for stubborn. "So there's gossip about our relationship? So what? You said the main point was to make certain that everyone knew that I was your wife."

"I don't give a damn about the gossip. After that incident with the Riders this afternoon, we have to assume that not all of the bad actors are inside the organization."

Jolted, she stared up at him. "You think those guys who attacked me are somehow connected to the conspiracy?"

"I think we have to assume it's a reasonable possibility. Who else have you managed to piss off lately besides Jenner?" he asked.

She swallowed hard. "Not the Riders. I've never done a story on them. The management of Underworld Exploration wasn't too happy when I exposed their shady business ties with the Guild, but they complained the old-fashioned way. Their lawyers threatened to sue the paper. I can't see a big company like that hiring a bunch of low-life gang members to get rid of one measly little tabloid reporter."

"I think you're in more trouble than you realize. Until we know what's going on, you won't be spending the night alone."

"Why your place?" she muttered.

"You'll be safer at my house. I installed a state-of-the-art ambertronics security system shortly after I bought it last month. No one can even get on the grounds without triggering the alarms."

She thought about the strange restlessness that had kept her awake last night. Her intuition had told her that someone was watching. Her intuition was usually right. Maybe the Riders had been stalking her.

She made her decision.

"You're right," she said, rezzing the Float's little flash-rock engine. "I need to pick up a few things at my place."

Chapter 8

SHE EMERGED FROM THE BEDROOM, AN OVERNIGHT CASE in her hand, and found Fontana studying the miniature star dressing room on the coffee table. He looked deeply intrigued.

"Where did you get this?" he asked.

"An ex-hunter named Jake Tanner built it for Elvis. Poor Jake is a juice addict who lives in an alley a few blocks from here. When he's not in a juice dream, he makes the most amazing miniatures out of discarded items and materials that he scrounges from garbage bins. Elvis's dressing room is his latest masterpiece."

"It's incredible."

She smiled. "Yes, it is."

The dressing room was a marvelously detailed work of art. The walls stood some ten inches high. There was no ceiling, so you looked straight down into it.

The room was complete, right down to the dressing table covered in red velvet and the mirror surrounded by tiny lights. There was also a little guitar. The walls were paneled and set with hooks designed to hold the costumes that Jake had made for Elvis. In addition to his sparkling white cape, there was a short-sleeved shirt printed with exotic tropical flowers. A tiny lei hung next to the tropical shirt.

Elvis popped into the dressing room using the little door. He puttered about briefly, checking to be sure that nothing had changed since he had left it. Satisfied, he came back out and chortled at Sierra.

"The guitar actually works," Sierra said. "Listen."

She reached down into the dressing room and used her fingertip to pluck one of the strings on the small instrument. There was a faint but distinct twang.

Fontana smiled. "Amazing."

She straightened and tightened her grip on the handle of the rolling suitcase.

"I'm ready," she said.

"You don't have to look as though you're going to a funeral."

"Sorry. It's been a long day. I'm exhausted."

He took the suitcase from her and went toward the door. She picked up Elvis and followed.

"So, are you going to work out or something?" she asked, trying to sound casually unconcerned.

"At this hour of the night? I don't think so."

If she had any sense, she would keep her mouth shut, she thought.

"I was under the impression that de-rezzing ghosts had some side effects," she said cautiously. "Or is it different when you manipulate dark light?"

"It's all dissonance energy," he said. He opened the door. "Same side effects."

"I see." She didn't know where to go with that.

Fontana closed the door and turned around to face her. She was forced to halt directly in front of him. He did not touch her, but she noticed that it was suddenly very hard to breathe.

"Something you should know," he said. He used the edge of his hand to tip up her chin.

She managed to rez up a bright, polite smile. "Yes?"

"A man doesn't get very far in the Guild if he can't handle a little afterburn."

Heat suffused her face. "I didn't mean to imply that you were, uh—"

"That I might be crazed with lust because I rezzed those five little ghosts?"

She blushed. "Never crossed my mind."

"Is that right? It crossed mine. The answer is yes, by the way."

"Yes, what?"

"Yes, I'm crazed with lust. Doesn't mean I'm out of control."

"Oh. Good. Well, that's just great. Glad to hear it."

"I'll prove it," he said.

She was transfixed. "How?"

"Like this."

He bent his head and took her mouth. Heat flashed through her, just as it had in the registrar's office. Energy crackled in the atmosphere. Dazed from her own volatile response, she swayed a little, leaning into him. She felt Elvis scramble up onto Fontana's shoulder so that he wouldn't get crushed. It was a smart move. Fontana's chest was quartz-hard, and she was pressed very tightly against him.

She wanted the kiss to go on forever, but Fontana ended the reckless plunge into passion a moment later. He raised his head and set her gently away from him.

"Time to go home," he said.

Chapter 9

FONTANA EASED THE RAPTOR TO A HALT IN FRONT OF A pair of massive gates and punched a code into a small device on the dashboard.

The gates were fashioned in an elaborate design that made them appear more like large works of metal art than a security feature, but Sierra had a hunch they were probably made of mag-steel. A high stone fence surrounded the property.

The gates swung open, and she saw the mansion. It loomed like a fairy-tale castle in the glowing green fog. Not the home of the handsome prince, she decided, more like the ominous domain of a sorcerer.

"Must take a big staff to run this place," she observed, trying to make herself focus on small talk.

"I believe in delegating. I have a household manager. She comes in five days a week and oversees whatever is needed. I let her take care of hiring gardeners, housekeepers, and any other services she thinks are necessary."

"But she doesn't live here?"

"No. I like my privacy. When I come home at night, I want to be alone."

The drive was so choked with luminous mist she could barely make out the dark shapes of the trees that lined the approach to the big house.

Fontana eased the Raptor along the paved lane and into a garage. The door of the garage locked behind them with the rumbling clang of a bank vault. Sierra collected Elvis and got out of the car. Together they waited while Fontana extracted her small suitcase from the trunk.

He used another code to rez a second vaultlike door.

"Okay, I see what you mean about your security system being a bit more elaborate than mine," she said. "Do all Guild chiefs feel that it's necessary to invest in such sophisticated equipment, or is there something about being the boss of the Crystal Guild that makes it a good idea?"

"Are you implying I might be a trifle paranoid?"

"Just a touch."

"It's a good character trait in a Guild boss."

"I'll take your word for it," she said.

They entered the mansion through a back hall. Fontana turned on a few lights. She looked around as they moved into the house.

"It's beautiful," she whispered.

"Not quite the kind of place you expected a Guild man to own?"

"Don't start with me, Fontana. I've had a very long day."

"Sorry."

He paused. She got the feeling he was regrouping, searching for a way to get the conversation back on track.

"The house dates from about fifty years before the Era of Discord," he said. "The inlay work and the mosaics are all original."

"Beautiful." She studied one of the dark blue, yellow, and white mosaics on the floor. "There is so much history in this house."

"That was the attraction," he said. He looked at her. "I don't have a family history of my own, so I bought one."

"What do you mean?"

"I'm a bastard."

"You mean your father never married your mother." She brushed that aside with a small move of her fingers. "Yes, I know. I found that out when I did my research on you."

She could tell that she had finally caught him off guard, but he covered his reaction swiftly with a wry smile.

"Ray did warn me about the dangers of marrying a journalist," he said.

"It wasn't the circumstances of your birth that I found interesting," she continued. "It was your reputation. When hunters talk about you, they always cite Fontana's First Rule: Never leave a man behind for ghost bait."

He shrugged. "It's an old story."

She watched his face in the shadows. "I gather it goes

back to your work in the tunnels. There was an incident. Someone tried to hijack a shipment of artifacts. You were in charge of the expedition that was attacked. You and your men fought off the pirates and got the civilians out of harm's way, but some members of your crew were taken hostage by the hijackers. You went back down and single-handedly rescued your men."

"That was a long time ago."

She smiled. "That's the thing about reputations, isn't it? They hang around for a long time."

He led her into a room lit with faint, luminous green light. She recognized the source of the illumination. It came from the array of alien antiquities massed inside. Countless vases, urns, and exquisite little jars were displayed on various tables and pedestals. Most of the artifacts were crafted of the ubiquitous, indestructible quartz that the craftsmen of the vanished civilization had used to build everything from their utensils to great cities. The psi that emanated from the quartz was the source of the eerie green glow.

Having concluded that they were going to hang around awhile, Elvis scampered down from her shoulder and began exploring. He soon disappeared into the deep shadows of the gallery.

Sierra went to stand in front of a selection of quartz plaques engraved with strange designs.

"This is a very fine collection," she said. "Museum quality."

"It came with the house." He walked toward her and

halted directly behind her, not quite touching. "The former owner was a collector. When he died, the heirs wanted to sell the collection to a museum. I offered to buy it instead."

"That must have tacked quite a bit onto the purchase price."

"Yes." He rested his hands on her shoulders. "But it was worth it."

A case full of artifacts that were not made of green quartz caught her eye. It was the one cabinet in the room that had artificial lighting.

"Good heavens," she whispered. "Is that real dreamstone?"

"Do you really think I'd have any fakes in here?"

She flushed. "No. My father has a couple of pieces, but I've never seen that much of it outside a museum."

No one knew why the aliens, who had used quartz for virtually everything else, had fashioned some items out of the mysterious dreamstone. The experts could not even decide if the exquisitely beautiful substance was native to Harmony. No naturally occurring deposits had ever been found.

Unlike quartz, dreamstone did not glow with its own natural illumination, but in the subdued case lighting, each item shimmered and shifted and swirled with fabulous colors that had no names. Dreamstone was solid to the touch, but to the eye it had the properties of a liquid, ever changing and endlessly, fascinatingly beautiful.

She looked at Fontana, a little awed in spite of herself.

"I take back what I said about you being a trifle paranoid. The dreamstone alone justifies all your security."

Another kind of energy shimmered through the room.

"I protect what is mine," Fontana said.

Chapter 10

HIS NAME WAS HANK, AND HE HAD BEEN LIVING ON THE streets in the old Quarter for nearly a year. Before that he had spent nearly two decades as a Guild man working underground until he'd been ghost-fried so bad he'd been forced to retire. He had seen a lot of weird things in his time but never anything like the four-foot-wide beam of ultraviolet energy sweeping slowly down the alley.

The beam appeared impenetrable at first, but as it got closer, he could see shadowy shapes moving about on the other side. It was impossible to make them out clearly, but he thought he caught glimpses of dark figures that resembled two-legged, fishlike beings with bulbous heads.

He crouched behind the large metal trash container, knowing it would provide no protection from the moving beam. Dissonance energy crackled invisibly in the atmosphere, a lot of it. His para-rez senses had been dulled by a steady diet of Green Ruin for a long time now, but the hunter in him could still recognize alien psi when it was this heavy. It was ghost energy but not like any he had ever encountered down in the tunnels. For one thing, it was the wrong color. For another, it was too well-controlled. No hunter could shape and focus ghost light that cleanly. The stuff usually flared and flashed in violent waves, no matter how good you were at handling it.

He should be on his feet, running for his life. Hunters had some natural immunity to green ghost light, but he was sure that no one could survive a brush with this ultraviolet monster. Nevertheless, some instinct warned him that his only chance was to remain concealed behind the trash container.

The beam halted a short distance away near the doorway where Jake Tanner had his crib. There was no sound from Jake. The guy was probably lost in a juice dream.

The fish-headed shadows on the other side of the wall of energy moved about with a purposeful air. He couldn't see what they were doing. But after a few seconds, the wide beam of ultraviolet shifted.

He figured there was some important stuff a man ought to think about at a time like this, but he couldn't seem to recall anything he really wanted to dwell on in his last moments. He'd said his good-byes to the real world and his life when he'd crawled into the endless bottles of Green Ruin.

Might as well go out on a rush of heavy diss light. Probably as good a way to die as any.

But the energy beam was no longer moving toward him. Instead, it retreated swiftly back toward the opposite end of the alley. After a moment it suddenly vanished, as if someone had rezzed a switch to turn off a flashlight.

Hank realized his heart was pounding harder than it had the time he'd encountered his first big ghost down in the tunnels. He started to reach for another bottle of Green Ruin with shaking fingers and then hesitated.

After a moment he made himself get to his feet. He didn't want to do this, but Jake had been the closest thing he'd had to a friend since he'd discovered the magic of Green Ruin.

He picked up his flashlight, switched it on, and made his way toward Jake's crib. He wasn't surprised by what he found. Some part of him had known that the bedroll would be empty.

The bastards had taken Jake.

Chapter 11

FONTANA SAT ALONE IN THE DARKENED BEDROOM, A glass of brandy in one hand, and contemplated his wedding night. Sierra was asleep two doors down the hall. This was the first time since he had bought the mansion that anyone other than himself had slept here.

It felt good to know that she was in his house. He would have preferred that she slept in this room; nevertheless, she was under his roof, and that was enough for now.

The stunt with dark light at the party had been a dumbass move. Why the hell had he done it?

Because he had been unable to resist the hunters' traditional wedding night challenge, that's why. Damn it, for a while there tonight he'd actually let himself believe that he really was a newly married man.

Growing up a bastard, his mother dead in a car accident when he was fifteen, he'd had very little in the way of traditions. When he joined the Guild, it was as if he had finally found a family. He had embraced the organization and everything about it, including all the old traditions, with the fervor of a new convert.

Tonight Sierra had become his wife—a Guild wife—and he had been overcome with a fierce desire to prove himself to her in the traditional Guild way.

He should have known better than to expect an outsider to be impressed with such an archaic tradition, especially a woman like Sierra, who had been born into an upper-class family.

The social status of the Guilds had always been an uneasy one, at least as far as mainstream society was concerned. Sure, high-ranking Guild members and their wives got invited to celebrity parties and elegant charity fund-raisers. A lot of people found raw power of any kind fascinating. They enjoyed rubbing shoulders with members of their local Guild Councils in certain social circles. Politicians and CEOs courted the top people in any Guild because the organizations possessed the kind of cash that could bankroll a campaign or invest in a hedge fund.

But if you were a part of the elite of mainstream society, you didn't want your daughter to marry a Guild man, not even if the marriage was a short-term MC with no lasting status. A Covenant Marriage between a high-ranking member of a Guild and a woman with Sierra's social background was so rare as to be the stuff of legend. Such marriages did occur from time to time, but they were usually the result of financial considerations. A once-wealthy mainstream family seeking to recoup its fortunes might contemplate such an alliance, but only as a last resort.

He wondered what Sierra's classy parents would say when they discovered that she was in a Marriage of Convenience with a Guild boss who was also a bastard. One thing was certain: they would not be happy about the situation.

He drank some of the brandy and wondered how long his marriage would last.

Chapter 12

"I DON'T BELIEVE IT," SIERRA SAID. "YOU ACTUALLY SUBscribe to the *Curtain*?"

They were in the breakfast room. She had made an old family favorite, Earth toast. There was also orange juice and coffee. Elvis was perched on the windowsill, nibbling on the small slice of toast that she had given him. A cup of coffee sat beside him.

"Well, sure," Fontana said. He slapped the day's edition down onto the breakfast table. "Figured it was in my own best interest to know how a certain investigative journalist was going to come at the Guild next. I was a Hunter Scout. *Be prepared* is my motto."

"I thought *Never leave a man behind for ghost bait* was your motto."

"That one came later." He looked at the plates in her hands with interest. "Is that real Earth toast?"

"My mom's recipe." She set one of the plates in front of him. "Hope you like it."

"Oh, yeah." He surveyed the egg-battered toast as though it were one of the priceless pieces of dreamstone in his collection. "Haven't had it in years." He reached for the butter.

His enthusiasm warmed her for some reason. She sat down across from him and picked up her glass of orange juice.

"Let me see the headline," she said.

"Brace yourself."

"How bad is it?"

He swiveled the paper around so that she could read it. "Got to give Runtley high marks for creativity."

Sierra looked at the screaming headline.

GUILD BOSS WEDS MYSTERY BRIDE
IN SECRET HUNTER CEREMONY

Beneath that was a second banner line in a slightly smaller font.

COUPLE GOES THROUGH
SECRET HUNTER WEDDING-NIGHT RITUAL
IN ALIEN TEMPLE OF LOVE

Two photos accompanied the short piece. The larger shot was a tight close-up of Fontana and herself coming out of the registrar's office. There was no mistaking the big Guild seal ring on her finger. She appeared somewhat the worse for wear, but it was the cool satisfaction on Fontana's austere face that gave her a chill.

"I think we lucked out," she said, going for a positive spin. "There's nothing in the piece about vampires."

"Don't miss the description of the secret wedding-night ritual. It's on the next page. Your friend Kay has a vivid imagination."

Sierra turned the page reluctantly.

". . . The mysterious rites associated with the consummation of a high-ranking Guild marriage are conducted in an alien temple of love that is concealed deep within the catacombs. The alien temple is said to resonate with a form of strange psi that greatly enhances the satisfaction of both bride and groom . . ."

Sierra cleared her throat. "I'm afraid Kay went a little over the top."

"You think so?" Fontana's mouth kicked up in a wicked grin. "Don't know about you, but speaking personally, I'm sorry we missed that secret alien temple of love. Sounds interesting."

Aware that she was blushing, Sierra hastily closed the paper.

"Normally the mainstream media doesn't pay a lot of attention to what we print at the *Curtain*," she said. "But it won't be able to ignore a Guild boss wedding. That kind of thing is always news. And the *Curtain* got the scoop. Runtley is probably rubbing his hands together with glee as we speak."

Fontana checked his watch. "The other newsrooms will have hit the phones as soon as the day's edition of the *Curtain* hit the street. Guild headquarters will have confirmed the story by now. It's probably gone out on the major wire services. I'll bet we're on the morning news in the other city-states."

"Good grief." Sierra gripped her fork very tightly. "Do you really think the news of our marriage will get beyond Crystal City?"

Fontana raised his brows. "Don't tell me you've been laboring under the illusion that our wedding would be nothing more than a local story."

She swallowed. "It's just an MC, not exactly earth-shaking news."

"Trust me, when a high-ranking Guild man from any of the big cities gets married, its news. You're a journalist. You should know that."

"I think I've been in denial."

"I can see that."

As if on cue, Sierra's personal phone rang. She jumped a couple of inches. Annoyed with herself, she reached into her pocket, took out the small device, and glanced at the incoming number. She groaned and answered.

"Hi, Mom."

"What in the world is going on, Sierra?" Marilyn McIntyre demanded.

Her voice was crisp, authoritative, and deeply concerned. Sierra was also pretty sure she detected an underlying edge of panic.

"I can explain, Mom."

"Your father just called. He said that his executive assistant heard a news report about a woman with your name marrying the CEO of the Crystal City Ghost Hunter's Guild. I assume its some sort of mix-up."

"Not exactly."

"Please don't tell me you let the editor of that dreadful tabloid you work for talk you into printing a ridiculous story like this just for the sake of boosting circulation."

"It wasn't Mr. Runtley's idea," Sierra said.

"Just tell me it isn't true."

Sierra realized that something had changed in Fontana's expression. It was a subtle shift, nothing more than a faint tightening at the corners of his mouth. The warm, intimate heat that had been in his eyes a moment ago had disappeared.

"Mom, it's only a Marriage of Convenience," she said, trying to project the calm, cool air of an adult woman who is entirely capable of choosing her own lovers.

"MCs are so tacky." Marilyn's voice rose. "Sierra, how could you? How in the world did you ever come to meet a Guild boss in the first place, let alone get intimately involved with him? You've only been in Crystal for six months."

"It's complicated."

"Don't you realize how this will look?" Marilyn said tightly. "We haven't had a Marriage of Convenience in this family since your grandmother Larken entered into one with your grandfather. And that MC only lasted a few weeks before they came to their senses and converted it into a Covenant Marriage."

Sierra seized on that. "Speaking of which, did Grandmother ever tell you why she and Grandpa chose an MC first?"

"She said something once about wanting to be sure because she didn't trust her intuition when it came to love. But that's ridiculous. Your grandmother's talent is legendary in this family. I've never known her to be less than absolutely positive about anything."

Her grandmother had been right to be wary, Sierra thought. When it came to love, things got very murky, even for those with keen intuition.

"Mom, don't worry about me. I'm fine. It's just a simple Marriage of Convenience. People go in and out of them all the time."

"Not people in this family," Marilyn shot back. "What about Jonathan?"

For some reason the mention of Jonathan's name was one button too many.

"You know, Mom, I don't really give a flying chunk of untuned amber what Jonathan thinks."

"How can you say that?" Marilyn's shock reverberated through the phone. "You loved him. You were engaged to him. He called just the other day wanting to know when you planned to return to Resonance."

"Whatever I felt for Jonathan ended the day I found him in bed with Adrianna Silbury."

"Good grief, you never said anything about that when you called off the engagement."

"You're Jonathan's mother's best friend. I didn't want to muck up your relationship with Mrs. Pemberley."

"I . . . don't know what to say. I'm dumbfounded. I thought Jonathan loved you. He was one of us, a member of the Society. You were *matched*."

"Jon was fond of me. We were friends. But it turned out that he was primarily interested in me because he saw me as a business asset."

"You mean because you're a McIntyre?" Marilyn asked sharply. "But that's nonsense. His family name carries just as much weight in this city and in the Society as yours does."

"No, Mom." She glanced at Fontana and let her eyes slide away. "Because of the other thing. You know."

Marilyn was no fool. "Your intuition?"

"Uh-huh."

There was a long silence on the other end of the line.

"I'm stunned," Marilyn said finally. "Your father and I had no idea. But if Jonathan's feelings for you weren't genuine, why didn't you sense it? Why didn't the matchmakers pick it up?"

Fontana ate his Earth toast with a grim air. She knew he was listening to every word she said.

"I really can't explain right now, Mom. Let's just say that the experience taught me a lesson. I had a very close call with Jonathan. I'll never contemplate another

Covenant Marriage without a trial Marriage of Convenience first. It's just too risky."

"Obviously you didn't need an MC with Jonathan to discover that he was cheating on you," Marilyn pointed out smoothly.

Sierra wrinkled her nose. "You know, that's the problem with having a mom who is a philosophy professor. You're always pulling the logic card on me. Okay, you win that one on points. Nevertheless, you can see why I'm feeling a little skittish about the whole concept of a Covenant Marriage these days. It's a dangerous institution, as far as I'm concerned."

"So you plunge straight into a Marriage of Convenience with a Guild boss, instead?" Marilyn shot back. "That doesn't sound a great deal safer."

Sierra caught Fontana's eye. She couldn't tell what he was thinking, but for some reason the short-term vows they had made to each other yesterday popped into her head. *"I promise to remain faithful so long as we both are bound by this agreement . . ."*

She also remembered the strong currents of psi that had accompanied the promise. She had known in that moment that, whatever else happened, Fontana intended to keep his end of the bargain. The MC might not last longer than a week, but for those few days, he was hers. And she was his.

"Got to go, Mom. I'm in the middle of fixing breakfast. Give my love to Dad, and tell him not to worry. Everything's under control."

"You always say that, but things never quite work out that way," Marilyn retorted. "And what about your grandparents' anniversary next month?"

"I'll be there."

"With or without your new husband?" Marilyn asked ominously.

"We'll see," Sierra said airily.

She ended the connection before her mother could respond and turned off the phone.

"Sorry about that," she said briskly. "My mom just heard the news."

Fontana poured more coffee into his cup. "I get the feeling your folks aren't too thrilled to hear that you're in an MC with me," he said, his voice exquisitely neutral.

"It isn't you. It's the whole MC thing. In my family they're considered sort of, well—"

"Lower-class?" he suggested with a cold smile. "Something a Guild man might do, for instance?"

Anger flashed through her. She raised her fork in warning. "Stop right there, Fontana. I've had enough high drama with my mother this morning. Understood?"

His eyes tightened at the corners, and his jaw looked as if it had been carved from stone. She almost smiled. He wasn't accustomed to having people tell him to shut up. Somewhat to her surprise, however, he changed tactics.

"Who's Jonathan?" he asked.

"Don't play the innocent with me. I'm sure you know all about Jonathan Pemberley." She forked up a bite of the toast. "You would never have gotten involved with me unless you had done a very thorough background check."

"I did come across the announcement of your engagement to Pemberley. Also noticed that it had been ended quietly and abruptly about eight months ago."

"Is there any other way to end an engagement?"

Fontana ignored that snappy little riposte.

"Well?" he said.

"Well, what?"

"Are you going to tell me about Pemberley?"

She concentrated on her coffee. "You heard me explain to Mom that I found him in bed with someone else."

He waited. She did not volunteer anything further.

"That's it?" he said after a while.

"That's it."

"Why do I have this feeling that there's more to the story?"

"Beats me." She smiled. "Possibly because you are suspicious by nature?"

"Possibly. I heard you tell your mother that Pemberley viewed you as some kind of business asset."

"Uh-huh."

"Because of your family's power in Resonance?"

"Not exactly." She put down her coffee cup. "Look, I really don't want to talk about Jonathan. Let's change the subject."

"Fine. You want to change the subject, let's get down to business."

"Business?"

"It's time you kept your end of the bargain. I want to meet your source, the one who told you about the alien abductions and the discovery of a secret alien lab."

Her end of the bargain. Well, what had she expected? That's what this marriage was all about, after all: a bargain.

"Okay" she said, "but there are no freebies here, Fontana. I'll introduce you to Jake, but in exchange I want the complete file on Jenner."

"What makes you think there's a file?"

"You know, there are a lot of things you do well, but looking innocent is not one of them. You're a planner. I'm betting that when you decided to take down Jenner, you compiled a file."

"You're right. There's a file."

"Do I get it?"

"Yes."

Chapter 13

THE ALLEY WAS IN ONE OF THE SEEDIEST NEIGHBORHOODS of the Quarter, a narrow lane formed by buildings with boarded-up doorways and empty windows. The structures would have been real firetraps, Fontana thought, if it weren't for the fact that the First Generation colonists had built them out of native stone and a lot of high-tech, fireproof materials imported from Earth before the closing of the Curtain.

"Jake will probably still be asleep at this hour," Sierra said. She had her purse slung over one shoulder. Elvis, nattily attired in his white cape, was perched on the other shoulder. "He's not what you'd call an early riser."

Fontana surveyed the alley. The lane smelled like a lot of other alleys he'd had occasion to visit, an aromatic mix of stale garbage, stale urine, and stale booze. Shards of broken bottles glittered on the ground.

"Great location for a mugging," he said, checking windows and doorways. "Come here often?"

"As a matter of fact, yes." Sierra sounded irritated by the question. "It's safe. Jake and his friend Hank have staked out this alley as their personal turf. They were both powerful hunters once upon a time. They can still defend their territory when necessary."

"The fearless lady reporter."

It took every scrap of his considerable powers of self-control not to start yelling at her. What the hell did she think she was doing meeting washed-up hunters in grimy alleys?

He knew that Sierra sensed his simmering anger. She tightened her grip on the sack of cookies she had brought with her.

"As it happens, I'm an excellent judge of character," she said. Every word was iced with invisible frost.

"Yeah?" And then, because he couldn't help himself, he added, "if that's true, what went wrong with Pemberley? Why didn't you figure him out right away?"

She gave him a repressive glare. "I've always heard that it is not a good idea for a couple to dissect prior relationships."

A couple. She'd referred to the two of them as a couple. Maybe that was a good sign.

Elvis was excited. He clung to Sierra's shoulder and leaned forward with an air of anticipation.

"Looks like the bunny enjoys strolling through dark alleys," Fontana said.

"Elvis knows this particular alley. He and Jake are buddies. Jake makes toys for him, and we give Jake cookies in return. Works for both of them."

"But not for you?"

"Let's just say that I blame the Guild for not taking better care of its men. Jake should not be living in this alley. He needs rehab and counseling to get off the juice, and then he needs a job. He's very good with his hands. In another life I think he could have been an artist."

"Instead, he came to a bad end as a retired ghost hunter, right?"

"You have to admit that, while the benefits are great, a lot of hunters end up drifting like Jake after they leave the catacombs. The Guilds take them in young, use them up, and then toss them out onto the street. They don't do a good job of preparing them to lead productive lives in mainstream society."

"You made your point in that series on burned-out hunters that you did for the *Curtain*," he said.

"You read that series?" She looked pleased.

"Hell, yes. Everyone on the Council, including Jenner, read it. Caused quite a rumble in management."

"Evidently not enough of one. Nothing was done about the problem."

"Jenner was still in charge at the time. He saw the series as just another PR issue. He figured he took care of it by giving the *Herald* an exclusive interview that highlighted all the work the Guild Foundation does with teenage boys."

"Hah. All those Hunter Scout programs are nothing more than thinly veiled recruitment operations for the Guild, as far as I'm concerned. It is a totally self-serving charity."

"The Guild sees the programs as a way of keeping young dissonance energy para-rez talents from experimenting recklessly with their budding ghost-rezzing abilities."

"In other words, you don't want a bunch of young hoodlums forming gangs and using their talents to intimidate people, because it would be bad for the image of the Guild."

He smiled. "You've got it."

"All that those scout programs do is glamorize life in the Guilds. I doubt if any of the troop leaders bother to tell the boys that it would be smart to get some higher education under their belts before they go underground or maybe even consider a real profession instead of ghost hunting."

"You've made your negative opinion of the Guild's outreach efforts crystal clear in the *Curtain*," he said.

"I've certainly tried."

"Speaking of outreach, how did you meet Jake Tanner?"

"I told Simon and the men at the Green Gate that I wanted to talk to any hunter who could tell me about the alien abductions and the secret lab rumors. They suggested Jake because he was a juicer who had recently retired from the Guild. I tracked him down."

He decided it would be better for his nerves if he did not ask her exactly how she had set about tracking down a burned-out hunter.

"I'm surprised that Tanner was willing to talk to a reporter," he said instead.

"He and Elvis took to each other right away. Jake trusts me because he likes Elvis. The problem is that because Jake uses juice, you never know how much of what he says is a fantasy from his most recent juice dream and how much is real."

Elvis muttered uneasily. Fontana glanced at him. The dust bunny was no longer a scruffy fur ball. He was partially sleeked out, all four eyes showing.

Sierra stopped abruptly.

"Something's wrong," she said.

Elvis stared intently at a doorway halfway down the alley. He muttered darkly.

Fontana followed his gaze and saw what looked like a portion of an old blanket or sleeping bag sticking out of the entrance.

"That's Jake's crib?" he asked.

"Yes," Sierra said.

She started forward, her face urgent and intent. Elvis chattered unhappily. She stopped again.

"This doesn't feel right," she said, talking so softly that she might have been speaking to herself.

Elvis mumbled, clearly disturbed.

This doesn't feel right. Fontana made a mental note to go over that odd comment at a later date.

"Wait here," he said, automatically sliding into the voice he always used when he wanted instant and unquestioning obedience. It was the voice he had employed underground when the safety of a team was at stake.

Somewhat to his amazement, Sierra obeyed. Elvis appeared strongly disinclined to move forward, too. Maybe Sierra was simply trusting the bunny's instincts instead of actually following a Guild man's orders. Then another thought crossed his mind. Maybe Sierra was trusting her *own* instincts. Now, that was an intriguing thought.

He walked to the grungy bedroll and looked down.

"It's empty," he said. "Probably ran out of juice and went looking for a dealer."

"No," Sierra said with shattering conviction. "He's gone. Just like the others."

"You don't know that. Not yet."

"Yes," she said. "I'm sure of it. Come on, we've got to see if they took Hank, too."

"See if who took Hank?"

"The aliens."

"Tell me you don't really believe Jake was abducted by aliens."

She did not respond. Instead, she rushed toward the large trash container at the far end of the alley. Fontana followed. By the time he got there, she had disappeared behind the container. When she reappeared a few seconds later, her face was stark with dread.

"He's gone," she said. "I've got to find him."

"What makes you think he wasn't abducted, too?" Fontana asked.

"Because his bedroll is gone. He packed up and moved, maybe because he saw what happened to Jake."

Chapter 14

AT THREE O'CLOCK THAT AFTERNOON, IVOR RUNTLEY charged into the newsroom bellowing and waving his hands. Accustomed as everyone was to his frequent bursts of excitement, nobody looked up.

Elvis, hovering above the coffee machine in his balloon craft, was the exception. He responded with his customary enthusiasm. He chortled and bounced up and down, nearly toppling out of the cardboard basket.

"Listen up, everyone," Runtley shouted, "the day's print run is sold out. We're getting flooded with requests for more details on the alien temple of love. Kay, I need another story about the secret hunter wedding-night rituals for tomorrow's edition."

"Ask Sierra." Kay did not take her eyes off her computer screen. "She's the one who actually experienced the secret rituals in the alien temple of love."

"Forget it," Sierra said. "I'm working on the alien abductions story. I've got some hot new leads."

Runtley stopped, briefly stymied. Both stories promised to be grabbers. He made an executive decision.

"Kay, you'll have to do the secret wedding-night rituals piece. That's final."

Matt grinned at Kay. "Surely you got some inspiration last night when you went home with Ray Takashima. I saw the way you two were eyeballing each other."

"All I got last night was a hangover," Kay said primly. "There was no inspiration of the sort to which you so crudely refer."

"Maybe you just don't remember it," Phil suggested.

Kay narrowed her eyes. "In case you haven't read it, *Ten Steps to a Covenant Wedding: Secrets of a Professional Matchmaker* strongly advises against sleeping with anyone on a first date or a second or third, for that matter."

Phil rolled his eyes. "Don't tell me you're reading some dumb dating manual."

"As it happens, my mother gave me the same advice," Kay said in an acid tone.

"So did mine," Sierra volunteered. "It's very sound advice, if you ask me."

They all looked at her.

"What?" she said.

Matt gave her an evil grin. "Is that how you got Fontana to marry you? By holding out until after the third date?"

"Maybe you should write your own dating manual," Phil said. "*Ten Steps to Marrying a Guild Boss.*"

Sierra glared at each of them in turn. "One more word out of either of you, and there will be no more cookies, ever."

"Just trying to be helpful," Phil said.

"That's enough, people," Runtley snapped. "This is a newsroom. Kindly act like professionals. Phil, get me a photo of the alien love temple."

"Gee, boss, I dunno," Phil said. "According to Kay, the alien love temple is hidden away in some secret underground tunnel."

"You're a photographer, damn it, I expect you to get creative. How hard can it be to figure out what an alien love temple looks like?"

"Well, I might be able to do something with the coffeepot and a couple of doughnuts," Phil conceded. "I'll get my camera."

Sierra's phone rang. She pounced on it.

"I think we found Hank for you," Simon said on the other end. "Rumor is he's holed up in a bar on East Wall Street. Place called the Firewall Tavern."

"Thanks, Simon. I really appreciate this." She ended the call, yanked her purse out of the bottom desk drawer, and got to her feet. "Got a lead on my missing source. I'll see you all later."

She paused long enough to collect Elvis from the balloon basket and then flew out the door.

The last thing she heard was Phil making his customary announcement in a deep, resonating voice.

"Elvis has left the building."

FONTANA LOOKED AT THE FILE SPREAD OUT ON THE DESK.

"Tanner's service records for the last six months of his Guild career are missing," he said.

"Yeah, I can see that." Ray flattened his palms on the desk and surveyed the file, grimly thoughtful. "Occasionally paperwork goes astray, but under the circumstances, I've got to admit this looks a little strange."

Fontana engaged the intercom. "I need you in here, Harlan."

The door opened. Harlan Ostendorf appeared, looking seriously concerned. It was an expression he did well, because it came naturally to him. Fontana suspected that he had probably been born looking seriously concerned. Harlan was now in his midfifties, and the lines engraved by his serious view of life had become indelible.

Harlan's serious approach to his work was one of the two reasons Fontana had pulled him out of the accounting department and promoted him to chief executive assistant immediately after Jenner had been forcibly retired. The second reason was that he hadn't trusted the man Jenner had installed in the position.

"Any reason why the file of a retired hunter named Jake Tanner might be missing the records for his last six months of service?" Fontana asked.

Harlan frowned, looking more serious than ever. "No, sir. That doesn't sound right. But there are duplicates of all service records in Benefits. I'll send Dray down to get them for you."

"Thanks."

Harlan disappeared, closing the door quietly behind him.

"There's something else that happened six months ago that's starting to bother me," Ray said. He opened another file. "A hunter named Cal Wilson was killed in an apparent jungle accident. He evidently fell into a ghost river whirlpool. Could be a coincidence. There was an investigation, but—"

"But Jenner signed off on the report declaring it an accident," Fontana concluded, "so we should take the results with a grain of amber."

"I think so, yes."

"We need to find out if there's any connection at all between Jake Tanner and Cal Wilson."

Twenty minutes later, Harlan stuck his head around the edge of the door. His expression had moved from serious to somber.

"The duplicates in Benefits are missing as well, sir," he said. "I had Dray check the computer archives. They've been deleted from there, too."

"Had a hunch that might be the case. Thanks, Harlan."

Harlan retreated into the outer office, closing the door behind him.

Fontana considered the file. "Damn, she was right."

Ray's brows rose. "Who was right?"

"My wife."

It felt good to say that. *My wife*. The beginning of a real family of his own. *No, don't go there. Too soon. Too many things can go wrong.* Starting with the fact that her real family probably considered him no better than a mobster.

The door opened again.

"Sorry to interrupt, sir," Harlan said. "But I thought I'd better remind you of the annual Crystal City Charity Ball event tonight."

"That damned fund-raiser. I'd forgotten about it. Thank you, Harlan."

"Also, there was another phone call from Mr. Burns."

"You told him I was unavailable again?" Fontana asked.

"Yes, sir."

"Thanks."

The door closed again.

Fontana reached for the phone. "I'd better tell Sierra about the charity ball."

Ray lounged back in his chair, looking amused. "You mean she doesn't know yet?"

"Not like I haven't had a few other things on my mind." He dialed Sierra's number.

Ray gazed at the ceiling. "Got a feeling this is going to turn ugly fast."

"What the hell are you talking about?"

"You can't drop a bombshell like this on a woman." Ray checked his watch. "Not when she's only got a few hours to shop."

"I don't see any major problem here. It's just a fancy party."

"Obviously you've got a lot to learn about marriage," Ray said.

"You're an expert? You've never been married."

"At least I had the common sense to acknowledge my lack of expertise and buy a manual on the subject."

Fontana looked at him. "There's a manual?"

"*Ten Steps to a Covenant Marriage: Secrets of a Professional Matchmaker* by Celinda Ingram."

"Don't tell me you're reading a book on how to get married."

"Bought a copy this morning."

"Why in hell did you do that?" Fontana asked.

"Because Kay is reading it. Figured it would be a good idea to keep one step ahead of her."

"Damn. You can't be serious. It doesn't happen that fast."

Ray spread his hands. "Says the man who got married within hours after meeting the lady."

Before he could think of a rational response to that remark, Sierra answered her phone.

"Hello?" She sounded distracted.

He heard muffled traffic noises in the background. "Where are you?"

"In my car. Simon found Hank. I'm on my way to talk to him."

A strange sensation exploded in his gut. Not panic, exactly, but something very close to it.

"No," he said. With superhuman effort, he managed to keep his voice calm and controlled. "You are not going anywhere."

There was a short, brittle silence.

"I'll pretend I didn't hear that," Sierra said quietly.

He didn't need Ray's elevated eyebrows to realize he was not handling this well.

"Listen closely, Sierra. I don't want you meeting Hank alone."

"Why? What's wrong?"

"I think Jake Tanner was involved in something very dicey, and I don't want you following him down the same dust-bunny hole. Understood?"

"You found something?" she asked quickly.

"It's more like what I haven't found. Look, where are you supposed to meet Hank?"

"East Wall Street. Place called the Firewall Tavern."

"Hell. Trust you to find your way to the Firewall. Out of all the dumps in the Quarter, you picked that one to walk into alone."

"What's wrong now?" Sierra asked, sounding bewildered.

"Don't go into that place without me," he said, keeping his voice very even.

"Why not?"

"It's a dive."

"That's okay, I do dives."

"Not like the Firewall. Pay attention, Sierra. I repeat, do not go into the Firewall without me."

"You know, Fontana, we really must have a little talk soon. Just because you're my husband for a while, that doesn't give you the right to order me around as if I were one of your hunters."

Well, at least she had referred to him as her husband, not as her partner in the investigation. He set his back teeth. "*Please* don't go into that tavern until I get there. It isn't just any Quarter dive. People have been known to disappear into the catacombs or get permanently ghost-fried when drug deals go bad there. Last I heard, journalists don't have any special immunity to a mag-rez or a ghost."

She exhaled slowly. "Okay, those are all good, logical reasons for waiting. I'll meet you outside the Firewall."

He allowed himself to breathe again. "One more thing."

"If this is another warning about the Firewall, you've made your point."

"This isn't about the Firewall." He was on his feet, taking his black jacket off the wall hook. "I forgot to tell you this morning that we've got a social engagement tonight."

"What kind of social engagement. Your family?"

"I don't have any family, remember?"

"You never told me that. I know your parents were never married, but that doesn't automatically imply that you don't have a family."

"It does in my case. The social engagement I'm talking about is the annual Crystal City Charity Ball. The head of the Guild always attends. I need a date. In light of recent events, that would be you."

"Are you kidding?" She sounded outraged. "I can't go to the Crystal Ball with you."

He winced and held the phone some distance away from his ear. He noticed that Ray was smiling.

"Why not?" he asked cautiously.

"You need a ball gown to go to a ball. I don't have one in my wardrobe. Didn't think I'd need one here in Crystal."

"So? Go shopping this afternoon. The Guild will pick up the tab."

Ray winced.

"Damn it, Fontana," Sierra said tightly. "You can't just spring something like this on a woman—"

Out of nowhere, inspiration struck. "Donovan Corley will be there," he said.

"Corley?" Sudden interest replaced the annoyance in her tone. "Are we talking about the same Corley who is the CEO of Underworld Exploration?"

"The very same."

"You'll introduce me?"

"Sure."

"You've got a date."

He ended the connection and gave Ray a satisfied smile.

"I'm a fast learner," he said.

Chapter 15

HER PSI SENSES SHRIEKED A WARNING WHEN SHE WALKED through the door. Not that she needed her intuitive talent to know that the Firewall was the kind of place that gave hunter bars a bad name, Sierra thought. She doubted if even the most thrill-seeking coeds or bachelorette parties would schedule an evening of fun here. Dark, dingy, and reeking of stale booze, it smelled a lot like the alley where Hank and Jake had made their homes.

The ambient underground psi was very strong. Fontana was right; the establishment was probably sitting on top of a hole-in-the-wall. She didn't doubt that he'd been correct about the drug dealing in the basement, either.

With the exception of a couple of tough-looking types dressed in faded khaki and worn leather, the place was nearly empty. The bartender gave Sierra and Fontana a hard look.

"Got a feeling the service is not great here," Sierra said quietly.

"That's okay," Fontana said. "I don't plan to leave a tip." He took her arm in a proprietary manner. "I see someone in the last booth. Is that Hank?"

She peered through the gloom. There was a shadowy figure at the back of the room. "Yes, I think so."

"Keep moving."

She did, but it wasn't easy. Her intuition was shrieking at her to turn around and run. The only thing that kept her going forward was the knowledge that Fontana was by her side.

Elvis wasn't happy, either. He rumbled softly, not in a good way, and went sleek. His second set of eyes appeared.

One of the men gave Sierra an assessing look and leered. "Well, well, well, Chuck, look what just walked in. Kind of classy for this part of town, ain't she?"

Evidently this pair didn't read newspapers or watch television, Sierra thought. They hadn't recognized Fontana.

"I do believe that what we have here is a nice uptown couple that wandered into the wrong place at the wrong time," the second man said. When he leered, he displayed a lot of bad teeth.

His companion guffawed at the witticism. "I'll bet the pretty lady would be real nice to us if we did her a couple of favors first."

"What favors you got in mind, Chuck?"

"I think we should singe the guy in the suit first. Teach him some manners. This is a hunter bar. Outsiders ain't welcome. Then we burn the little rat on the lady's shoulder. It's a pest-control issue."

"Whatever you say, Chuck." The first man got to his feet. He stepped directly in front of Sierra. "I'll bet you came here looking for a good time, didn't you, honey? Chuck and me, we'll be glad to show you one. Ain't that right, Chucky?"

"Damn right," Chuck agreed.

He, too, was on his feet. He started to circle around behind Fontana.

"Hang on to Elvis," Fontana said quietly to Sierra. "I don't want him to get hurt."

Sierra grabbed Elvis in both hands and clutched him tight. Elvis wriggled in annoyance, but she did not release him.

Fontana looked at the two men. "We won't be staying long. If you're smart, you'll sit down, finish your beers, and leave us alone."

The man who was trying to get into position behind Fontana grinned, showing off his really bad teeth again.

"We can always drink beer. Right now, the lady looks like more fun. Ain't that right, Joe?"

"She sure does," Joe agreed. "I'll get her out of the way. Don't want her to get fried when you take care of the suit."

He reached for Sierra's arm. Elvis snarled, showing his own impressive array of teeth. Unlike those of the hunters, his were in excellent condition. Joe retracted his arm instantly, reddening with anger.

"I'll wring its neck," he vowed, retreating to a safe distance.

"This is not a good idea," Fontana said, his voice calm and just slightly edged with irritation.

"Sure isn't a good idea for you," Joe agreed.

Acid-green fire pulsed. Two ghosts coalesced rapidly out of the heavy alien psi that permeated the atmosphere of the tavern, one in front of Fontana and one behind him.

More energy swirled in the shadowy space. A rippling, whirling, churning river of energy the color of midnight rapidly took shape. It formed a barely visible whirlpool that shimmered fiercely in the gloom. The nearest green ghost was sucked into it and vanished. The second one quickly disappeared as well.

The two hunters were still trying to adjust to the realization that their ghosts had ceased to exist when Chuck realized that the dark waves of psi were headed toward him.

He screamed and ran toward the front door. The dark light pursued, brushing him ever so gently. He collapsed to the floor, unconscious.

The river of night turned toward Joe.

"No." Joe threw up both hands in a useless attempt to ward off the dark energy. *"No."*

But his back was to the bar. There was nowhere to run. The black wave touched him lightly. He jerked like a puppet on a string and then sprawled on the floor.

The darkness vanished. Fontana looked at the bartender, who seemed to have been flash-frozen.

"Will there be any further objections to our presence in your establishment?" Fontana asked politely.

The man shook his head. "Nope. You're the new Guild boss, aren't you?"

"Yes."

The bartender nodded. "Thought so. Saw your picture in the *Curtain* this morning. Chuck and Joe, they don't read the papers. They gonna be all right, or do I have to dump 'em into the catacombs?"

"They'll wake up in a couple of hours," Fontana said. "But they may not be feeling perky."

"Not my problem. That was dark light you zapped 'em with, wasn't it?"

"You're a former Guild man, aren't you?" Fontana asked.

"Damn straight."

"Then you know that officially speaking, there is no other kind of dissonance energy except green light."

"Right. Understood. Can I get you a beer?"

"No, thanks," Fontana said. "We won't be staying long."

He drew Sierra past Joe's still form. She was shivering with reaction to the violence. Adrenaline, she thought. Elvis, however, was fully fluffed again. Only his daylight eyes were visible in his tatty fur.

Hank was still in the booth at the rear, looking bleary-eyed and a little stunned. Both of his hands were wrapped around a bottle of Green Ruin.

Sensing the panic that was only partially dulled by the alcohol, Sierra spoke gently.

"Hank?" She slid into the booth across from him. "Are you all right? I've been very worried about you."

"What are you doing here?" Hank asked, but his attention was riveted on Fontana. "That was dark light, wasn't it?"

Fontana sat down beside Sierra. "Name's Fontana."

"Yeah, I recognized you even before you used the dark psi. You're the new Guild boss. What do you want from me? I'm retired."

"Information is what we want from you," Fontana said.

Hank's gaze went to the two men on the floor. "I don't know anything."

"We know that Jake disappeared," Sierra said.

Hank licked his lips and drew a shaky breath. "This is about what happened to Jake?"

"Yes," she said. "You saw what happened to him, didn't you?"

"I was sleeping off a lot of booze." Hank rubbed the back of one hand across his mouth. "I don't know what I saw."

"Please tell us, Hank," she said.

Hank sank in on himself, looking a lot older. "You wouldn't believe me if I told you."

Elvis fluttered down from Sierra's shoulder. He bobbed and weaved across the table and stood up on his hind legs in front of Hank.

Some of Hank's tension seemed to ease. "Hey, there, little buddy. How you doin'?" He patted Elvis.

Elvis chortled a greeting. Hank seemed to relax a little.

"Tell us what happened to Jake Tanner," Fontana ordered quietly.

Hank tightened his grip on the bottle. "If I tell you what I saw last night, you'll figure that I've been fried." He took a gulp of Green Ruin and lowered the bottle. "I'm tellin' you right now, I'm not goin' to no hospital. I'd rather go down into the tunnels and start walking without amber."

In other words, he would rather commit suicide, Sierra thought. She reached out to touch his arm.

"No one's going to force you into a hospital, Hank," she said. "Please tell us what happened to Jake. You saw something, didn't you?"

Hank fixed her with a grim, haunted look. "You want to know what happened to Jake? The aliens got him, that's what happened."

Chapter 16

FONTANA FOLLOWED HER BACK TO HER APARTMENT BEcause it was closer and because they needed a place where they could talk privately.

"Okay, let's see what we've got," she said, dropping her purse and coat on the hall table.

He followed her into the kitchen. Elvis was already there. He had taken up a position in front of the refrigerator.

"We've got nothing except the Green Ruin fantasies of a burnout," Fontana said. He lounged against the counter, folded his arms, and watched her open the refrigerator. "Fish-headed creatures operating a giant beam of ultraviolet energy."

"Hank saw something." She removed a loaf of bread and a jar of peanut butter from the refrigerator. "I agree his recollections are garbled because of the booze, but whatever he saw scared the heck out of him last night."

"Aliens." Fontana grimaced.

"He was very clear about the fact that the ultraviolet light didn't pulse and flare the same way that green ghost energy does. He said it was steady, the way a flashlight beam is steady until you move the flashlight."

"Dissonance energy is highly unstable. It always pulses and flares." Fontana paused. "Maybe what he saw wasn't diss light."

"He said he could feel it, remember? He was sure it was dissonance energy, just not the usual kind." She spread peanut butter on two slices of bread. "Hank may be a burnout, but he worked the tunnels for a lot of years. He knows ghost energy."

"You believe he was telling us the truth?"

"Absolutely. At least he was telling us what he believes to be the truth."

Fontana rubbed his jaw, eyes narrowing. "I've never heard of ultraviolet psi light."

She put the lid back on the peanut butter jar and took a plump, yellow banana out of the basket. "Until I met you, I never knew there was such a thing as dark light."

"That's because you're a civilian," he said. "There are a lot of things civilians don't know about what goes on underground."

She gave him her steely smile and started to peel the banana. "That's because the Guilds like to keep secrets. Well, here's the thing about secrets, Mr. Guild Boss. You can't keep them forever. Sooner or later, there's always a leak."

"And there's only one surefire way of taking care of that kind of leak."

She went very still, her eyes stark with dread. "Dear heaven. Do you think someone killed Jake? Maybe he was murdered because he talked to me about the rumors of an alien lab."

The guilt and dread in her eyes bothered him. He walked around the counter and gripped her shoulders very tightly.

"All we know for certain is that Jake has disappeared, possibly for the same reasons that those other hunters vanished from the streets. Whatever is going on, it started before you began your series of reports on the alien abductions, remember?"

She relaxed a little. "Yes."

"That means that nothing that has happened is in any way your fault."

"But what is going on?" she whispered.

"I don't know yet, but I think the timeline can be narrowed down to something that happened about six months ago."

"How do you know that?" she asked eagerly.

"Jake's service records covering the last six months of his employment with the Guild have vanished. I think that someone, presumably Jenner, made sure they disappeared."

"That was right around the time that I went to work at the *Curtain*," she said. "Shortly after that, I picked up the rumors about Underground Exploration's sweetheart deals with the Guild. A couple of months later, I heard the first reports of homeless men in the Quarter being abducted by aliens." She handed the peanut butter and banana sandwich to Elvis. "We have to find out what happened to Jake."

"Yes."

"I want justice for him and for all the others who disappeared."

"We'll get it."

"It's all so damned unfair." She wiped her eyes with a tea towel. "He was just a burned-out hunter trying to get by. He loved making that miniature dressing room for Elvis. I think he could have had a life if the Guild hadn't abandoned him to the streets."

Fontana said nothing.

Sierra suddenly lowered the tea towel. "Good grief. Aliens."

"Not you, too. I've got enough problems on my hands. If you are about to tell me that you actually believe the aliens have returned to Harmony—"

Her expression lit with zeal. "I saw them."

"What?"

She tossed the towel down onto the counter and dashed out of the kitchen. She went into the small front hall. When she returned, he saw that she had her notebook in hand. She flipped it open.

"This is the picture of the aliens moving around behind the ultraviolet beam that you asked Hank to draw for us," she said.

She unfolded the sketch and put it on the counter. Two diverging parallel lines indicated the energy beam. There were also a couple of stick figures representing the aliens.

"What about it?" he asked.

"The heads of the aliens." She was practically glowing with excitement. "What do they remind you of?"

He studied the bulbous, slightly elongated shapes. "Fish heads?"

"That's not what they look like to me," she said.

He looked up, aware of the energy shimmering in the air around her. "What?"

"Motorcycle helmets," she said.

Chapter 17

KAY STARED, GOGGLE-EYED, JAW ALMOST ON THE FLOOR. "You're going to the Crystal Ball tonight? With Fontana?"

"Well, it's not as if I'd go on my own," Sierra said. She lounged on the corner of Kay's cluttered desk. They had the newsroom to themselves. Matt was out chasing down a story about a rez-screen star who was rumored to have checked into rehab for the twentieth time. Runtley was in his office, and Phil was in the men's room. Everyone else was out to lunch.

"Okay, I'm seriously impressed," Kay said. "That is so exciting. Everyone who is anyone in Crystal will be there. Just think, you'll be hobnobbing with all the most important, most influential movers and shakers in town."

"This isn't going to be a social event for me. It's purely business. Donovan Corley will be there. Fontana promised to introduce me to him. With luck, I'll be able to zing him with a couple of questions about UEX's deals with the Guild."

"Oh, that should go over like a rat in a punch bowl. Sierra, the Crystal Ball is *the* social event of the year. You can't just barge in and grill powerful men like Corley while they're swilling champagne."

"Why not? I've had a hunch from the beginning that Corley and his company are somehow involved with the juice dealing."

"Is that so? Why?"

"There are a couple of reasons. First, those cozy deals UEX has with the Guild."

"So what? A lot of big companies have sweetheart contracts. It's understood that if you want to extract valuable resources from underground, you have to give the Guild a piece of the action. That's true for all the organizations, not just the Crystal Guild."

"Second," Sierra continued, undaunted, "ghost juice started hitting the streets within weeks after UEX abruptly halted what was supposed to have been its biggest exploration venture into the rain forest to date. I don't think that was a coincidence."

"You still believe there's a conspiracy going on, don't you?"

"Yes, I do."

"Look, even if you get a crack at Corley tonight, you don't really think he's going to confess to being a drug lord, do you?"

"I just want to see his reaction when I ask him a few questions."

"If I were you, I'd worry more about getting a dress," Kay said. "You can't wear one of your business suits and a pair of pumps. You're Fontana's wife. You have a responsibility to look *good*."

"I realize that. I made an emergency call to a certain fairy godmother, and she came through for me."

"You've got a fairy godmother now?"

"My cousin, Tamsyn. She's the fashionista in my family. Lives in Cadence, but she knows where to shop in every one of the city-states. She gave me the name of a boutique on Amber Lane and made a phone call. I'm supposed to ask for Doris."

"Amber Lane? I can't even afford to park on that street, let alone shop there."

"Fontana said that the Guild would pick up the tab. Business expense."

"Think Fontana has any idea of how expensive things are in Amber Lane?"

Sierra smiled. "I doubt it."

"Oh, wow," Kay breathed, "this is simply too cool for words."

Runtley stuck his gleaming head through the doorway. "What's going on here?"

"Sierra's going shopping," Kay said.

Predictably, Runtley turned a vivid shade of purple. "I don't pay my reporters to shop in the middle of the afternoon."

"Got to buy a dress for tonight," Sierra explained smoothly. "Turns out I'm going to be covering the Crystal Ball."

Runtley's eyes glittered. "Fontana got you a press pass?"

"Well, actually, I'm going as his wife."

"Oh, yeah, right," Runtley said. "I keep forgetting. I want photos."

Phil sauntered toward them from the direction of the men's room. "What's going on?"

"I'll tell you what's going on," Runtley said, glowing with triumph. "The *Curtain* is covering the Crystal Ball. You're the official photographer."

"Woo-hoo," Phil said. "Just like a real newspaper, huh?"

Chapter 18

THE CRYSTAL PAVILION WAS AN OVER-THE-TOP TRIBUTE to the twin forces of architectural exuberance and the generous financial backing of the city's wealthiest and most powerful citizens, businesses, and organizations. The interior of the grand ballroom was a glittering, decadent fantasy of sparkling mirrored walls and gleaming marble-and-amber floors. A glass dome arched high overhead. The countless lights of a couple dozen massive chandeliers illuminated the expensively dressed crowd.

Sierra paused in the hallway outside the ladies' room. Her gown was a deceptively simple column of dark green that flowed from throat to ankle, a perfect example of understated elegance. An ingenious arrangement of hidden pleats and a discreet slit allowed freedom of movement. Just the right amount of skin was on display. Tamsyn's contact, Doris, had not failed her.

She was a McIntyre. Because of her family's standing in Resonance, she had attended a great many social events over the years. She knew how to dress for this kind of occasion, so she hadn't been worried about showing up in the wrong gown. But for reasons she could not explain—or perhaps did not want to examine too closely—she had wanted to do Fontana proud. The chiefs of the Guilds always had an uneasy relationship with the mainstream upper crust. Some of them, like Jenner, deserved their unsavory reputations. But her intuition told her that Fontana was a good man. He deserved the respect of his peers here in Crystal.

She spotted him a short distance away, waiting for her. He was talking to a well-dressed, distinguished-looking man in his early forties. Donovan Corley was even more aristocratically handsome in person than he was in newspaper photos and on the evening news. From the discreet touches of gold at his cuffs to his air of bone-deep self-assurance, he practically screamed old money. Corley knew his place in the social order: the top.

Fontana made a fascinating contrast. His formal black and amber evening clothes were every bit as expensively tailored as Corley's. His tux could well have come from the same exclusive shop. But somehow it made him look like a well-dressed assassin rather than a soft, pampered member of the social elite.

At that moment, he glanced toward the doorway and saw her. He smiled; an intimate, possessive, wholly masculine smile of sensual appreciation and pride.

She suddenly felt light and beautiful and utterly feminine. Champagne seemed to be flowing in her veins. She went toward him with a sense of gathering excitement. When she got close, he reached out and pulled her closer still.

"Sierra, I'd like you to meet Donovan Corley," he said. "Donovan, my wife, Sierra."

"A pleasure, Sierra," Donovan said in a voice laced with a prep school accent.

She would have forgiven him the accent if he hadn't leaned on it so deliberately. Two could play at this game.

"Good evening," she said coolly, letting her own polished heritage gleam through the words. She knew her parents and her brothers would have groaned if they had heard her. "I've been looking forward to meeting you. Are you enjoying yourself?"

She didn't need her psychic intuition to know that she had succeeded in startling Donovan.

Out of the corner of her eye she saw Fontana's mouth twitch. He swallowed some champagne to drown his amusement.

Donovan recovered immediately.

"I'm enjoying it about as much as I did last year and the year before that," he said, injecting dry amusement into his ever-so-cultured tones. "What can one say about the Crystal Ball? It is what it is."

"Very true." She tucked her hand under Fontana's arm. "Events like this do have a certain sameness about them, don't they? My father complains every year when Mother drags him out to the usual round of charity auctions and fund-raisers."

Donovan's eyes tightened a little at the corners. "Do your parents live here in Crystal?"

"No, Resonance."

"I know a lot of people in Resonance," Donovan said. "And McIntyre is a fairly common name."

She smiled and said nothing.

Donovan frowned. "I don't suppose there's any connection to Jason McIntyre of McIntyre Industries?"

"My father."

"I see." Donovan flicked a quick glance at Fontana. Then he switched his attention back to Sierra. "My apologies. I was under the impression that you were the Sierra McIntyre who works for the *Curtain*?"

"You know my work. I'm flattered." She gave him her brightest smile.

"No offense, but you aren't quite what I expected."

"I get that a lot."

She believed him. He certainly had not expected Fontana to be married to the daughter of a member of his own social class. But she could tell that he was adjusting swiftly, reassigning her to another familiar category, that of a shallow, superficial, self-absorbed woman raised with too much money and indulgence who had decided to entertain herself with a joke of a career and an exciting, dangerous lover. Not an uncommon species in his world.

"You, on the other hand, are exactly what I expected,"

she said smoothly. "Care to comment on the rumor that your company discovered an alien lab in the jungle?"

For an instant, Corley simply looked stunned. A second later, his anger sparked. Unfortunately, so did her intuition, warning her that she had been wrong. She hated when that happened.

"That ridiculous, totally unfounded rumor was started by your paper," he snarled softly. "I believe our lawyers made our position clear."

"Yes, they did," Sierra said. "And I apologize for the misunderstanding. However, given UEX's extremely close ties to the former head of the Crystal Guild, I'm sure you can see how such speculation could arise."

"I don't think I'll dignify that with a response," he said coldly. "If you'll both excuse me, I'm going to join my wife."

He turned on his heel and walked off through the crowd.

Fontana raised his brows. "You know, I was getting along fine with Corley until you showed up. What's your secret for pissing people off?"

"It's a talent."

He snagged a glass of champagne off a passing tray. "What's wrong?"

"Nothing."

"Don't give me that." He handed the champagne to her. "You were humming with excitement when you asked Corley for a comment. But as soon as he denied the alien lab rumor, you looked like a kid who just opened a birthday present and discovered a pair of socks."

She wrinkled her nose. "Sadly, I don't think he's involved in the conspiracy."

"Don't tell me you believed him."

"Yes, as a matter of fact, I do."

Fontana turned watchful. "Why?"

"Just a feeling," she said carelessly. *The same reason I know you're not involved,* she thought.

A man spoke behind her.

"Good evening, Fontana. Congratulations on your marriage. I hope you will introduce me to your new bride?"

The sudden surge of dark, ominous energy came out of nowhere, searing her senses. For a couple of heartbeats, the glittering room blurred around her. She swayed a little. She had been living with her talent all of her life, but never had she experienced a reaction like this. It was as if someone had suddenly shut her up inside a very small spacc; a coffin for example.

Breathe.

Terrified that she might lose her balance, she gripped Fontana's arm very tightly with her free hand. His fingers closed over hers instantly, steadying her.

He gave her a quick, searching glance and then turned her slowly to face the newcomer, giving her time to put on a polite smile.

"Sierra, this is Troy Patterson," he said. "Troy is a member of the Guild Council, as I'm sure you're aware."

Only years of learning how to control her talent saved her from running, screaming, for the nearest exit. Troy Patterson certainly did not look like a man with cold-blooded murder on his mind. He was handsome in a superficial rez-screen star sort of way: tall, lean, and square-jawed, his smile an engaging cross between sexy and charming. His high, sharply defined cheekbones emphasized gray eyes.

"A pleasure," she murmured.

Mom, you would be proud. All those years of drilling good manners into your offspring just paid off.

"Can we dare to hope that the *Curtain*'s coverage of the Guild will become a little more positive now that you're a Guild wife?" Troy asked. His engaging grin belied the darkness underneath.

She managed to keep her own smile in place. "I must admit that I'm gaining a new perspective on the organization."

"Glad to hear it," Troy said.

Fontana moved slightly. "If you'll excuse us, I'm going to dance with my wife."

"Of course." Troy inclined his head graciously to Sierra. "Welcome to the Guild family, Sierra."

An icy chill flashed through her, leaving all of her senses taut. There was an old saying that described the sensation perfectly: *Like someone just walked across my grave*. But in this case, the grave in question was not her own.

Fontana steered her through the crowd. She did not resist, but she was not in the mood to dance. What she really wanted to do was go back into the ladies' room and throw up. But that would cause gossip. *"Guild Boss's Bride Ill at Ball. Pregnant? Covenant Marriage on Fontana's Agenda?"*

Fortunately, the band was playing a slow number that did not require any complicated maneuvers. She could not have handled a tango at that moment.

Fontana pulled her into his arms and guided her into the pattern of the dance.

"Are you all right?" he asked quietly.

"Yes." She took a deep breath and forced herself to look like the happy bride. "How long have you known Troy Patterson?"

"Jenner appointed him to the Council a year ago. Before that, he was with one of the smaller, outlying Guilds. Why?"

"Because I'm pretty sure he wants to murder you."

Chapter 19

"HOW DID YOU KNOW?" FONTANA ASKED. HE SOUNDED interested but not alarmed.

That was not quite the reaction she had expected. She stared at him, aghast.

"You *know* he wants to kill you?" she finally managed in a low whisper.

"Let's just say I know he isn't fond of me. Smile. People will think we're arguing."

"What's going on here, Fontana?"

"Patterson was Jenner's man from the start. I'm almost certain that he was involved in Jenner's scheme, whatever it was."

"But you told me that every member of the Council voted to allow you to fight that duel with Jenner. That means Patterson agreed to it, too."

"The rumors circulating about Jenner's corruption were starting to cause real damage to the organization."

"You mean the Council actually took my stories seriously?" she asked, thrilled.

"You and your paper were considered a nuisance. What really had the Council worried was the fact that the Chamber was looking into the gossip."

"Oh." So much for her investigative reporting.

"Everyone knew we had to get rid of Jenner. Any Council member who tried to protect him would have run the risk of being viewed as being as corrupt as Jenner."

"In other words, Patterson threw his pal Jenner under the bus."

"Well, sure," Fontana said. "That's what guys like that do."

"I know I certainly wouldn't want to depend on Patterson in a pinch."

"He'd leave a man behind for ghost bait, all right," Fontana said.

She shuddered. "You're the head of the Guild now. Can't you get rid of him?"

"Forcing a man off the Council is almost as tricky as taking out a Guild boss. It can be done, but I'd rather have him where I can watch him."

"Ah, yes, the old 'Keep your friends close, but keep your enemies closer' rule."

"That's the plan at the moment." His hand tightened at

her lower back, pulling her closer. "You haven't answered my question."

"What question?"

"You didn't meet Patterson until this evening, and you only exchanged a few words with him. How did you know he was dangerous?"

A little jolt of unease flickered through her. She'd known this was coming. Fontana saw far too much. He noticed the little things. Still, she might be able to finesse it.

"As I'm sure you're well aware," she said coolly, "I don't hold a high opinion of anyone on the Guild Council."

"Sorry, I'm not buying that explanation. You reacted to Patterson before you even saw him. I was holding your arm, remember? I felt the shock that went through you. You picked up something about him on the paranormal plane, didn't you? You're psychic."

"You say that so casually. As if everyone has some weird psi talent."

"At the rate para-talents are appearing in the population, that may soon prove to be true."

"Being weird is not, generally speaking, a good thing," she said crisply, "especially when it comes to psychic senses. In case you hadn't noticed."

"You're talking to someone who works dark light, remember?"

"Working dark light may be a rare and unusual talent, but it is, at least, a recognizable para-rez ability associated with alien energy. Furthermore, you need amber to use it."

"You don't use amber."

"No." She hesitated. "I can use it the same way everyone else does to rez a car engine or turn on a lamp, but I don't need it for my talent, so I don't carry it. My parasenses are different from yours and those of most other people, because they aren't linked to alien psi or something in the environment here on Harmony. There have been various kinds of psychic talents in my family for generations. The records indicate that some of my ancestors who came through the Curtain possessed them."

"What is your talent? Some kind of high-level intuition?"

"Yes." She frowned. "You seem to be taking this rather calmly."

"I'm a Guild boss. We're supposed to be unflappable."

"Do you actually believe me?"

"Yes."

"Oh."

He smiled. "What did you expect?"

"That you'd think I was either a little strange or that I was faking it."

"Is that how people usually react?"

"I don't go around advertising my talent. Historically, people in my family have kept quiet about their psychic natures."

"If your intuition is so damn good, how did you manage to get engaged to Pemberley?"

She made a face. "My intuition works very well, but it isn't always as simple to interpret a reading the way I just did with Troy Patterson. Some things, like immediate danger, come through loud and clear. Others are murky."

"Pemberley fell into the murky category?"

"I knew he wanted me. I sensed that he felt he needed me. I took that to mean he was in love with me. And since I was attracted to him . . ." She moved one hand a little on Fontana's shoulder. "It was easy to convince myself that we were a good match."

Fontana frowned. "You said he wanted you. Needed you. Sounds like love to me."

"The problem was that Jon's feelings for me were so closely interwoven with his passion for something else that I couldn't tell the difference. To be fair, I don't think he could, either."

"What was that something else?"

"What Jon wanted was my talent," she said quietly. "His real passion was his family's business empire. It's in trouble. He believed that he could use me to regain control."

Fontana understood.

"You would have made the perfect business wife," he said. "You would have been able to read his competitors and business associates. You could have told him when someone was trying to maneuver against him or when someone could not be trusted. You could have given him unparalleled insight into everyone he dealt with. Talk about having a competitive edge."

"Yes." She sighed. "Jonathan wanted to marry me because he thought I would be incredibly useful to have around."

"Whereas you know I find you to be a frequent pain in the ass, but I like having you around, anyway."

Chapter 20

THE SHIVERING SENSATION WAS GETTING WORSE. GOING downstairs into the depths of the Crystal Pavilion's parking garage did not improve the situation.

Fontana gave her a concerned survey when he tucked her into the passenger seat of the Raptor.

"Are you okay?" he asked.

"Yes."

"Gee. Now my lowly male intuition is telling me that you're lying through your teeth."

"Just a little tense, that's all."

He closed the door, circled the vehicle, and got in behind the wheel. "Is it always like this for you?"

"I've had strong reactions in the past, but it's never been as bad as this. Something about Troy Patterson really rezzed my senses and triggered the old claustrophobia feeling. I don't understand it."

She'd been certain that the worst was over when Troy Patterson disappeared into the crowd. She'd been wrong. On some very primitive level, not being able to see him had proved even more unnerving than being in his presence. Her brain would rather confront the danger face-to-face than flinch at every fleeting shadow.

"Think about something else," Fontana said.

"Like what?"

"Like me." Fontana put the Raptor in gear and drove out of the garage. "What does your intuition tell you about me now, tonight?"

Her mouth went dry.

"I realize there's an . . . attraction," she said cautiously.

"I want you. Given your special intuition, you know that already."

She didn't know what to say.

He slowed for a light. "I'd also like to make it clear that my feelings for you have nothing to do with any scheme to use your talent. Hell, I didn't even know you were psychic until tonight."

"I know."

He drove through the intersection and turned toward the Quarter. "I can't claim to be highly intuitive, but I've had the feeling from the beginning that the attraction between us goes both ways. Am I wrong?"

"No." She took a shaky breath. "I'm just not sure it's a good idea."

"What are you afraid of?"

"I'm not afraid," she said quickly.

"Yes, you are. I can feel it."

The fog was growing heavier as they drove deeper into the Quarter. Infused with the psi that emanated from the great quartz wall around the ruins, it glowed a luminous green.

"Okay," she said. "Maybe I am a little afraid."

His jaw hardened. "Of me?"

"No. Of myself. I nearly made a disastrous mistake with Jonathan. I don't want to repeat it."

"We're married, Sierra. I know that as far as you're concerned, it's just a business arrangement, but I'm taking it seriously. What about you? Can I expect you to honor those vows we made yesterday? Or are you brooding about Pemberley?"

Anger pulsed through her, sharp and driven by pain. She had just opened a vein for him, and he had the nerve to mention Jonathan.

"No, I am not brooding about Jonathan," she said. "But that doesn't mean I'm interested in a short-term affair with you or anyone else."

He opened the massive steel gates and drove up the long drive in front of the mansion. "I'm not looking for short-term, either."

"Don't try to tell me you're looking for long-term. We just met yesterday, remember? We hardly know each other. Besides, your first priority at the moment is the Guild."

"So much for your great intuition."

She folded her arms around herself. "What's that supposed to mean?"

"It means that right now my top priority is you. You are one badly rattled reporter."

"I'm not *rattled*," she said through her teeth. "I just need some time to recover from the psychic shock I got when I met Troy Patterson."

He drove into the garage, de-rezzed the engine, and turned in the seat to face her.

"Any idea why Patterson had such a strong effect on you?" he asked quietly.

She stared straight ahead through the window. "Yes."

"Care to explain?"

"I don't think this is a good time. I need sleep."

For a moment she thought he was going to keep her prisoner in the front seat of the Raptor until she told him why she had overreacted to Patterson. But to her great relief, he finally nodded once and opened the door.

"Let's go inside," he said. "I've got what you need. My special tonic."

"What?" she asked.

"You'll see."

Elvis greeted them when they came through the back door. He bounced around, muttering cheerfully. He still wore the white cape she had put on him earlier before leaving the mansion.

Sierra scooped him up. "Did you miss me?"

Elvis rumbled happily and scrambled up to her shoulder.

Fontana crossed the room and opened an ornately designed cupboard. He took out a bottle and two glasses. She smiled a little.

"Brandy is your special tonic?" she asked.

"Works wonders."

He splashed some into each glass.

She accepted one of the glasses from him and took a swallow. Then she immediately took another. The heat felt good. Restlessly, she started to prowl the room. Fontana drank some of his own brandy and watched her.

She stopped in front of a display of radiant green urns and took another sip.

Fontana propped one shoulder against a paneled wall, saying nothing.

Gradually, the tension within her began to fade. Perspective, or what felt a lot like it, returned. When she reached the opposite end of the gallery, she came to a halt. She held up her half-empty glass and examined it closely.

"You know, Fontana, I think you may have something here."

"Thanks. But I should warn you that the brandy can hit hard when you're rezzed on psi and adrenaline."

"Hmm. You think that's what got me tonight when you introduced me to Patterson? A heavy dose of adrenaline?"

"That and a strong shot of whatever biochemicals are involved when your psychic senses get stressed to the max. Probably not that much different from what happens to a hunter who melts amber."

"I don't think it's quite the same thing," she said

smoothly. "I've heard tales about what happens when hunters melt amber."

He smiled. "Is that right? What have you heard?"

She drank some more brandy and leaned down to study the glowing objects in a display case.

"First you get really, really lusty," she said. Good grief. Was she flirting with him?

"There is a strong afterburn effect," he conceded.

She straightened and looked at him. "I've heard that not every hunter is powerful enough to rez the kind of energy it takes to actually melt amber."

He swirled the brandy in his glass. "That's true."

"Can you do it?"

"What do you think?"

She smiled. "Oh, yes. My intuition says you're definitely strong enough to do it."

He drank a little more of his brandy.

"So, do you do it a lot?" she asked, going for wide-eyed innocence. It was a look her brothers assured her that she did very well.

"Melt amber?" Fontana shook his head. "As infrequently as possible."

"Really? Why?"

"There are a couple of major downsides to using the kind of energy it takes to burn through a chunk of tuned amber."

She leaned one hip against the corner of the display case, letting the slit in the green gown fall open along the length of one thigh. "Such as?"

"Well, for one thing, it makes the amber unusable until it can be retuned." He studied her thigh. "When you're underground, you don't like to lose good amber."

"What else?"

"The burn stage doesn't last long. Less than an hour."

She smiled knowingly. "An hour is a long time when it comes to some things."

"Yes, but you pay a heavy price for the good time. After the burn comes the crash. It can last for several hours."

"You mean you go to sleep afterward? I've heard that's pretty common with men."

"It isn't an ordinary sleep. It's more like going unconscious. Nothing can keep you awake." He examined his brandy. "When you're out like that, you're . . . vulnerable."

"Vulnerable," she repeated, tasting the word. She no longer felt like flirting. "As in, someone like Troy Patterson could sneak up and kill you?"

"As in."

"Okay, I can see why you wouldn't want to go out of your way to burn amber." She looked down at her own glass. "I think I can go to sleep now."

He came toward her through the glowing shadows of the gallery. He looked wonderful in this room, she thought; a man of power surrounded by objects of power.

She smiled again. "You know, you are the sexiest man I've ever met."

"Try to remember that in the morning."

She pouted. "You think I'm drunk?"

"No. I think you're about to crash."

He picked her up in his arms and started toward the door. She rested her head against his shoulder and inhaled his scent.

"You smell good, too," she whispered.

"So do you."

She was vaguely aware of being carried up the grand staircase. She snuggled closer, wondering if he was taking her to his room. She did not know whether to be relieved or disappointed when he walked into the guest bedroom.

He set her on her feet, turned her around, and unzipped the green gown.

"You're undressing me," she said, watching the satin pool at her feet.

He picked up the gown and put it carefully across the back of a chair. "This is as far as I go."

"Oh. Well, I suppose it's for the best."

"That's what I'm telling myself."

She kicked off her shoes and sank down onto the bed, yawning. He pulled a quilt up to cover her. She closed her eyes. Elvis hopped up beside her and settled down at her feet.

"I lied when I said I didn't know why I freaked out so badly after that encounter with Patterson," she confessed.

She did not open her eyes, but she felt Fontana go still beside the bed.

"Did you?" he asked.

"The reason I had that little panic attack was because of you."

"I caused it?" His voice was perfectly neutral, utterly drained of all emotion.

"Well, sort of." She turned on her side and pulled the quilt to her chin. "When I realized how much of a threat Patterson was to you, I understood something else, as well."

"What was that?"

"How much I'm attracted to you, even though I swore I'd never get involved with a man who was so much like everyone else in my family. I can't seem to help myself. It wasn't the thought of Patterson wanting to murder someone that gave me a panic attack. It was the realization that he wanted to murder *you* in particular that did it."

"Sierra."

"Good night, Fontana."

She thought she heard him say something else, but it was too late. She was already plunging down into the warm oblivion of sleep.

Chapter 21

SHE CAME AWAKE ON A SURGE OF ADRENALINE. HEART pounding, she sat straight up in bed, trying to shake off the sense of disorientation. *Get a grip. You're in Fontana's house. That's why the room doesn't look familiar.*

But common sense wasn't having any effect on her intuition. Everything inside her was shrieking at her to get out of the room, or, if all else failed, to hide under the bed. *Run.*

Evidently the medicinal effects of the brandy had worn off. This panic attack was worse than the one she'd had earlier at the Crystal Ball. She was practically jumping out of her skin. Every hair on the back of her neck was standing on end. She could hardly breathe.

A familiar rumbling sound caught her attention. In the luminous light that filtered through the windows she saw

Elvis. He was at the foot of the bed, fur sleeked, all four eyes gleaming.

The bedroom door opened with terrifying softness; a figure glided silently through the opening. She would have screamed, but her throat was paralyzed.

"Get up," Fontana said very softly. "We have to get out of here. Now."

Dazed, she shoved aside the covers. Fontana was dressed in what looked like a black T-shirt, black trousers, and black boots. He gripped a short, cylindrical object in one hand.

"What is it?" she whispered. "What's going on?"

"Someone got through the security system. More than one person, I think." He opened her closet. "They're on the grounds and moving toward the house. If they got this far, they'll be able to get inside. Since I have no way of knowing how many of them there are, we're leaving. Here, put these on."

He tossed a pair of jeans, a turtleneck sweater, and the casual loafers she had brought with her to the mansion down onto the bed. Then he went to the window, flattened himself against the wall, and looked out into the green mist.

She realized that she was still wearing her lacy black bra, panties, and panty hose. The panty hose had to go. You couldn't run for your life in panty hose.

She got rid of the panty hose, pulled on the jeans, and then jerked the turtleneck down over her head. She shoved her feet into the loafers.

"Okay," she said. "I'm ready." Since when had she started sounding breathless? "Where are we going? The garage?"

"No."

"A safe room?" Her heart plummeted. She couldn't stand the thought of being locked up in some tiny space while they waited for the cops to arrive.

"There is no safe room. But don't worry; there's a way out."

He went toward the door. She got a closer look at what he held in his hand. It was a wicked-looking mag-rez.

"I can't tell you how happy I am to hear that," she said.

Instinctively, she grabbed her glasses, her purse, and Elvis, and followed Fontana out into the unlit hall. There was enough vague light coming through the clerestory windows to illuminate the corridor.

"I didn't hear any alarms," she said.

"The entire ambertronic system is down."

"You mean *none* of that fancy security stuff is working?"

"I'm definitely going to have a few words with the company that installed it when this is finished."

Another icy shiver slipped down her spine. "The whole house is wide open?"

"Not yet. In addition to the high-tech stuff, the doors have old-fashioned mechanical locks. But if they got this far, it's safe to assume they'll be able to get through the bolts."

"If the security system is out, how did you know there were intruders on the grounds?"

"The heavy psi. Can't you feel it?"

"Sorry, all I can feel is my own pulse," she said.

"I'm a hunter. I'm especially sensitive to dissonance energy. Trust me when I tell you there's a lot of it in the vicinity."

"What's so unusual about that? There's always plenty of background energy here in the Quarter."

"Not this much." He halted at the window at the end of the hall. "Take a look."

She hurried forward. Heavy fog cloaked the gardens, but the mist wasn't glowing with the usual green psi.

"What in the world?" she said.

"You're looking at ultraviolet psi energy," Fontana said. "Someone is generating a wide beam of it. That's what knocked out my security system."

Figures moved in the glowing mist; shadowy forms with two legs and bulbous heads.

"Hank's fish-headed aliens," she said. "Night Riders. But how are they managing to pull so much dissonance energy?"

"You know those rumors in the *Curtain* about the discovery of a secret alien lab? Got a hunch there might be something to them."

"I was afraid you were going to say that."

"Let's move. They'll be inside any minute now."

She pushed hard to tamp down her rising panic. "Any

chance this could be about stealing your antiquities collection?"

"I don't think so."

"They want us dead, don't they?"

"I think we'd better assume that, yes."

"So much for your theory that the threat of the Chamber coming down on the Crystal Guild would provide protection for both of us."

"Those guys are Night Riders, not Guild men," Fontana said. "Evidently they don't know enough to be afraid of the Chamber."

He opened a nearby door, revealing a narrow, tightly wound spiral staircase. An awful, sinking sensation that had nothing to do with aliens and Night Riders seized her.

"Ah, jeez," she said. "Please don't tell me we're going down into the catacombs."

"Safest way out. One of the reasons I bought the place. Never know when you're going to need an escape route."

He started down the staircase, descending into darkness.

"No offense," she said, gripping the banister, "but does it strike you that your statement might make you sound a trifle paranoid?"

"A healthy dose of paranoia is part of the standard Guild boss job description."

"I can understand that."

"Close the door and throw the lock. I've got a flashlight."

She swallowed hard and locked the door behind her. With Elvis on one shoulder and her purse slung over the other, she started down into the inky depths. She heard a small snick. The narrow beam of Fontana's flashlight shafted through the darkness. She got a little dizzy when she realized she could not see the bottom of the stairwell.

Don't think about it, just keep moving. That's the key.

Elvis clutched her shoulder with his hind paws, holding on tight but not sinking his tiny claws into her. She sensed his highly rezzed, battle-ready tension. It wasn't all that different from what she was picking up from Fontana. Males. Always ready to rumble.

Halfway down, she heard a muffled explosion overhead. A low roaring followed.

"What in the world was that?" she whispered.

"Sounds like the bastards just set fire to my house."

"Oh, my God."

"That's probably what my insurance company is going to say, too. It wasn't easy talking them into giving a Guild boss a policy in the first place."

"But if the house is on fire, that means we can't go back up these stairs," she wailed.

"Don't worry, there are other ways out of the catacombs."

But to get to one of those exits, they would have to travel underground, perhaps for a long distance. On the surface, the next hole-in-the-wall or an official gate might be only a couple of blocks away. But in the underworld, things were different. She'd heard enough about the strange maze of tunnels to know that there were no direct routes anywhere. Furthermore, only a tiny percentage of the vast network of catacombs had been charted. To say nothing of the hazards of illusion traps and drifting ghosts.

"You okay?" Fontana asked.

She took a deep breath. "I'm okay."

Suck it up, woman, you're an investigative reporter. Act like one.

The staircase wound deeper beneath the old mansion. She was getting dizzy watching Fontana's light spiral endlessly away into the shadows. She tried not to think about the tomblike darkness that surrounded her.

Eventually the twisting beam of light halted. Her head was spinning so badly she had to grip the metal banister with both hands to keep from stumbling into Fontana.

"You sure you're okay?" he asked, steadying her.

"Touch of vertigo," she admitted, closing her eyes. She was trembling, and they weren't even inside the catacombs. Dear heaven, how was she going to get through this?

The answer was simple. She was going to get through whatever came next because there was no other option.

"Take a couple of deep breaths," Fontana said. "Don't pass out on me."

It was an order, given with all the icy assurance of a man who expected to be obeyed. Well, he was a Guild boss, she reminded herself. They weren't known for their compassion and consideration.

Oddly enough, although she resented the brusque command, it had a bracing effect. *Like a splash of cold water,* she thought. She took some slow, deep breaths. Her head seemed to clear a little.

"I told you, I'm okay," she said.

If he suspected that she was lying through her teeth again, he did not let on.

"Stay here while I de-rez the door into the tunnels," he said instead.

She felt him move away from her. When she opened her eyes, she saw that the beam of his flashlight was shining on a massive plate of solid mag-steel. It looked like the door of a bank vault. She watched him enter a code.

"Who installed that?" she asked.

"The former owner."

She glanced back over her shoulder. "I suppose the good news is that, if the house is going up in flames, the Riders aren't going to be coming down that staircase behind us."

"That's it, think positive." He reached for the steel door handle. "If it makes you feel any better, there's no way they can know about this hole-in-the-wall. But even if they did, I doubt that they would follow us into the tunnels."

"Why?"

"Because they have to know that once we're in the catacombs, they'll be on my turf. Everything's different underground."

Chapter 22

THE HEAVY DOOR OPENED WITH PONDEROUS SLOWNESS, revealing a jagged tear in the tunnel wall. Fontana felt the familiar rush of psi first. It flowed out of the catacombs, an invisible wave that stirred his already rezzed senses. Next came the acid-green light. He turned off the flashlight. There was no longer any need for it. Down here everything was made of quartz, and the stone glowed the same psi green night and day.

No one knew when the aliens had left Harmony. Some experts believed they had been gone for at least a thousand years. Others put the date much further back, maybe five or even ten thousand years. There were a few archaeologists who were convinced they had never left at all, just died out. Whatever the case, they had left the lights on.

He looked into the large rotunda that lay on the other side of the tear in the quartz. Half a dozen vaulted corridors branched off the circular space. He knew that there were an endless number of intersections leading off each of the branches and so on throughout the vast maze.

Here and there vaulted doorways opened onto strangely shaped chambers. No one knew what purpose the rooms had once served. Some were empty. Others contained the mysterious artifacts and relics that fueled the thriving antiquities trade.

The architecture of the catacombs was slightly disorienting to the human eye. The proportions never seemed quite right. Compounding the problem was the fact that the energy that emanated from the quartz had a subtle effect on the normal as well as the paranormal senses. His hunter para-rez talents gave him an advantage over people like Sierra, who lacked the ability to resonate with alien psi, but that didn't mean things ever felt normal down here. That, of course, was one of the big attractions for him.

Sierra followed him through the doorway. She looked around, her eyes a little haunted. He hated having to put her through this, but there was no alternative.

Elvis showed no qualms at all. He leaned forward eagerly, fully fluffed again.

The thick, mag-steel door closed with an ominous, reverberating clang. Sierra jumped a little and looked back over her shoulder.

"This way," Fontana said. He moved through the hole-in-the-wall into the tunnel. "I keep a utility sled down here. We'll use it to get to the nearest exit."

"Sounds like a good plan."

Something in her voice made him look back at her. She was clearly very tense, but she didn't look like she was going to faint. Still, he did not like the dread in her eyes.

"Don't worry," he said, trying to project a little reassurance. "I've spent a lot of time down here. I know my way around, and I've got plenty of amber and a compass. We won't get lost."

"Glad to hear that."

He realized now what was wrong with her voice. It was flat, almost a monotone. It was as if she was fighting to keep all emotion out of it. She was hanging on to her self-control with willpower alone, he thought. Good thing she had a lot of it. Dealing with her unusual talent all these years had probably gone a long way toward developing that core of inner strength.

The sled was right where he had left it. He got behind the wheel. Sierra climbed quickly up onto the bench seat beside him. He rezzed the simple, amber-based motor, one of the few kinds of low-tech mechanical devices that worked underground.

Sierra gripped the edge of the bench seat very tightly on either side of her thighs and stared straight ahead. Elvis muttered into her ear, as though he, too, was trying to assure her that everything would be okay.

"How far is the next exit?" she asked in that too-even tone.

"The nearest official gate operated by the Guild is only

about a mile away from the mansion aboveground, but down here it would take us a couple of hours. These sleds are slow. Top speed is just a little faster than the average person can run. The real problem is that there are no direct routes between any of the entrances."

"We're going to be down here for the next *two hours*?"

"Take it easy," he said. "I know another hole-in-the-wall. It's only about twenty minutes away. It opens under an old, unused warehouse."

She nodded once, but she did not relax her grip on the edge of the seat.

"How's the claustrophobia?" he asked.

"Is my face the same color as the tunnel wall?"

"Not quite."

"Take that as a good sign. I should be okay as long as we're in motion."

"I'm not planning to hang around down here for any length of time, believe me."

She seemed to relax a little. "I trust you won't tell any of your Guild pals about my little problem. It's embarrassing to be married to the boss and not be able to go underground without having a panic attack."

He smiled. "Don't worry. It'll be our little secret."

He punched the coordinates of the hole-in-the-wall into the amber-rez locater. Out of long habit, he also checked his compass. You couldn't be too careful underground.

He steered the sled down one of the hallways. The locater flashed. He made another turn.

"Good heavens, this place really is a maze, isn't it?" Sierra whispered. "I wonder how the aliens navigated it."

"We'll probably never know, but it must have had something to do with their paranormal natures. They obviously needed a psi-heavy environment in which to live, so they must have had a lot of ways to manipulate that kind of energy."

"Compared to them, we humans barely dabble our toes in psychic waters," she said softly. "We live mostly through our normal senses, not our para-senses."

"On the other hand, we're still here, and they aren't."

"Good point. We must be doing something right."

"I'm not sure that's the explanation," he said. "The thing humans have going for them is that they are just flat-out stubborn when it comes to stuff like surviving."

That got a tiny smile from her. "I believe the experts refer to it as an ability to adapt to changing conditions."

"Right." He nodded. "Stubborn. Like I said."

The heavy push of raw dissonance energy struck hard an instant later. He eased his foot off the sled's accelerator.

Sierra reacted immediately, stiffening.

"What's wrong?" she asked tightly. "Why are we slowing down?"

"Ghost coming up. Big one."

She gave him an anxious glance. You can de-rez it, I assume?"

"Let's review. What do I do for a living?"

"Oh, right." She drew a breath. "Sorry. I'm a little tense."

The tunnel curved sharply to the left. He slowed the sled to a crawl. The last thing he wanted to do was blunder into a ball of ghost fire.

But it wasn't the familiar acid-green of normal ghost light that confronted them. Instead, a hot barrier of tightly seething ultraviolet energy blocked the corridor.

Two shadowy figures with bulbous heads were just barely visible on the other side of the wide beam.

"They found us," Sierra said without inflection.

He brought the sled to a halt and studied the rippling, pulsing barrier of ultraviolet light. "How the hell can they keep dissonance energy so symmetrical? The stuff is inherently unstable."

"It's so strong that even I can feel it," Sierra whispered, amazed. "It's like a psychic storm."

He glanced at her and saw that her hair was lifting and stirring in response to the energy in the atmosphere. Elvis's fur was sticking straight out in a spiky halo. The dust bunny gazed straight ahead at the wall of light, watchful and cautious, just as they were.

"Oh, jeez," Sierra whispered. "The beam is moving. They're coming toward us."

"We've got a problem," he said.

"You *can* deal with that thing, right?"

"Maybe. Assuming it responds to dark light the way regular ghost light does."

"That is not reassuring, Fontana."

"The problem is that even if I can de-rez it, I'd have to pull a hell of a lot of psi to do it."

"So?"

"So, I won't have much in the way of reserves left afterward to deal with whoever they'll have waiting for us in the warehouse."

"How did they know that we would come this way?" she whispered.

"Good question. But this isn't the time to answer it." He turned the sled around and started back the way they had come. "Sorry, but there's no choice now. We're going to have to head for the official Guild gate. It's a two-hour run. Can you handle it?"

She reached up to touch Elvis. "I'm a Guild boss's wife. I can handle anything."

"Right answer."

She twisted in the seat to look back the way they had come. "The energy beam is picking up speed. The two Riders just climbed into a sled."

"Can you tell how many of them there are?"

"Just the two of them, I think, but I can't be absolutely certain. It's like trying to look through a waterfall."

He glanced back and saw that she was right. The beam of ultraviolet psi was pursuing them down the corridor at sled speed.

"We've got a lead on them," he said. "We should be able to maintain it. With luck, we may even be able to lose them in the catacombs."

"Can't they track us with one of those new amber-rez locaters?"

"Yes, but I know a few tricks that can fool a locater."

"I thought those things were supposed to be foolproof."

"The Guilds like to keep a few secrets."

"Remind me to ask you about that later," she said.

"A Guild boss is always happy to grant interviews to members of the press."

He was halfway around the curve in the tunnel when his over-rezzed senses picked up another blast of alien psi. The low growl to his right told him that Elvis had sensed it, too.

"I think we've got another ultraviolet ghost coming up ahead," he said.

She gripped the edge of the seat. "Ambush."

"I take back everything I said about how no one else could possibly know about my private escape route." He did a quick survey of the curving tunnel in front of them. "A million intersecting hallways down here, but never one nearby when you need one. Probably why they chose this section. Okay, we've run out of options. I'm going to have to de-rez one of these monsters."

"Which one?"

"The one up ahead. No point going back the way we just came, because even if we make it through, there's still the problem of dealing with whoever will be guarding the warehouse exit. By the time we get there, I'll be only half conscious."

"So we go forward."

"There's a shovel in the back. Get it."

She looked at him, startled. "Why?"

"It's the closest thing we've got to a weapon besides the jungle knife under the seat. Better dig that out, too. If we make it past that energy barrier, we're going to have to face whoever rezzed it."

Without another word she turned in the seat and reached back. Elvis scrambled off her shoulder and bounded up onto the dashboard where he had an excellent view.

There was a clang and a couple of thuds from the rear of the sled. A few seconds later, Sierra turned around. She gripped the long handle of the shovel.

"If you have to use it, think of it as a lance," he said. "If it gets snagged on the other vehicle or if someone tries to pull it out of your hand, let it go immediately. Otherwise you'll be yanked out of the sled."

"Okay."

"Don't forget the knife."

Obediently she reached under the seat and came up with the jungle knife. She slid the long, heavy blade out of its sheath and placed it on the dashboard next to Elvis.

She was pale and tense, but he could literally feel the hot force field of determination that blazed invisibly around her. A strange thrill flared deep inside him. He was torn between the need to protect her and a soul-stirring pride in her courage. His woman, his wife.

The ultraviolet waterfall was waiting for them when they came out of the curve. He slowed the sled a little and started summoning dark light, as much as he could pull.

A whirlpool of pulsing midnight swirled into existence in the passageway ahead of the sled. He had intended to try to tackle the monster by attacking its tightly whirling core. That was standard practice for dealing with UDEMs, both the kind that floated at random through the tunnels and those that were human-generated.

But the energy barrier did not have an obvious core. The intricately churning psi looked as strong and tight at the outer edges as it did at the center. He aimed his flaring vortex of dark energy at the side of the waterfall.

Dark light slammed into ultraviolet near the point where the energy veil met the tunnel wall. There was an explosive sound not unlike a burst of fireworks.

"Look," Sierra said. "You sliced off a piece of the ghost."

His first salvo had taken a big bite out of the monster. But the gap disappeared almost instantly. Within seconds the veil repaired itself.

He could punch through it, but the hole would not last long enough for them to slip through the opening.

"I've got an idea," he said. "Move closer to me, as far away from the edge of the sled as possible."

She didn't ask any questions, just slid across the bench seat until she was only a couple of inches away from him. There was so much psi in the atmosphere now that her hair swirled around her face as though she were swimming in a pool of invisible water. Impatiently she pushed a few tendrils out of her eyes and held the shovel at the ready.

The moving dam of energy behind them was getting close. He didn't have to look back to know it was there. He could feel the stuff coming toward them like a tsunami. Time had run out.

"Looks like we do this now," he said.

He pulled more midnight energy, more than he had ever summoned in his life. The waves of darkness pulsed and churned. When they were big enough, he threw everything he had through his amber and divided the night ghost at its core. Two whirlpools of highly volatile night fire appeared directly in front of the sled.

Instead of using the twin ghosts as battering rams, he positioned one on the front of the sled and the other against the passenger side of the vehicle. He had to maintain exquisite control. The slightest brush would sear their psychic senses. He might make it because he had some natural immunity, but with this much energy involved, he would likely be a candidate for a nice quiet parapsych ward afterward. He doubted that Sierra would survive. As for Elvis, who knew? Dust bunny paraphysiology was a mystery.

He drove toward the ultraviolet waterfall, aiming to get as close to the tunnel wall as possible.

Light and colors from across the spectrum flashed and

flared as the churning night in front of the sled smashed into the ultraviolet beam. An opening just large enough to accommodate the sled appeared.

He floored the accelerator. Metal screamed when the left fender of the sled scraped against the tunnel wall. Ultraviolet energy surged, seeking to plug the opening, but the whirlpool of darkness that he had stationed on the right-hand side of the sled held the beam at bay for the seconds they needed to get through.

And then they were on the other side.

He saw another sled. A man in a motorcycle helmet, visor raised, sat in the front of the vehicle. He held a small device in both hands. There was no way he could swivel the gadget around, because the action would cause the ultraviolet beam to sweep over his two companions who stood beside the sled.

"They made it," one of the Riders yelled. "Turn this thing around and follow them."

"Shit, here come the others," the man inside the sled shouted. Panic lanced through his words. "They can't see us through that beam they're generating. They'll run right over us. We'll be fried."

The second man outside the vehicle ignored him. He jerked a long-bladed knife out of a belt sheath and lunged forward. His trajectory took him straight toward Sierra's side of the sled. He managed to grab the edge of the door opening, clearly intent on vaulting up into the cab.

Sierra aimed the shovel at his chest and shoved. The attacker screamed, lost his grip, and fell back onto the floor of the tunnel.

Fontana checked the locater and took a hard left. The shouts and curses of the men faded quickly into the distance behind them.

Chapter 23

"WE CAN OUTRUN THEM, RIGHT?" SIERRA ASKED.

She felt strangely, unnaturally calm now that there was a genuine reason to panic. Either her overcharged senses had finally succumbed to the stress and burned out altogether or else being chased by a bunch of guys who wanted to kill you was a sure cure for claustrophobia.

"It will take them a while to regroup back there," Fontana said. "We should be able to put some distance between us."

Something about his tone of voice warned her that the situation had improved only moderately in his view. He was driving with a hard efficiency, glancing frequently at the dashboard instruments, pushing the little vehicle to its limits.

Elvis, still perched on the dash, was fully fluffed again and leaning forward excitedly, clearly enjoying this new game of tunnel chasing. Nevertheless, he still had all four eyes open.

She twisted in the seat and looked back. Behind them the branching corridors were empty. "You lost them."

"Not for long," Fontana said. "All we can do is stay ahead of them. Their sleds can't move any faster than ours."

"I thought you knew some tricks for throwing off their locaters."

"I do, but they aren't guaranteed to work. The real problem is that we haven't got time to make it to the main gate."

"You said it was only a couple of hours away."

"We don't have a couple of hours now. I burned a lot of amber getting us through that ultraviolet ghost beam. In less than an hour, I'm going to go out like a de-rezzed light."

A chill shot down her spine.

"The burn-and-crash thing?" she asked.

"I told you there were some major downsides to melting amber. It's a huge psychic energy drain. Takes time for the body to recover. I'm going to need at least three or four hours of sleep, and I'm not going to have any choice about it when the crash hits."

She cleared her throat. "I, uh, thought there was a period of increased excitement following a big burn. That adrenaline-testosterone rush business."

He gripped the wheel. "What do you think is keeping me awake and driving right now?"

She drew a deep breath. "I see. Well, I'm sure I can drive the sled."

"But can you use an amber-rez coordinator or a compass to find the gate?"

She winced. "No."

"Remind me to teach you one of these days. Every Guild boss's wife should learn how to navigate underground."

"I'll be sure to put it on my to-do list."

"Meanwhile, we haven't got an option; we're going to go into the jungle."

"What?"

He glanced at the sled's locator. "There's a gate into the rain forest not far from here. The Riders won't know about it."

"No offense, but that's what you said about the warehouse exit."

"This is different," Fontana said. "This is mine."

The intensity of his words made her look at him.

"Yours?" she repeated.

"I found it a week after I moved into the mansion. Turns out one of the things dark light is good for is opening gates into the rain forest. I never told anyone that I discovered and opened this particular gate."

"Not even your friend Ray?"

"Not even Ray."

He turned a corner so sharply Elvis had to scramble to keep his perch. Sierra seized the grab bar and steadied herself.

"What if they figure out that we went into the jungle?" she asked. "Won't they just use another gate and come looking for us with their locaters?"

"The new locators work fairly well in the catacombs but not in the rain forest. Too much strange psi floating around in there. Plants, trees, animals, ghost rivers, all kinds of things give off energy in there. The only ways to navigate are the old-fashioned ways."

"By amber compass?"

"And by using the position of the sun and the two moons, if you know how to do it. Most people don't."

She was stunned. "There's a real sun and a couple of moons in the jungle?"

"No, of course not. They're artificial, created by some kind of alien energy source that we haven't been able to locate. No one knows how the system works, but it seems to do the job. The bottom line is that if we get into the jungle before those guys find us, we'll be safe. We can go to ground while I sleep off the burn."

She looked down one of the seemingly endless corridors of green and felt the edgy prickle of panic spark inside her again. She tried not to think about the hours of being trapped in a strange jungle that awaited her.

"What's it like in the rain forest?" she asked, unable to help herself.

"Like nothing you've ever seen."

The quiet wonder in his voice made her turn her head very quickly to look at him.

"You *like* going into the rain forest?"

"Yes. But generally speaking, I prefer to go in under different conditions."

He checked the instrument panel again, turned sharply into a strangely vaulted chamber, and brought the sled to a halt at what appeared to be a blank quartz wall.

"This is it," he said. "We can drive through the gate and get the sled out of sight, but we won't be able to take it more than a few feet inside."

"Why not?"

"You'll see."

Elvis suddenly seemed to notice that the tunnel chase game had taken a new twist. He muttered enthusiastically and tumbled down from the dashboard. The next thing Sierra knew he was out of the sled, fluttering eagerly toward the chamber wall.

"Elvis, come back here," she called. "Where are you going? This is no time to run off."

He gave her a cheerful, chittering response, but he did not dash back to the sled. Instead, as she watched, amazed, a small, dust-bunny-sized section of the wall dissolved. Elvis dashed through the opening and promptly disappeared. The wall shimmered and became solid once again.

"*Elvis,*" she cried, horrified. "Where are you?"

The little hole reopened. Elvis popped out, chortling happily at the new game. He scurried back across the floor and up into the sled.

She clutched him. "Please don't do that again."

"Now, that is very interesting," Fontana said, suddenly thoughtful.

"What?" she demanded.

"Elvis just opened and closed a jungle gate."

"Maybe that's where he goes when he disappears occasionally at night. I've always assumed he was out trolling for girlfriends in unsavory dark alleys."

"Probably out hunting. What better place to hunt than a jungle? Okay, listen closely. I've got just enough power left to open and close a gate large enough for us, but after that, I'm going to be very close to finished."

Alarmed, she held Elvis very still.

"Finished?" she repeated. "That doesn't sound good."

"I'll probably be unconscious within minutes. After I go out, you'll be in charge."

She glanced at the knife on the dashboard. "I should probably tell you that I don't know diddly-squat about surviving in a jungle."

"The rain forest is fairly safe so long as you don't go stumbling around or try to move after dark. It's an artificially constructed environment, remember? The aliens probably didn't want to fill it full of dangerous critters. As far as we've been able to figure out, the biggest hazards are the ghost rivers."

"But what about poisonous insects? Snakes? Predators?"

"There aren't many that are dangerous to humans, and those that are tend to avoid us."

"I have to tell you I'm not sure I can do this," she whispered.

"You're a Guild boss wife. You can do anything, remember?"

He leaned forward abruptly and kissed her. It was a hard, fast, rough, thoroughly possessive kiss, and it told her just how much sexually charged tension was zapping through him.

He broke off the kiss an instant later. Heat and regret burned in his eyes.

"Sure hate to waste the afterburn like this," he said. "But we've got priorities here."

He turned to face the quartz wall. She was still trying to catch her breath when she realized that dark light was once again swirling in the atmosphere. Where was Fontana getting the energy to do this? He had to be pulling on the last of his reserves.

The waves of night fire formed a now-familiar whirlpool in front of the wall. With disconcerting suddenness, a large section of solid quartz seemed to dissolve.

Elvis bounced up and down, delighted that Fontana knew how to play this game, too.

A fantastical scene appeared as the gate opened. She had seen photographs and rez-screen videos of the alien rain forest, but viewing it in person was something else entirely.

Her first impression was of a mass of impossibly verdant foliage. Giant ferns, spectacular palm fronds, and trees choked with vines and leaves loomed in the opening. The hues and intensities varied, but all of the plant life she could see was infused with the unique psi green that characterized virtually everything else the aliens had constructed.

Fontana drove through the opening into the jungle. It was as if they had entered another dimension. Heat, humidity, and the rich smells of a giant greenhouse enveloped them.

"Nothing gets out of here into the tunnels," Fontana explained. "The gates have some kind of invisible barriers that keep jungle life inside."

He de-rezzed the sled and turned in the seat. Once again energy pulsed.

Sierra looked back and saw that the tunnel wall had re-formed.

"We're going to have to move fast," Fontana said. "I've got maybe ten, twelve minutes, max. Grab one of the supply kits in the back. I'll take the other."

He climbed out of the cab, gripping the edge to steady himself. There were grim lines at the corners of his mouth. His jaw was rigid. She knew that he was operating on willpower alone now, but he seemed to have a lot of that particular commodity. A born leader, she thought. But more than that, a man who protected others. Her intuition rezzed faintly, making her understand that Fontana's only objective now was to see her safe. He would keep going until he accomplished that goal or until he dropped in his tracks.

When he reached into the back of the sled and picked

up one of the kits, she saw his knuckles whiten with the effort.

She scrambled out and grabbed the second kit. Turning, she saw that he was already heading into the jungle, moving at a steady slog. Elvis scampered along at his heels. She hurried to catch up.

"Where are we going?" she asked.

"Where else?" Fontana said. "The secret alien temple of love."

Chapter 24

HE KEPT CHECKING AND DOUBLE-CHECKING THE COMpass, aware that in his present state of exhaustion it would be all too easy to make a mistake. He had been this way several times in recent weeks, but he knew he couldn't trust himself to recognize the path. Nothing ever looked the same two days in a row in the jungle. New growth was always taking the place of old, altering the landscape. And then there was all the damned psi to contend with. The plants and trees gave off even more energy than quartz, probably because they were living things. The swamp of paranormal waves played tricks on the normal human senses.

His feet felt as if they were made out of solid mag-steel now. It was all he could do to get one thousand-pound boot in front of the other. The effort required to keep his eyes open was painful. The postburn rush was fading fast.

Fortunately, his destination was not far. He pushed through one last web of cascading vines. The alien ruin was there, right where the compass said it should be. Relief nearly overwhelmed him. Sierra would be safe here while he slept off the afterburn.

She came up beside him and halted suddenly, staring in amazement at the strange structure.

"Not a cave," she whispered, sounding vastly relieved.

"No," he said.

"I was so afraid it was going to be a cave. This is incredible."

"I know."

The ruin was unlike any other that he had ever seen. It was made of quartz but not the usual opaque green variety. Instead, the graceful, circular pavilion was fashioned entirely of a transparent, emerald-tinted stone. Seven clear stone pillars supported the elegantly vaulted, crystal-clear quartz roof. On an earlier visit he had measured the diameter of the transparent floor. Fifteen feet. Plenty of room for both of them.

"You'll be safe here," he said, aware that he was starting to slur his words. He managed, barely, to haul himself and the emergency kit up onto the transparent floor.

"The clear quartz must have some special properties," Sierra said, following him. "This place should have been buried by vegetation centuries ago. Instead, it's as clean as the day it was built."

"Like the tunnels," he said. He crouched to open the supply kit. "You can leave the pavilion, but don't go out of sight of it. Understand? You won't be able to find your way back."

"Don't worry, I'm not going anywhere down here without you."

He pulled out the bedroll. "There's water in the supply kits, but feel free to drink from the stream over there. I tested it."

"I've heard that all the water that has been found in the jungle so far is safe to drink."

"So far. Down here you don't make too many assumptions." He kicked the bedroll open and stretched out, yawning. "I'll wake up in about three, maybe four hours."

She was as safe as he could make her for now. He sprawled on the bedroll, turned on his side, and let the weight of sleep take him.

THE HUMIDITY WAS INCREASING EVEN AS THE LUMINOUS green sky darkened with ominous peridot clouds. The long-sleeved turtleneck Fontana had pulled out of the closet and told her to put on before they escaped the mansion had proved to be an exceptionally bad fashion choice. She was so hot in it that she began to worry that she might suffer from heatstroke. To be fair, Fontana had never intended to take her into a jungle tonight.

She opened one of the supply kits. There was a variety of neatly packed items inside, including some energy bars and what looked like one of Fontana's shirts. The shirt was typical Guild boss black with amber buttons. There were also several chunks of amber in the bag. All of it tuned, no doubt.

She started to remove the suffocating turtleneck and then paused self-consciously to make sure Fontana wasn't awake. But he was sound asleep on the bedroll, his back to her.

Hurriedly she removed the garment and tossed it aside. After a moment's thought, she took off her perspiration-dampened bra as well. Constricting undergarments were not comfortable in the jungle.

The shirt was much too big. It hung to her knees and kept sliding off her shoulder, but when she rolled up the sleeves, she was pleased with the result.

"Much cooler," she said to Elvis. "Here, let me take off your cape. It can't be very comfortable in this heat."

He didn't pay any attention when she slipped the rhinestone cape off over his head. He was too busy checking out the contents of the supply kit.

She folded the little cape and tucked it into her purse.

"Hungry?" she asked.

He rumbled.

She removed one of the energy bars, unwrapped it, and handed it to Elvis. "It's no peanut butter and banana sandwich, but it's all we've got."

He took it eagerly and crunched the bar with evident enjoyment.

She unwrapped a second bar and tried it warily. It wasn't bad.

"Not very tasty, but definitely edible," she declared.

She surveyed her surroundings while they ate. The first thing she noticed was that, unlike the tunnels, the rain forest was a noisy place. Birdcalls echoed endlessly through the leafy canopy. There were occasional flutterings and skittering sounds in the undergrowth. Each time she heard something, she glanced at Elvis to see if he looked alarmed. He remained fully fluffed.

She looked at the stream Fontana had indicated earlier. It emanated from a small, plant-choked grotto. Water bubbled out of a rocky green pool and flowed away, disappearing into the undergrowth.

"Wonder what this place looks like at night," she said to Elvis. "Sure hope we don't have to find out."

On the positive side, the oppressive sense of claustrophobia was gone. The tunnel walls were no longer closing in on her. There was one thing to be said about the jungle: it was big; so big that if she hadn't known she was underground, she could easily have believed that she was in a real tropical rain forest. Except for the green-tinted artificial sunlight, of course. That was just plain alien-weird.

No one knew how far the jungle extended. Exploration had barely begun, but the most popular theory at the moment was that the eerie, underworld rain forest linked all four of the dead cities that had thus far been discovered and the ruins of the smaller outposts as well. Unable to live in the aboveground environment, the aliens had been forced to construct an underground ecosystem that could sustain them.

They had done an impressive job. Their bioengineering work had survived and was still flourishing long after the builders themselves had vanished.

A sharp, shrill shriek somewhere nearby startled her so badly she dropped what was left of her energy bar. She looked at Elvis, who showed no indication of going on alert status. Instead, he scampered across the clear stone floor, picked up the uneaten portion of her energy bar, and finished it off.

"Guess the five-second rule applies here as well as anywhere else."

She folded the wrappers from the two energy bars very neatly and stashed them in the supply kit.

There was no sound from Fontana. After a while, she got a little worried. She rose and leaned over his still form to check on him. He was sleeping deeply, but his breathing sounded normal, slow and even.

She absolutely had to stretch her legs. Cautiously she stepped off the strange floor and onto the ground.

Elvis chattered excitedly, sensing a new game.

"You're my early warning system," she reminded him. "I'm counting on you to let me know if there's trouble in the vicinity."

He fluttered off the circular floor and bounced up onto an emerald green rock near the stream. He began to investigate a vine full of green orchids that hung from a tree limb.

She wandered over to a nearby palm and availed herself of the privacy offered by the broad, fluted fronds. Fontana might be out like a light, but it was the principle of the thing. She hardly knew the man. Sure, they were married and he had just saved her life and the sexual chemistry between them worked both ways and she was definitely falling headfirst into love. Still, you just didn't pee in front of a man you had only known a couple of days.

When she was finished, she washed her hands in the little stream and went to join Elvis on his rock. She leaned forward and plucked one of the emerald orchids.

"It's gorgeous," she said.

In fact, now that she'd had a chance to grow accustomed to the sights and sounds, she was beginning to relax and take in the sheer, otherworldly beauty of the rain forest.

"It's not so bad," she said to Elvis. "Magical, in fact."

He clutched the dangling vine in all six paws and pushed himself off the edge of the rock. The makeshift swing carried him out over the grotto pool in a graceful arc. When the return arc brought him back within reach, Sierra caught him, much to his delight.

Laughing, she launched him into another swing. He chortled gleefully.

"When we get out of here, I'll ask Jake to build you your very own swing," she said. Then she stopped. Jake was gone, possibly dead. Why was she suddenly thinking about him?

In fact, now that his name had popped into her mind, she could not *stop* thinking about him. A little rush of intense awareness shot through her. She knew this edgy sensation well. It was her intuition kicking in, warning her to pay attention. There was something Jake had said . . .

And then the storm broke. Green lightning flashed. The rain hit. She grabbed Elvis and hurried back into the crystal gazebo.

Chapter 25

FONTANA CAME AWAKE TO THE FAMILIAR LOW ROAR OF A jungle downpour. He sat up abruptly and shoved his fingers through his hair. He contemplated the rain with grim resignation.

The warm deluge was coming down the way it always did in the jungle, in a relentless torrent. The atmosphere bordered on steamy. He couldn't see more than a couple of feet beyond the edge of the gazebo.

"Figures," he said. "Given my luck lately."

"You're awake." Sierra came toward him, holding out an energy bar. "How do you feel? Are you hungry?"

She had put on his shirt. It looked good on her. Not that she wouldn't look good in anything or, preferably, nothing at all, but the fact that it was *his* shirt that she was wearing gave him a sense of satisfaction. His woman in his shirt. And he was stuck here with her in the crystal ruin while the rain forest did its thing. Maybe his luck wasn't so bad after all.

"Starved," he said. He took the energy bar, ripped off the wrapper, and ate almost half of it in one bite. "I'm always hungry after a heavy burn," he explained around the mouthful.

Elvis chortled a greeting and scampered over to say hello. Fontana patted him in the vicinity of what should have been the top of his head. "How's it going, King?"

Elvis bounced a little.

Fontana popped the last of the energy bar into his mouth, got to his feet, and stretched.

"How long has it been raining?" he asked.

"An hour, maybe longer," Sierra said.

"Well, one thing's for sure. We're going to be here for a while. You can't move in the jungle in these conditions. The really bad news is that by the time the rain lets up, it will probably be night. We sure as hell aren't going to try traveling after dark."

"But it was nearly three AM when we left your house. It's late morning now."

"Not down here, it isn't. This place is on a different, artificial schedule. I'll be right back," he added, stepping off the platform into the rain.

"Wait, where are you going?" she asked anxiously.

"Where do you think I'm going? I need to take a leak."

She turned pink. "But you'll get soaked. You're already soaked."

"I'll dry off fast once I'm back in the gazebo."

He didn't have to go far to find the privacy he thought he probably needed, not for his sake, but for hers. You just didn't take a leak in front of a woman you had only known a couple of days, especially a classy lady like Sierra.

When he returned a moment later, she was sitting cross-legged on the second bedroll, a can of Curtain Cola in her hands. She had poured some of the cola into a cup for Elvis.

"Want some?" she asked. She held up a second can. "It's the only caffeine I could find."

"Underground you can't keep a fire going long enough to heat water for coffee," he explained. "Another side effect of the heavy psi."

He stepped up onto the platform and took the can of cola she offered. By the time he was halfway through with it, his clothes were almost dry.

"Wow." Sierra watched the process with amazement. "I don't believe it. A minute ago you were drenched to the skin. Now your shirt isn't even damp."

"Another weird effect of the quartz," he explained.

He sat beside her. Together they watched the rain come down in sheets. An unfamiliar sensation settled softly on him. He had to search for the word, but when he found it, he knew instantly that it was the right one: *contentment*. He could not recall ever having felt content before in his entire life. It was a strange but surprisingly pleasant feeling. Wholly unwarranted, too, he reminded himself. He still had a drug ring to take down, a bunch of guys in motorcycle leathers had tried to roast them alive in his own house tonight, and there were at least two seriously dangerous alien devices floating around that could generate controlled beams of ultraviolet dissonance energy.

Still, sitting here with Sierra, watching the rain, he felt a soul-satisfying sense of contentment. He could stay here with her forever, he thought.

"How did you find this place?" Sierra asked.

"After I bought the house, I started spending as much of my spare time as possible down in the catacombs. The former owner was obsessed with charting the sector near his personal hole-in-the-wall. He left maps in his journal. He was a tangler, so he had already cleared the illusion traps. That meant I didn't have to bring one in to do the job."

She nodded. "I have a friend who is a tangler. She's a para-archaeologist. She loves going down into the tunnels."

Tangler was the common term for an ephemeral-energy para-resonator, a person who possessed the psychic ability to resonate and control ephemeral energy.

Ephemeral energy was another form of alien psi. It was found in the catacombs in the form of illusion traps. For reasons known only to themselves, the aliens had set dangerous psychic snares throughout the tunnels. The shadow traps were frequently found in doorways and the entrances to chambers.

"The experts think the traps were intended as security devices," Fontana said. "If you don't have a natural talent for sensing them the way a tangler can, they're damn hard to spot. The only visible evidence is a faint shadow."

"That's all?"

"It's usually enough, if you know what you're doing. The ambient psi light in the tunnels creates no natural shadows."

"So if you see one, beware?"

He nodded and drank more cola. "The problem is that shadows in the catacombs are easily missed, because we're all so accustomed to seeing them aboveground. People tend not to notice them in the underworld environment."

She looked out at the driving rain. "Are there any illusion traps in the jungle?"

"None have been found so far. Good thing, too, given that it would be impossible to spot them visually. The jungle is full of shadows."

"You said you found the rain forest gate a few weeks ago. When did you discover this ruin?"

"I stumbled across it a few days later while exploring," he said.

She gave him one of her deep, knowing looks. "This place is very special to you, isn't it? That's why you haven't told anyone, not even Ray, about it."

"I don't want to give it up to the para-archaeologists," he admitted.

"It's a place of retreat for you."

He thought about that. "In a way, yes."

"I think that's what it was for the aliens, too."

Something in her tone made him look at her. "Is that guesswork or your intuition?"

"Intuition."

"I thought that only worked with people."

She drew up her knees and wrapped her arms around them. "Sometimes it also works in spaces in which people have invested a lot of emotion."

"If there's any emotion left in this place, it's old. Maybe a few thousand years old."

"I know."

"And it would be *alien* emotion."

She shrugged. "I realize that. All I can tell you is that this little gazebo feels like a place meant for quiet contemplation and reflection. Maybe someone built it so that he or she could come here to meditate on nature."

"A bioengineered nature?"

"But it's real. And don't forget, all the evidence indicates the aliens couldn't enjoy the nature on the surface. This was all they would have had."

He lounged back on his elbows, intrigued by her quiet certainty. "You think that the aliens who built all those sterile tunnels actually felt the need to commune with nature once in a while?"

She smiled. "It makes them seem more human, doesn't it?"

Chapter 26

NIGHT FELL AS HARD AND FAST AS THE RAIN HAD EARLIER. Sierra immediately discovered why Fontana had included a simple amber-crank lantern among the sled's emergency supplies. Unlike the opaque quartz that lined the tunnels, the crystal gazebo did not give off any illumination. Other things did, however.

The rain forest was drenched in night, but here and there a few small animals and certain plants glowed, glittered, or gleamed psi green.

Sierra sat on her bedroll and watched, fascinated, as a small, iridescent lizard slithered past the ruin. Its eerily shining body vanished into the undergrowth. Elvis watched, too, but not in wonderment. His attention was that of a hunter considering its prey. His second set of eyes popped open.

"Oh, jeez," Sierra said. "I think I'm about to witness the dark side of dust-bunny life."

"They are predators," Fontana pointed out.

He was sitting with his back propped against a pillar, one leg stretched out in front of him, the other drawn up. In the pale light of the lantern, his strong face was etched in savage shadows.

"Yes, I know," she said. "But I prefer that Elvis got his protein the same way I do, from a supermarket." She picked up an energy bar and waved it invitingly at Elvis. "Hey, King, how about another one of these tasty treats instead?"

Elvis considered the bar and politely declined. He chortled cheerfully and then hopped off the edge of the gazebo and disappeared into the undergrowth.

Sierra shuddered. "I can only hope he doesn't feel the need to drag back a trophy to show me what a great hunter he is."

"Has he ever done that before?" Fontana asked.

"No."

"Then he probably won't do it tonight."

"I'll cling to that logic."

She looked at Fontana. He seemed a little remote and distant, as though his thoughts were a million miles away. Which was probably the case, she concluded. Some very nasty people had tried to kill them earlier. That kind of thing gave a person a lot to contemplate.

"Any idea how the Riders got their hands on that ultraviolet generator?" she asked after a moment.

"No, but I can tell you this much, it didn't come from the Guild labs."

"And here I was getting ready to write an exposé on the secret weapons research being conducted by the Guild," she said.

"Not us. Not this time."

"Do you think maybe some hunters with some highly unusual talents have joined the Riders?" she ventured.

"That would be the simplest explanation, but I'm inclined to doubt it."

She shivered. "What if someone really has discovered an alien lab filled with infernal devices?"

"I'm not sure if an entire lab has been uncovered, but it sure looks like someone found a couple of very interesting alien gadgets. Wouldn't be the first time that's happened."

"A few months ago there were reports in the press about some kind of parapsych medical instrument that was discovered in the rain forest. It's being used on an experimental basis to treat hunters who have been severely psi-burned."

"They're getting good results, too," Fontana said. "Takes someone with a special talent for rezzing the device, but it works."

"A door has been opened down here in the jungle, hasn't it?" she said quietly. "If one alien machine has been found, it's only reasonable to assume that more may have been discovered or will be."

"Yes."

"But what about the disappearances of the homeless men? And the juice dealing in the Quarter? My intuition tells me that they're all connected, but I can't see how."

"I agree, there's some kind of link." He was silent for a moment. "One thing interesting came out of Jake's file."

"You mean aside from the fact that the last six months of his service records were missing?"

"Aside from that. Jake can work, or, rather, could work, ghost river energy. The rivers are a major problem down here. Hunters who can handle them are valuable."

"Any chance you'll find out what Jake was doing during the last six months of his professional career?" she asked.

"Ray is piecing it together. He'll identify and talk to people who worked with Jake. Eventually we'll get the answers."

"Unless all of the men who worked with him during those last six months are on the list of those who disappeared," she said.

"Even if that were the case, there are still all of the members of the exploration teams that Jake accompanied. Trust me, if someone was going around kidnapping a lot of pricey scientists and para-archaeologists, it would have been noticed."

"True."

"Ray came up with something else that may or may

not be important. A hunter named Cal Wilson was killed in a jungle accident about six months back. Turns out he was one of the men assigned to the UEX venture."

"You have to admit that UEX keeps coming up in this thing."

"Yes," he said. "It does."

Silence fell again. Sierra listened to the sounds of the night-darkened jungle. She was tired, but she knew she was too highly rezzed to sleep.

After a while, Fontana spoke out of the shadows. "Tonight when I carried you upstairs to bed, you said something."

"Did I?" She smiled a little. "I have to admit that things became a bit of a blur after you poured the brandy down my throat."

"You said that I was like everyone else in your family."

She winced. "I didn't mean to insult you. Being an aggressive, goal-oriented, talented overachiever isn't necessarily a bad thing."

"That's not what I meant."

"What did you mean?" she asked, baffled now.

He looked at her very steadily. "I'm not like everyone else in your family, and we both know it."

"You're going to try to argue that you aren't an aggressive, goal-oriented, talented overachiever? That's a difficult position to defend, given the facts, isn't it?"

"You know what I mean. We both know I'm not the kind of man your family expects you to marry."

"Ah, so we're back to that, are we?"

"I overheard that conversation with your mother, remember? She was horrified because you'd married a Guild man."

"You overheard one side of that conversation. If you'd heard both sides, you would know that Mom was horrified because I'd gotten myself into a Marriage of Convenience. People in my family don't do MCs."

"Everyone in your family goes straight into a full-blown Covenant Marriage, is that it?"

"When they find the right person, yes."

"That's a little risky, isn't it?"

"Mistakes are uncommon," she said quietly.

"Neat trick." He looked coldly amused. "How are they avoided?"

"Mostly, people in my family rely on professional matchmakers. It's an old tradition that dates back to our ancestors on Earth."

He frowned. "Your family has always used matchmakers?"

"For generations. But our matchmakers are a little different."

"How?"

"They're all psychic." She smiled. "You could say they have a special talent for the work."

"How in hell did you all find psychic matchmakers?"

She looked at him. "It's a family secret. If I tell you, you have to promise to keep it."

His mouth quirked a little at the corner. "One thing I'm good at, sweetheart, is keeping secrets."

"Yes, I know. Okay, here goes. Ever heard of an old Earth group called the Arcane Society?"

"It's an old-world legend. I came across it when I did some research on my own talents. It was supposed to have been a secret organization of people who had paranormal talents."

"The Arcane Society really did exist on Earth."

He watched her closely. "And?"

"And a lot of my ancestors were members. They came through the Curtain along with all the other colonists two hundred years ago. They brought their matchmakers with them. We've continued a lot of the old traditions."

"You've *continued* the traditions? Are you telling me the Arcane Society still exists and that it is operating here on Harmony?"

"Yes. For a lot of reasons, we keep a very low profile."

"Son of a ghost," he said softly. Then he laughed. "I've married a woman who has more secrets than a Guild boss."

"The odd thing is, no one thought we would need the Society after we came through the Curtain, at least, not after psychic talents started appearing in the population here on Harmony. But it soon became clear that some things hadn't changed. People like us who possessed unusual or very strong psychic talents that were not associated with alien psi or accessed with amber faced the same problems on this world that they had on Earth."

"People get nervous around you?"

"Or else they think we're charlatans and con artists.

Worse yet, some people want to turn psychics into money-making stage acts. So, yes, the organization continues to exist."

"What about Pemberley? Were the two of you matched by your Society's matchmakers?"

"Yes."

"So they aren't infallible?"

"No," she said. "They aren't infallible. What I'm trying to tell you is that my family is a little different. We understand what it is to be different. It's true that at this point they don't know you. Naturally they've got questions and, as I explained, they don't approve of MCs. But they judge people as individuals, not according to where they went to school or their social connections."

He got slowly, deliberately to his feet, crossed the short distance between them, and reached down to clasp her wrists. He hauled her gently upward and then caught her face between his hands. Everything about him was intense and focused. Invisible energy—the energy of desire—swirled in the atmosphere around them.

"I'm damn sure that if you ever do introduce me to your family, they're going to have more than just a few questions," he said. "But they aren't here right now. You're the one who's here. All I care about is what you think of me."

She reached up and put her arms around his neck. Maybe it was the aftereffects of the danger they had shared during the past few hours, or maybe it was because she had been fascinated by him from the moment they had met. Maybe it was simply her intuition. Whatever the reason, she did not even try to suppress the truth.

"Okay, Fontana, I'll tell you exactly what I think." Her voice sounded low and sultry, even to her own ears. "I think that you are everything I've been raised to expect in a good man. Honorable, centered, strong, and decent. And I think that I want you more than I have ever wanted any other man in my life."

"Sierra."

He captured her mouth with his own, heat, hunger and need fusing in a kiss that stole her very breath. He crushed her to him, and she held on for dear life, for the sheer, glorious thrill of a searing intimacy unlike anything she had ever experienced.

Psychic energy flashed. She was aware of it with all of her senses, normal and paranormal. She knew that he was responding to it, too.

Slowly, reverently, he unfastened the black shirt she wore. It fell to her feet. His hands glided over her, learning the shape of her. He was very careful of her bruised arm. When he stroked her breasts, the rough, masculine skin of his palms excited her nipples.

She freed her mouth to kiss his throat, inhaling his scent. He uttered a deep, hoarse groan. When she unbuttoned his shirt, her fingers trembled. It took forever to get the garment open, but finally she was able to spread her hands across his chest. Everything about him was hot and hard.

He removed her glasses and set them on top of one of

the emergency kits. Then he sank to his knees in front of her and undid the fastening of her jeans. Shivers of anticipation flickered through her. She gripped his sleek, powerful shoulders to steady herself, hardly daring to believe that this was really happening.

He tugged the denim down to her ankles. She stepped out of the jeans. Now she was clad only in the delicate panties she had worn to bed, but she did not feel awkward. Instead, she felt like a goddess. He was making her feel this way.

When he kissed the sensitive skin of her belly, liquid heat pooled deep inside her. She knew she was already wet. She sucked in her breath when she felt his fingers slide between her thighs. A moment later she was trembling so hard she thought she might collapse.

He rose and kicked open the bedroll that she had been sitting on a few minutes earlier. He sat down, cross-legged, and opened his trousers, freeing himself.

"Come here," he said. "I need you so much."

He drew her down until she was straddling him, her knees cushioned on the fabric of the bedroll on either side of his thighs. He teased her with his hands, teased her and coaxed her and urged her until nothing else mattered but the exquisite tension building inside her.

This was what it was supposed to feel like, she thought, dazzled with the discovery. She had never realized how intoxicating sex could be.

"Yes," she whispered, suddenly desperate. Her nails dug into his shoulders. "Yes. Now. *Hurry.*"

"There's no rush." He watched her with half-shut eyes. "We've got all night."

"I don't," she said fiercely. "I've never been this close."

She reached down, took him into her hand, and tried to fit herself to him.

He sucked in a sharp breath. "I get the message. But we need to do this slowly. You're so small and tight."

He eased himself into her, stretching her, filling her impossibly full.

"It's not that I'm so small," she whispered. "It's that you're so big."

He laughed a little, and then he groaned as she clenched around him. He made another sound: a man in the grip of torment or rapture. She could not tell. She was too busy concentrating on her own reaction to the deep invasion.

The hot, tight sensation was almost unbearable. She began to move, tentatively at first and then with increasing speed and confidence.

"I said slow," he reminded her, smiling a little.

He flexed his fingers on her derriere, squeezing gently, controlling her headlong rush.

She bent her head and sank her teeth into his earlobe.

"Well, if you feel that strongly about it," he said.

He moved his fingers into her cleft. She did not think she could tighten herself any more snugly around him, but she was wrong. Her body reacted to the intimate caress by ratcheting up the coiled tension within her, drawing all her inner muscles ever more taut.

"Yes," he breathed. He let her feel his own teeth now, on her throat.

The sensual storm broke over her in an irresistible wave of unfurling energy. Helpless, she abandoned herself to the release.

He followed her over the edge, pulsing heavily into her, his breathing harsh in her ear. He gave a husky, exultant roar of satisfaction.

When it was over, he fell back, pulling her down across his chest.

"CLOSE ENOUGH?" FONTANA ASKED A LONG TIME LATER.

"Hmm?" She snuggled deeper into the bedroll they shared.

He levered himself up on one elbow. "You said something about never having been that close. Just wanted to be sure you made it."

She blushed and opened her eyes to find him looking down at her. There was a subtle difference about him, she thought. She tried to come up with the right descriptor. Pleased? Relaxed? Satisfied? Happy? There was a bit of all of those things in his hard face, but something else as well. She wondered if he felt what she was feeling, a sense of connection between them. It was more than just the great sex, she thought. There was a shimmering, psychic element to it. Her intuition told her that it could be the most wonderful thing that had ever happened to her. Or the most painful.

"Yes," she said. "Definitely close enough. Right on top of it, actually."

He kissed her bare shoulder. "Because I'll be happy to keep trying until I get it right."

She giggled. "It couldn't have been any more right; trust me."

He kissed her, a long, indulgent kiss, savoring her.

After a moment he raised his head slightly.

"Feel something?" he asked.

Her heart leaped. He sensed the psychic link the sex had established between them. Joy sparkled through her.

"Yes," she whispered.

"Me, too." He looked toward the foot of the bedroll. "Thought so. Elvis is back."

So much for pillow talk with a Guild boss.

Elvis rumbled a cheery greeting. She was relieved to see that there was no evidence of the iridescent lizard or anything else that he might have dined on. She reached out to pet him.

From out of nowhere Jake's name flickered through her mind again, accompanied by a sense of urgency.

She looked at Fontana.

"That reminds me," she said, "while you were sleeping off the afterburn, I remembered something Jake Tanner told me when he gave Elvis the dressing room. I doubt if it means anything in light of Jake's drug issues, but it might be worth checking out when we get back to my apartment."

Chapter 27

THE TREK THROUGH THE RAIN FOREST TO THE NEAREST official Guild-sanctioned gate took several hours because of the rough terrain. Fontana knew that he could have made it in half the time, but Sierra was a novice in the jungle. She was healthy and in excellent condition, but she lacked training and experience.

"You know, this would have been a lot easier and faster if we could have used the sled," she said at one point. "Maybe the Guild should consider putting some roads in down here."

"That was tried." He used the heavy steel blade to hack through a maze of vines. "Lasted about three days."

"What happened to it?"

"The jungle reclaimed it. Most of it was gone within twenty-four hours. By the third day you couldn't even tell where the construction crew had cleared the path, let alone see any signs of pavement. The only way we can keep the clearings around the official gates is by maintaining them every day."

"You mean stuff down here grows that quickly?"

"Yes, but only under certain conditions. The vegetation recovers fast when you try to destroy some portion of the landscape, but otherwise everything down here remains in balance."

He heard a muffled thud.

"Ooomph," Sierra said.

He turned and saw her sprawled facedown on a mass of vines. Elvis scuttled around her, cooing anxiously.

She looked up with a mournful expression. "Remind me to cross jungle exploration off my list of possible future career paths."

He walked back a few steps and helped her to her feet. "You've got a list of career paths?"

"When you come from an overachieving family, you're expected to have a career path early on. Like from about age ten. I'm still looking for mine."

"Ten is a little young to be making that kind of decision isn't it?"

"Oh, I don't know," she said sweetly. "When did you decide to join the Guild?"

He scooped up Elvis, stepped over a fallen log, and moved forward again. "At the age of eight on my first day as a Hunter Scout."

She laughed. "And now you're running the Crystal organization. See? You've been focused for years, just like the others in my family. Me, I'm still trying to decide what I want to do with my life."

"What have you tried besides journalism?"

"Well, there was a stint as a sales consultant in an art gallery. I enjoyed that quite a lot for a while."

"What happened?"

"Turns out I don't have a keen eye for modern art. Ever heard of Adam Bollinger?"

"Sounds vaguely familiar."

"He's famous for his life-sized sculptures of what he calls contemporary artifacts. His work forces us to confront the intrinsic shallowness of reality."

"And?"

"And when I arrived at the gallery one day, his new sculpture of a city garbage can had just been delivered and uncrated. It was still sitting on the sidewalk out front. I mistook it for a real garbage can and threw an empty coffee cup and a used tissue into it. Unfortunately, Adam Bollinger happened to be standing just inside the gallery doorway, supervising the unpacking of his piece. He saw me abuse his sculpture. The next thing I knew, I was looking for another position."

He hid a smile. "What was that?"

"I became a hotel concierge for a while."

"I take it that came to a bad end, too?"

"Let's just say that I learned a valuable lesson. When the CEO of a major corporation checks in and asks to have a private anniversary celebration arranged in his suite, it is not a good idea to assume that it is the anniversary of his

Covenant Marriage with his wife that he intends to celebrate."

"The anniversary was with the mistress?"

"Uh-huh."

"What happened?"

"The real wife showed up with the private investigator she had hired to tail her husband. There was a dreadful scene. The CEO was furious with me because he believed I'd tipped off his wife. The upshot was that the wife filed for divorce."

He whistled softly. "Was it granted?"

Divorce was rare, and it could be ruinously expensive, but adultery was one of the few grounds available to a couple that wanted to separate legally. Those grounds were allowed, however, only if all of the offspring of the union were eighteen years of age or older.

"The divorce was granted, yes, but it was very messy," Sierra said.

"Aren't they all?"

"Yes, but in this case the husband owned a high-flying computer company. The wife went after half the business. In the course of the trial it turned out that the firm was in bad shape financially. In the end, it went bankrupt."

He shoved aside a massive leaf. Something resonated somewhere in his brain. He had to fight not to grin.

"Are you talking about the Rensenbrier divorce?" he asked.

"You know about it?"

"It was in the papers for weeks. Not just the tabloids,

either. The business papers carried it as front-page news. I dumped my shares as soon as I heard the rumors, but I still took a hell of a hit."

There was an odd silence behind him. His amusement vanished. Grimly he tightened his grip on the emergency kit. He knew what was coming.

"You owned shares in Rensenbrier, Inc.?" she finally asked neutrally.

"Probably comes as a shock to find out that a Guild man occasionally thinks about things like long-term investments," he said.

"Don't you dare imply that I was questioning your financial sophistication." Temper crackled in her voice. "That's not what I meant. I was just a little surprised to hear that you owned shares in Rensenbrier, that's all."

"Why?"

She sighed. "Because most people who owned the stock get mad at me when they find out that I was sort of involved in the downfall of the company. You weren't the only one who lost money."

He stopped and turned around again. She looked miserable. Sexy as hell with his shirt falling off her shoulders and her nipples forming interesting little bumps in the fabric, but miserable. His irritation evaporated.

"You weren't involved," he said. "You were an innocent bystander. The company didn't crash because of the divorce. It was doomed when it came out in open court that Rensenbrier had been cooking the firm's books."

"Some people feel that if the divorce had never happened, the company's problems would not have been exposed, and they might have been able to bail before things went sour. Rensenbrier himself still insists that he could have saved the business if his reputation hadn't been smeared in court."

"Ghost shit. Rensenbrier was a house of cards just waiting to fall down. It was only a matter of time."

"That's what Dad said. The thing is, a lot of investors back in Resonance got the impression that I'd had a hand in the disaster. Gossip travels fast in business circles."

He searched her face. "Is that the reason you decided to move to Crystal?"

"Yes. I wanted to start over in a place where nobody knew me."

"So you came to a strange town where no one knows anything about you, and you proceed to do a series of exposés on the local Guild. You drag the corrupt chief right onto the front page of a tabloid newspaper. After he's out of the way, you marry the new Guild boss." He nodded. "That's the way to stay anonymous, all right."

She flushed. "Okay, so my plan didn't work out exactly as I'd intended. The thing is, after I met Jake and some of the other hunters in the Quarter and heard about the missing men, I had to do something. I couldn't ignore them. I felt like I'd found my calling at last."

He pushed through a heavy mass of leaves. "I knew it. A natural-born do-gooder."

"Hey, I resent that—"

He stopped. "Hush," he said quietly.

"Don't you hush me, Fontana." Then she, too, heard the voices in the distance. "The gate?"

"Almost there," he said.

He climbed up onto some exposed tree roots that were as thick as a man's body, pushed aside a monstrous, cup-shaped leaf, and saw the gate. It was wide open, revealing the glowing green quartz catacombs beyond. A large number of people were clustered around the entrance. They didn't look like the usual gaggle of explorers, archaeologists, biologists, and researchers that accompanied routine expeditions.

Most of the entire membership of the Guild appeared to be present in the clearing. The hunters were all dressed in jungle gear. Some milled about, waiting. Others unloaded equipment from two large sleds.

The man in charge turned to one of the hunters.

"Tell those damn reporters to get out of the way, or I'm going to let the next sled run right over them," Ray said in a voice that was meant to carry across the clearing.

"Yes, sir," the man replied.

Sierra clambered up onto the low mound of roots and surveyed the scene. "What's going on?"

"I think we'll be on the front page again tomorrow morning."

"What in the world?" Understanding lit her eyes. "They're getting ready to send out a search-and-rescue team. For us?"

"Touching, isn't it?" He jumped down from the roots

and reached up to give her a hand. "Let's go tell them that they really don't need to go to all that trouble."

He gave Elvis to her, took her hand, and started toward the busy gate. One of the hunters unloading a sled saw them first. A shout went up. Then the reporters and photographers realized what was happening. They poured through the gate in a wave.

"Sierra," Matt Delaney yelled. "Are you okay?"

Kay waved madly. "Don't say a word until we get back to the newsroom," she shouted. "This is a *Curtain* exclusive."

"The hell it is," a man in a sports coat and a very bad tie surged out of the pack. "When the Guild boss and his wife go missing, it's everybody's story."

"That's what you think," Kay shot back. She seized his coattails as he went past. "The wife in this case is a *Curtain* reporter. Get out of my way."

Somehow Kay's oversized tote connected with the other journalist's midsection. He grunted, staggered, and fell back a couple of steps. Kay rushed forward.

"Over here, Sierra," she yelled. "It's me, Kay."

Phil separated himself from the crowd. He bounded over a stack of supplies and equipment, camera aimed. "Do me a favor, Sierra. Undo another couple of buttons."

"Look," Sierra said. Her smile was a little misty. "Even Mr. Runtley is here. That is so sweet."

A moment later they were surrounded by the reporters. Leaving Sierra to fend for herself, Fontana pushed through the mob, delivering only a few clipped comments en route. Eventually he fought his way to where Ray stood, lounging against the side of a sled.

Ray folded his arms and grinned. "Should have known you'd pull off another chapter to add to the Fontana legend. You two okay?"

"We're fine. I'll be right back."

He walked to where the small army of hunters stood watching him and talking among themselves. They quieted when he approached.

"Thanks for coming out today, gentlemen," he said, shaking each hand in turn. "My wife and I appreciate it. Sorry to put you to the trouble."

The men grinned.

"Fontana's First Rule, sir," one of them said. "Never leave a man behind for ghost bait."

He stood and talked with them for a few minutes, and then he went back to Ray.

"What made you and everyone else think we'd disappeared into the jungle?" he asked.

"Your frequency didn't show up on the locaters. Figured the only other place you could be was in the rain forest." Ray paused. "I assume you know about the fire?"

"Yes. Anything left?"

"Not much. But the antiquities in the gallery are fine. Nothing can damage quartz and dreamstone. I've got a few men on guard at the scene to make sure nothing gets stolen until the relics can be recovered. The ashes are still too hot to search. The cops said someone used one hell of an accelerant."

"How did you know we went underground?"

"The authorities assume they'll be looking for two bodies in the ashes. But I figured that if you'd had any warning at all, you would have used your hole-in-the-wall. I asked for volunteers." He angled his head toward the group of hunters. "Every damn Guild man showed up. You're a popular guy. The ones you don't see here are either on assignment and didn't get the word or keeping watch over what's left of the mansion. What the hell happened?"

"Almost got abducted by aliens."

Ray nodded. "Knew it would be a good story."

Chapter 28

SIERRA PAUSED IN THE ACT OF POURING COFFEE INTO three mugs. "There's nothing left at all of your beautiful house? How dreadful."

They were in her apartment. Fontana and Ray were at the small table, poring over notes and files. Fontana had his phone out, about to make a call.

"The antiquities collection was the only thing that would have been hard to replace," Fontana said absently. "It's all fine." He entered a number into his phone and waited for the other party to answer. "As for the house, it can be rebuilt."

"But you can't duplicate that gorgeous old woodwork or those incredible mosaics," she insisted. "They were museum quality. Craftsmanship like that just doesn't exist anymore."

"Maybe not, but fireproof building materials sure do. I intend to use them when I rebuild."

Ray winked at Sierra. "Fontana's not what you call the sentimental type."

Probably because he was so goal-oriented, she thought. The only thing that mattered to Fontana was the future.

He spoke into the phone.

"Davis? Fontana." There was a short pause. "You heard about that already?" Fontana shot an unreadable look at Sierra and then got to his feet and walked to the sliding glass doors that opened onto the balcony. "Sure, I know the jungle is not your ordinary honeymoon venue, but things have gotten a little complicated. That's why I'm calling."

He talked briefly and then ended the call.

"Oakes finally turned up something interesting on Patterson," he said.

"About time," Ray said.

"Who is Davis Oakes?" Sierra asked.

"He's a PI in Cadence," Fontana explained. "He went the old-fashioned route and followed the money. He said it took a lot of digging, but it turns out Patterson has set up several accounts at a number of small banks and investment firms scattered throughout the city-states using phony names and IDs."

Ray whistled softly. "Patterson is using the accounts to launder the cash he's pulling in from his ghost juice business."

Fontana picked up one of the mugs. "Looks like it, yes."

"You no longer have a choice," Ray said. "You're going to have to force him off the Council."

Fontana shook his head. "He'll disappear, and we'll never find that alien lab."

Ray stilled. "What the hell are you talking about?" He glanced uneasily at Sierra and then turned back to Fontana. "Don't tell me you're actually buying into the *Curtain*'s theory that someone discovered an entire alien lab in the jungle."

"Maybe not a lab," Fontana conceded, "but that gadget the Riders used to destroy my security system and generate that ultraviolet ray is definitely alien technology."

"How do you know that? Maybe some hunter is working ultraviolet light naturally, the same way you and I work dark and green light."

"I don't think so. It was dissonance energy, but it was being generated at a very powerful level, a technologically enhanced level."

"He's right," Sierra said quickly. "They used small gadgets to create the energy beams. I saw one of them. It was about the size of a flashlight."

Ray rubbed the back of his neck. "We've always assumed that diss energy, hell, any alien psi for that matter, could only be manipulated by people with a lot of pararez talent. There's never been any technology that could turn it on and off. Even that artifact that they're using to heal the badly fried hunters at the Glenfield Institute has to be activated and focused by people with special psi abilities."

"It's possible that these ultragenerators require talent, too," Fontana conceded. "Either way, it produces very powerful rays that worked aboveground. The stuff knocked out my entire security system. Just think how useful that could be to someone who wanted to rob a bank or a house or immobilize an entire police station."

Ray exhaled slowly. "Okay, when it comes to the aliens, anything is possible, I guess."

"The generators came from somewhere," Fontana said. "I think the most likely explanation is that they were found in the jungle. Got a hunch that the discovery is part of what Patterson and Jenner were trying to cover up."

"Which reminds me, I've got some news of my own," Ray said. "While you two were frolicking on your eco-tour honeymoon trip, I located a couple of hunters who worked with Jake Tanner just before he suddenly retired."

Sierra was using a knife to scoop peanut butter out of the jar. She looked up quickly. "What did you find out?"

"The men I talked to recalled that Tanner's last job was a major corporate research-and-exploration expedition into the jungle. The project lasted a couple of weeks and then was halted abruptly. The official story is that the company concluded the venture was just one more dead-end exploration effort with no prospect of showing a profit."

"R-and-E projects are called off all the time," Fontana

said. "It's like prospecting for amber. Sometimes you get lucky. Sometimes you get nothing."

"Sure," Ray said. "But in this case the name of the company that funded the project that employed Tanner just happens to be Underworld Exploration."

Fontana raised his brows. "Even if Corley's company did turn up something valuable in the jungle, it's not a crime. That's what most rain forest exploration is all about, making money for investors. UEX is entitled to profit on anything it takes out of the jungle."

Sierra narrowed her eyes. "Unless it uses that discovery for illegal purposes such as forming a business partnership with the Riders in order to sell ghost juice on city streets."

"And therein lies the problem," Fontana said. "We've got zip in the way of proof that UEX is working with the Riders or anyone in the Guild, for that matter."

"Huh."

Frustrated, she finished the peanut butter and banana sandwich and gave it to Elvis. He carried it up to the windowsill and settled down to eat with his usual enthusiasm.

Fontana contemplated him for a moment, and then he turned to Sierra.

"I think it's time we took a look at Elvis's dressing room."

Ray gave them both a baffled look. "What's with the miniature room?"

"We're not sure," Sierra said. "It will probably turn out

to be nothing, but something Jake Tanner told me when he gave it to Elvis keeps going through my head."

They gathered around the coffee table and looked down into the dressing room.

Sensing a new game, Elvis muttered excitedly and scampered down from the windowsill, the unfinished sandwich clutched in one paw. He hopped up onto the coffee table.

"The detail is amazing," Ray said, bending down to touch one tiny lightbulb.

"Yes," Sierra said. "I hate to start tearing it apart when I don't even know what we're searching for."

Fontana looked at her. "Tell me again exactly what Jake said when he gave it to you."

" 'If Elvis ever wants to find me, all he has to do is look in the mirror,' " she recited carefully.

"I think," Fontana said, "we should start with the dressing table mirror."

Sierra hesitated, and then she reached down and tugged gently on the mirror. Elvis watched with great interest, but he did not seem alarmed.

The mirror did not budge.

"Looks like it's glued on," Ray observed. "Might be something behind it. You could try prying it off."

"No," Sierra said, very sure now. "If Jake wanted to conceal something in the dressing room, he would have done it in a way that did not require destroying the miniature in order to retrieve whatever was hidden. He was an artist. He wouldn't have wanted his work ruined."

She opened the drawer in the dressing table. The tiny comb was still inside, but that was all.

"It must be the mirror," Fontana said. "Let me see that thing."

He picked up the dressing room and examined the underside very carefully. Elvis watched, suddenly very intent.

"It's okay, King," Fontana said. "I'm not going to hurt your dressing room."

Satisfied that there were no hidden springs, locks, or levers, he set it back down on the coffee table. Gingerly he tugged and pressed each of the miniature lightbulbs that surrounded the mirror.

When he pushed the third one on the right, the mirror swung aside, revealing a thin little opening in the wall behind it. A piece of neatly folded paper was inside.

"Damn," Ray said softly.

Sierra leaned forward, thrilled. "Oh, my gosh, it's a message of some kind."

"Don't get too excited," Fontana warned. He removed the paper. "By all accounts, Tanner was a total burnout case, and he was into ghost juice. Everyone knows that juicers don't think or act logically."

He unfolded the sheet of paper and spread it out on the table. Disappointment flashed through Sierra when she saw that all that was written on the page were some numbers.

"Probably his lucky lottery ticket numbers," she said.

"Guess again," Ray said. He looked at Fontana. "Well,

what do you know? Looks like Tanner wasn't as far gone into dreamland as everyone thought."

"What do the numbers mean?" Sierra asked.

Cold satisfaction iced Fontana's eyes.

"They're coordinates pinpointing a position in the rain forest," he said. He met Ray's eyes. "I think it's time we went looking for Jake Tanner."

"Never leave a man behind for ghost bait," Ray said.

Excitement flashed through Sierra. "I'm coming with you."

Both men regarded her with faces that could have been carved from solid quartz.

"No," Fontana said.

Ray shook his head. "No."

Outrage burned through her. "This is my story, damn it, the one I've been chasing for months. I have a right to go with you."

"I'm sorry," Fontana said in his emotionless, utterly inflexible Guild boss voice. "Ray and I will be moving fast in the jungle. We don't know what we're going to find. We don't have time to babysit a civilian."

"Don't you dare call me a civilian," she shot back. "I'm an investigative journalist. What's more, if it hadn't been for me, you wouldn't even have those coordinates."

Elvis muttered unhappily, responding to her anger and frustration. He dashed across the coffee table, scampered up onto her shoulder, and murmured into her ear.

"I know we owe this break to you," Fontana said quietly. "The Guild won't forget that."

"Oh, great, now you're going to try to fob me off with that ridiculous line about how the Guild always repays a favor. Well, forget it. I don't want any favors from the Guild. I did this for all the men the Guild left behind as ghost bait on the streets of this city."

A crystalline silence gripped the room. No one moved. No one spoke. Even Elvis went very still.

After a moment, Fontana went to stand in front of her. He gripped her shoulders with both hands.

"I understand," he said. "I'm trying to make it clear that the Guild appreciates your work. But taking you with us is out of the question. You've only spent one night in the jungle. You've had no training or experience. We'd have to nursemaid you every step of the way. That would not only slow us down, it could jeopardize the mission. If Jake and the others are still alive, it might mean the difference between life and death for them."

Reality slammed through her. He was right. She had no business going into the jungle. Still, it was infuriating to be shut out like this when she could feel the story coming together.

"Okay," she said wearily. "Go find out what happened to Jake and the others."

"There's just one more thing," Fontana said.

"Don't press your luck."

"I want you covered by a security detail while Ray and I are gone."

"Is that a polite term for bodyguard?"

"Yes." He glanced at Ray. "But given the circumstances, I don't want to take the risk of arranging one through the Guild. It will start rumors that may give whoever is behind this a heads-up."

"You need some men from outside the Guild," Ray said. "Private agency, maybe?"

Fontana crossed to the window and stood looking down at the street below.

"I think I know where we can get some reliable men," he said.

Chapter 29

SIERRA GRIPPED THE ARMS OF HER DESK CHAIR AND gazed, stricken, at the copy of the *Curtain* Kay had just placed in front of her.

"Good grief," she said. "Did I really look that bad yesterday when you found us?"

"Hey, don't blame me for the picture." Kay angled one hip onto the corner of Sierra's desk. "Phil's the photographer. I'm just the ace reporter who got the exclusive honeymoon interview with the Guild boss's wife."

The cover photo showed her along with Elvis and Fontana emerging from the jungle. Fontana looked like he always did: cool, confident, and utterly in control of the situation. Elvis was as cute as always. But as for herself . . .

"I will never live this down," she declared. "I want

everyone to know that I'm holding Phil personally responsible for destroying what was left of my reputation. He can talk to my mother when she calls. And she will call, I can guarantee it."

"What's wrong with the shot?" Phil demanded. He wandered over to her desk, half of a doughnut in one fist. Elvis hovered nearby in his balloon basket, nibbling on the other half of the doughnut. "It's a masterpiece."

"Some masterpiece," Sierra said. "I look like a low-rent hooker who just spent the night entertaining clients in a dark alley."

"It's the hair," Kay said, commiserating. "The way it's all tangled up does have a certain after-the-fall quality."

"Nah," Matt said. "I think it's the way Fontana's shirt is hanging off one of her shoulders, and you can tell she's not wearing a bra."

"I look cheap," Sierra said flatly.

"No, really," Kay said quickly. "A woman dressed in a man's shirt looks sexy."

"Right," Phil said.

"Cheap," Sierra repeated.

"Well, sure, that, too," Phil agreed. "But take it from a man: cheap and sexy go together like chocolate sauce and ice cream."

"Thanks for that insight into the masculine mind," Sierra muttered.

Ivor Runtley loomed in the doorway of the newsroom. "What's going on in here? I want everyone back to work. Today's edition is almost sold out. I've got advertisers begging me for more space. Kay, I need another exclusive report on the jungle honeymoon. Matt, give me something else on the fire that destroyed Fontana's house."

"What do you want, boss?" Matt said. "I already used the arson angle."

"I don't want ordinary arson," Runtley bellowed. "Give me arson caused by aliens. Which reminds me. Sierra, I need something more on the secret alien lab."

She looked at him. "I think we should hold off on that for a bit, sir."

Runtley's brows shot skyward. "You've got inside information?"

"Let's just say that I'm hoping to have a major scoop for the *Curtain* within forty-eight hours."

"All right, sounds good. Meanwhile, you can work with Kay on the follow-up interview. Readers are really interested in the Guild boss's jungle honeymoon story."

"Yes, sir," Sierra said.

Runtley stormed off down thc hall loward Marketing.

Sierra looked at Kay. "Any bright ideas?"

"You're the one who spent the night in the jungle with Fontana," Kay reminded her. "Something exciting must have happened."

"Well, there was an incident with a lizard," Sierra volunteered. She was not going to tell anyone about the crystal alien ruin, let alone what had happened inside. The ruin had been Fontana's secret. Now it was hers.

"Lizards are boring." Kay tapped her pen on her notepad. "What do you say we go with a water feature this time? 'Guild Boss and Wife Bathe Nude in Hidden Lagoon.' "

"Oh, man," Phil said. "Does that mean I get to do a photo shoot of Sierra in the buff?"

Sierra gave him a warning glare. "Do not mess with me today. I am not in a good mood."

"Yeah," Phil said. "We noticed."

She picked up her coffee and started across the room to join Kay. She was almost to her destination when she noticed two men hovering in the doorway. One of them was Simon Lugg.

"Someone here to see you, Sierra," Simon said. "Mitch let him through downstairs because he says he's a relative. That right?"

Her security detail, which consisted of Simon, Mitch, Jeff, and Andy from the Green Gate Tavern, had taken to their assignment with enthusiasm. They had all been more than happy to do the new Guild boss another favor. Make that thrilled, Sierra thought. The fact that the chief respected them enough to entrust his wife's safety to their care had produced an immediate and transformational impact on the four. You could see it in the new spring in their step and the determination in their eyes.

The only problem, as far as Sierra was concerned, was that in their zeal to prove themselves, they had gone overboard. She was not even allowed to walk down the hall to the ladies' room without an escort.

She looked at the man standing beside Simon. He appeared to be in his early thirties, dressed in a high-end designer's notion of casual. His expensive trousers, open-throated blue shirt, and slouchy, cream linen jacket would have looked at home at the local yacht club. He gave her a tentative smile.

"There must be some mistake," she said gently. "I don't know you."

Simon's expression hardened. He jerked a thumb over his shoulder. "Let's go, pal."

"No, wait," the stranger said quickly. "My name is Burns. Nick Burns. I'm Fontana's brother." He tried another smile. "That makes me your new brother-in-law."

Chapter 30

"I THINK I'M SEEING THINGS." RAY LOWERED THE BINOCULARS, eyes narrowed. "Wouldn't be the first time in the jungle."

"That's no ghost river mirage." Fontana kept his glasses focused on the amazing scene. "I'm seeing the same thing."

They were sitting about twelve feet off the ground in the cradling limbs of a thickly leafed tree. It was difficult to get a clear view because of the foliage in the way, but he could see figures moving purposefully about near a large quartz ruin. The structure was not made of the clear, emerald-tinted quartz that had been used to fashion his little pavilion, but rather the ubiquitous, solid green rock the aliens had used to construct all their cities and the catacombs.

From the sliver-sized scenes he could see through the

vine-clogged trees, he could tell that the ruin was fairly large. It was about the height of a single-story human building at the outside walls, but the roof was wholly alien in design, ethereally arched and domed. There were no windows—another typical feature of alien architecture—only a small doorway. From his position he could not see through the opening but the familiar glow of green quartz emanated from it.

"The *Curtain*'s secret alien lab?" Ray asked.

"Looks like my wife was right yet again," Fontana said. "This could be a little embarrassing for the Guild."

"Time enough to worry about dealing with the PR problems after we figure out what the hell is going on."

"That's why we made you boss." Ray raised the glasses to his eyes again. "You know how to prioritize."

"I count five men."

"Got 'em. Number six is coming out of the building. He's carrying something. Looks like a big plastic water jug on his shoulder."

"I see him. There's another man behind him. Same kind of jug."

"Moving slowly," Ray said.

"Leg chains."

"Damn. Someone's got prisoners working down there."

Fontana lowered the glasses. "We need to get closer."

He followed Ray down out of the tree and then waited while Ray recovered the rope ladder, coiled it, and attached it to his utility belt.

The lively birdcalls and the fluttering in the canopy

provided some cover for them as they made their way through the undergrowth. The familiar noises also indicated that the creatures in the vicinity had grown accustomed to the presence of humans. That meant the operation, whatever it was, had been going on for a while.

When they drew closer, he uncoiled his own rope, snagged it on the wide branch of an emerald tree, and used it to climb up into the thick web of vines, limbs, and leaves. Ray followed him.

They were close enough now to have an almost unimpeded view of the alien ruin and the men moving around it. He took out his glasses again and studied the scene. Ray did the same. After a few minutes, they lowered their glasses and looked at each other.

He held up nine fingers. Ray nodded, confirming he had counted the same number. Four were obviously serving as guards. They were armed with knives and rez-ball bats. Not that they seemed to need them. The five prisoners all wore chains around their ankles that were secured to chains around their waists. No one would get far in the jungle dressed in that gear.

"Ghost juice," Ray said softly. "They're making it inside that building. Using prisoners to bottle it."

"Probably to transport it, as well. No other way to get those jugs back to the surface except to carry them out by hand."

"Think this explains those alien abductions we've been hearing about?"

"They needed labor. They took it off the streets of the Quarter. Men they thought no one would miss."

"Until a certain lady reporter came along," Ray said. "Now what?"

"We've got two options. Waste a full day going back to headquarters to put together a team and take the risk that Patterson will get wind of what's going on, or we do this the old-fashioned way."

"Just like the old days, huh?"

"We should be able to take the guards. Four of them, two of us."

"Odds change if they've all got those ultraviolet-generating gadgets you ran into in the tunnels," Ray pointed out.

"We've got this little thing called an element of surprise working for us. They aren't expecting trouble, and they sure as hell aren't expecting it to come at them from above."

"Probably morc guards inside the building," Ray warned.

"If we work fast, they won't know anything has happened outside until it's too late."

"Right." Ray took another look through the glasses. "Just out of curiosity, have we got a contingency plan?"

"Sure. A strategic retreat."

"Pretty basic sort of contingency plan," Ray observed.

"Usually the best kind. No way they can track us in the jungle. Their locators are useless. Doubt if they'd even try."

"But they'd probably manage to make all the evidence disappear while we're busy retreating. The cheap labor as well. If we start this, we'd better finish it."

"That's how we've always done things," Fontana said.

Ray slithered along the wide tree limb and disappeared into the mass of psi-green leaves. Fontana crawled out along his own limb until he found a place where he could transfer to another one that was even larger and closer to his targets.

When he was within range, he pulled dark light, working hard and fast. The whirling waves of night coalesced quickly here in the jungle.

He selected the nearest guard and sent the night ghost toward him from behind. At the last instant the man must have sensed the hot energy, because he tensed and started to turn around.

"Hey, Tony, you feel anything—?" he began.

He never finished the sentence. The dark whirlpool brushed against the back of his head. He jerked violently and crumpled, unconscious.

"Shit, Mac." The other man started forward. "What's wrong?"

Then he saw the whirling waves of night. He tried to run, but it was too late. The night fire touched him on the shoulder, a dark ghost come calling. He went down.

The other two guards had begun to realize that there was a problem. One of them raised a small device, but while he was trying to decide where to aim it, Ray's ghost, a bolt of green lightning took him out. He went down. The generator fell from his hands. Fontana quickly singed the other guard.

None of the guards had tried to rez their own ghosts, Fontana noted. They were Riders, not hunters.

He dropped from the tree and ran toward the two men he had fried. Ray did the same with his own targets.

Working fast and keeping an eye on the entrance to the ruin, they yanked knives, bats, and any amber they could find off the fallen men. Fontana found a key on one of the victims that looked like it could de-rez leg irons.

When he straightened, he saw the four chained prisoners watching him with expressions that ranged from amazement to wide grins. He motioned them to silence. They were hunters. They took his order immediately.

One of them jerked a finger toward the glowing entrance of the ruin and held up two fingers, indicating the number of guards inside the ruin.

Fontana tossed the key to the nearest prisoner and took up a position on one side of the opening. Ray flattened himself on the opposite wall.

Two more prisoners emerged from the building, leg chains rattling. They saw the downed guards and halted for a couple of seconds in confusion. One of the other four prisoners outside beckoned to them and made a zipping motion across his mouth.

The two men seemed to get the message immediately, just as the other four had. They started toward their companions.

Sensing something amiss, one of the two remaining guards came to the narrow entrance. He saw the four guards on the ground. Instead of retreating into the relative safety of the ruin, he leaped to a false assumption.

"You stupid juicers," he snarled at the prisoners, "you think you can get away with this? In case you haven't figured it out, you can all be replaced. Lots more where you came from."

He never noticed the shimmer of dark light in the air beside him, never saw Fontana and Ray.

He jerked once and dropped to the ground. Fontana grabbed the generator. Ray moved through the entrance, low and fast. There was a muffled shout. Green energy flashed once inside the alien structure, and then there was silence.

Ray reappeared. "All clear. Wait'll you see what's inside this place."

"Any more of these gizmos?" Fontana asked, holding up the two generators.

"No."

One of the hunters had succeeded in freeing himself from the leg irons. He handed the key to another man and limped toward Fontana and Ray. When he got closer it was clear that he was shivering; not from reaction, Fontana realized, but from a high fever.

"You're Fontana, ain't you?" he wheezed. "Heard 'em talkin' about the new boss."

"I'm Fontana. Who are you?"

"Arnie Lewis." Arnie broke off, coughing. When he recovered, he looked at the device, grimacing. "Nasty gadgets. You can set 'em for high, medium, or low. Low setting knocks a man unconscious for a few hours. Worse yet, it zaps your psi senses for at least two, sometimes three days. Makes it impossible to rez any ghost light. They used those things on us every forty-eight hours to make sure none of us could surprise 'em with some green fire."

Fontana studied the generator. "What do the other settings do?"

"Medium puts you into a coma." Arnie shrugged. "Sometimes you come out of it. Sometimes you don't. High kills you flat-out dead. They were fixing to use it on me in a day or two because I'm getting too sick to be of any use. Don't have what you'd call a top-notch Guild medical plan down here."

Fontana looked at the four fallen men. "All of these guys are Riders?"

"Yeah," Arnie said.

"How many of those ultraviolet generators are floating around?" Fontana asked.

"From what we can tell, they found six of them when they opened up this place. There's always two down here with the bastards who watch the bottling crew. The other two go with the sons of ghosts who guard the transport team. They're on their way back to the surface now. In between times they use those two to pick up fresh labor."

Ray looked at Fontana. "Probably the same two they used to ambush you in the tunnels."

"That's four," Fontana said. "What about the other two?"

A second man had unlocked his chains. His greasy, shoulder-length hair was tied back with a leather thong. Like the others, his clothes were ragged and filthy. But his eyes were clear and steady.

"I've been keeping track," he said. "The Riders have four in all. It was part of the deal Jenner cut with the gang. We're sure that Jenner himself kept one generator. Don't know what happened to it after he died, though."

"That's five," Fontana said. "What about the sixth?"

The man looked at the others. They all shook their heads.

Fontana examined the device. "Can anyone activate one of these things, or does it take a special kind of psi talent?"

"Anyone who can rez a toaster can use one of those damn ray guns," one of the men said. "The Riders love 'em. Said it meant that for the first time folks who couldn't work ghost light had some real firepower underground. Said it meant that the Guild no longer had a monopoly down here."

"The generators work aboveground, too," one of the men added.

"I know," Fontana said. "Found that out the hard way.

We're going to have to find the rest of these things as fast as possible. But first we have to get Arnie some medical attention and secure this place. Then we have to make arrangements with the Crystal police to pick up the transport team."

The rest of the hunters, freed of their restraints, gathered around.

"So you're Fontana?" The man with the tied-back hair surveyed him closely.

"That's right."

"I'm Tanner. Jake Tanner."

"Glad to meet you. The Guild owes you. If you hadn't left those coordinates in that miniature dressing room, we'd still be searching for all of you."

Jake grinned. "I was living in a juice dream at the time, but I figured that if I went missing like the others, Elvis and Sierra would get someone to come looking for me. Never expected them to send the big boss, himself."

A SHORT TIME LATER FONTANA STOOD WITH RAY AND Jake inside the alien ruin. Together they studied the five tall, ethereally graceful green quartz fountains that occupied the space. Each fountain was surrounded by a wide pool of sparkling, effervescent, psi-green water. There was so much hot psi in the chamber that the hair on the nape of Fontana's neck lifted. All of his senses were rezzed.

"What do you suppose the aliens did with the waters from those fountains?" Ray asked softly.

Jake shrugged. "Maybe they used it for the same reason I did."

"Why did you use the juice?" Fontana asked.

"To see things," Jake said. "Incredible things."

Chapter 31

"SORRY TO SURPRISE YOU LIKE THIS," NICK BURNS SAID. "I can see that Fontana hasn't told you much about his family."

"We haven't had a lot of time to get to know each other," Sierra said, choosing her words cautiously. "Ours was what you might call a whirlwind courtship. As I recall, he said something about not having any family."

Nick exhaled wearily. "You could probably be married to him for fifty years and not hear anything about us, at least not from him."

They were sitting in the small conference room adjacent to the newsroom. The door was closed for privacy, but Sierra could see her colleagues through the windows. They all appeared to be hard at work, but she knew that you could hear a pin drop in the outer room. Everyone was straining so hard to eavesdrop it was a wonder people weren't falling out of their chairs. The only one who appeared unconcerned was Elvis. He was in his balloon basket, floating toward the coffee-and-doughnuts table.

She lowered her voice. "Maybe you should wait until Fontana is back in his office. He's a little busy at the moment."

"I know. I went to Guild headquarters first. He's been ignoring my phone calls for a couple of weeks. I hoped to catch him off guard. But his executive assistant told me that he was unavailable."

"He's away on Guild business," she said somberly.

"Look, I'll be honest with you, there's a good chance he won't give me the time of day when he does get back from wherever it is he went. That's why I came here to see you."

"I really don't think he would refuse to see someone from his own family," she said quickly.

"You don't know him very well, do you? I suppose that's typical of Marriages of Convenience. People don't go into them for the long haul, so why check out the family?"

Enough was enough. "Let's get something straight here, Mr. Burns. I am Fontana's wife, and as such I am quite prepared to be polite to members of his family. I am not about to let said family members insult me or my husband or our marriage."

He blinked and then reddened. "Sorry. I didn't mean—"

"What you should keep in mind here is that, while I

know almost nothing about you, you, in turn, know very little about me or the reasons for my marriage to your brother." She smiled coolly. "Just what you've read in the papers, right?"

"Well, yes, but—"

"We all know how much you can trust the press."

Nick cleared his throat. He glanced uneasily at the copy of the previous day's edition of the *Curtain* lying on the table. The glaring headline read, "Guild Boss and Bride Vanish. Kidnapped by Aliens?"

"Right," he said.

"How did you find me?" she asked.

"Are you kidding? You and Fontana are headline news in the tabloids in Cadence as well as here in Crystal."

"I was afraid of that." She folded her hands together. "What can I do for you, Mr. Burns?"

His mouth tightened at the corners in a way that reminded her of Fontana.

"I won't play games, with you," he said. "My family needs Fontana's help, and they need it very badly. My mother is so desperate she tried to contact him herself several times in the past month. On each occasion Fontana's executive assistant made it clear that Fontana was unavailable to take the call."

"I see." This was worse than she had realized.

"If you knew my mother, you'd know how much pride she had to swallow in order to make those calls. Fontana is the result of an affair my father had years ago. She's always had a difficult time accepting him."

"I understand," she said quietly.

"Look, you're family now, so I'm going to tell you a big family secret." Nick leaned forward and spoke in very low tones. "Burns & Co. is in serious trouble. A year ago my father died. He stunned everyone when he left controlling interest to Fontana. But Fontana turned around and shocked everyone all over again when he declined his inheritance."

"Declined?"

"Just walked away from it." Nick waved one hand. "Blew it off. Cold as ice. Like Burns & Co. meant nothing to him."

"Well, maybe it doesn't. He hasn't ever been involved with the firm, has he?"

"No, but that's not the point. That company was my father's life. And he left Fontana in charge of it. That should have meant *something*, damn it."

"Please calm down," she said gently.

Nick took a visible grip on his emotions. His tone steadied. "At the time everyone in the family was enormously relieved to find out that Fontana didn't want the company. But then my brother, Josh, took over the firm, and we learned the truth. Burns & Co. is on the verge of bankruptcy."

"I'm very sorry, but I really don't know what you expect me to do."

"You've got to help me convince Fontana to save Burns," Nick said. "If he doesn't do something fast, a lot of people are going to get hurt."

"The members of your family?"

"Sure, but it isn't just my family that will take a hit. If the company goes under, several hundred people will lose their jobs. Look, we just need time. Fontana is the only one who can hold things together financially until Josh can get a handle on the situation."

"I realize you're desperate, but what, exactly, do you expect Fontana to do? I can tell you right now that he won't give up the Guild in order to run Burns & Co."

"Josh can turn the company around. He's brilliant. But he needs time and a large infusion of private capital to hold things together until he can restructure the business."

"You expect Fontana to pour money into the firm in order to save it for your family?"

"He's our only hope."

Chapter 32

TROY PATTERSON'S OFFICE WAS IN THE EXECUTIVE WING of Guild headquarters. Patterson was inside, seated behind his desk, signing some papers, when Fontana opened the door without warning.

Troy looked up. Cold anger glittered in his eyes before disappearing behind his genial mask.

"Fontana," he said easily. "What are you doing here? Figured you were still recovering from your honeymoon in the jungle."

"It's over, Patterson."

Troy cocked a brow. "The honeymoon? That didn't last long."

"Not my honeymoon. Your little rain forest drug factory."

Troy did not move, but something frantic flickered in

his expression. Like the anger, it vanished quickly. Cool outrage took its place.

"I don't know what the hell you're talking about." He gripped the arms of his chair. "I don't give a damn if you are the new boss of the Crystal Guild. I'm a member of the Council. I'm one of the people who helped put you into the CEO's office, remember? I and the others can kick you out of there just as fast as we put you in."

Fontana came to a halt in the middle of the room. It was raining outside. His black coat dripped water on the amber and granite floor.

"You had no choice but to vote with the rest of the Council, because you knew that if you didn't, everyone would wonder why," he said. "By the way, when the cops arrest you, it won't be only for running drugs. You're the chief suspect in the murder of Brock Jenner. There's also the little matter of kidnapping and unlawful imprisonment. We freed a total of twelve hunters, counting the additional men on thc transport team."

Troy gripped the arms of his chair. "You're crazy. I didn't touch Jenner. And there's no way you can pin a drug charge on me."

"Ray and I found the source of the ghost juice. We picked up the four guards at the scene. The police caught the others when the transport crew emerged on the surface with the fresh supply of the drug. They're all Riders, and it turns out they don't feel any loyalty to the Guild. They're talking as fast as they can."

Troy's eyes tightened. "You're bluffing. You haven't got proof of any of those charges. This is just a threat. You want me off the Council, and this is your way of forcing me to resign, isn't it? Congratulations on your more modern approach to running the organization. At least Jenner was honest about it. He got rid of people he didn't like the old-fashioned way. He made them disappear into the tunnels."

"I know about the bank accounts that you set up to launder your ghost juice profits. They all lead straight back to you."

"I've got a right to set up all the accounts I want."

"Sure, but not under a bunch of phony IDs," Fontana said. "The City-State Tax Service will want a detailed explanation of the source of your income. Things are going to unravel in a hurry when they start looking into your finances."

"That money came from selling antiquities that I found in the course of my own private explorations," Troy said.

"In which case the tax folks are going to want to see a hell of a lot of receipts. And they'll still want an explanation for the phony IDs used on the accounts."

"I can handle the CSTS," Troy said evenly. "If that's all you've got, you're about to find yourself unemployed."

"You're underestimating the CSTS, but that's your problem. As a matter of fact, I have got something more in the way of proof. I just came from an interesting conversation with Donovan Corley."

Troy stiffened. "The hell you did."

"Corley was a little annoyed to hear that his firm might have been connected to a drug operation, so he turned over all of the paperwork he had relating to a certain UEX project that took place six months ago."

"If anyone's running a drug operation in the rain forest, it's UEX," Troy said.

"According to the reports, they never found the alien ruin where the juice is produced. They didn't find a damn thing because on the advice of the hunter in command, they cut their losses and turned back before they stumbled onto the drug fountains. The hunter in charge was you."

"It's not unusual for a Councilman to work on an important joint exploration project; you know that," Troy said. "We had a deal with Corley's company. The Guild invested heavily in the venture. In situations like that, we always send a high-ranking member of the organization along to protect Guild interests."

"In this case, you protected your own interests—yours and Jenner's. Here's how it went down. At some point two weeks into the expedition, you and your second-in-command, Cal Wilson, went ahead on a routine scouting mission. You found the alien ruin, but you couldn't get inside because it was protected by the biggest ghost river either of you had ever encountered. Neither one of you could de-rez river light."

Troy's face twisted with fury. "You're making this up as you go along."

"You recognized the potential value of the discovery, and you didn't want to share it with UEX. You and Wilson made a deal. You noted the coordinates, and then you went back to the UEX team. You told them that the entire sector was blocked by a massive ghost storm. No one can work storm light. The team turned around and returned to the surface."

"If you think the authorities are going to buy this, think again."

Fontana thrust his hands into the pockets of his raincoat. "Here's where it gets really interesting. You knew that one of the other men on the UEX team could work river light. Jake Tanner. After the UEX people were safely out of the way, you and Wilson returned to the ruin with Jake. He de-rezzed the ghost river for you."

"Tanner's a juice dreamer," Troy said. "His testimony is worthless."

Fontana ignored that. "All three of you went into the ruin. You found the ultraviolet generators and the juice fountains. The waters in the fountains were obviously infused with a lot of unusual psi, but it tested clean just like all of the rest of the water sources discovered in the jungle."

"You're starting to irritate me, Fontana." Troy made a small move with one hand. A mag-rez gun materialized in his fist. "I mean, really irritate me."

"Jake and Wilson drank some of the water. Ten minutes later they were in dreamland. You couldn't wake them, so you were forced to sit there until they woke up.

While you waited, you experimented with the ultraviolet generators and discovered what they could do."

Troy smiled. "Those generators are incredible, Fontana. Absolutely amazing. There's no knowing what the aliens used them for, but I realized their potential as weapons immediately. It's the first reliable, sophisticated technology we've come across that can be operated both on the surface and underground in heavy psi conditions. What's more, you don't need a hunter's talent to activate them."

"You didn't tell Tanner and Wilson what the generators could do, did you?"

"Of course not." Troy's disgust was clear. "Tanner and Wilson came out of their dreams in a state of euphoria. They couldn't stop talking about their visions. I realized immediately that the fountains were a source of some kind of highly addictive hallucinatory drug."

"All you had to do was figure out a way to make the discovery profitable."

"Yes," Troy said. "There were some serious logistical issues to be resolved. I faced the same distribution obstacles as any other businessman trying to get a product to market. I also knew I couldn't hope to run the operation alone out of the jungle. So I brought Jenner in on the deal."

"Was it Jenner's idea to form a partnership with the Riders?"

Troy nodded. "Got to hand it to him. It was a brilliant move. He said we couldn't risk trying to recruit Guild men to sell and distribute the juice. He was right. You and some of the others on the Council would have heard the rumors. Also, it would have been a PR disaster if the cops had started arresting hunters and charging them with dealing the latest street drug."

"But everyone knew the Riders were already established in the drug dealing business. It's no big deal whenever one of them gets snagged by the cops."

"One of the problems we discovered straight off was that the juice only works well on people with strong para-resonating talents. That limited our market to hunters. We focused on retirees and guys living on the streets."

"At some point Cal Wilson proved to be a problem, didn't he?"

"The stupid son of a ghost tried to blackmail me," Troy said. "He wanted a bigger piece of the action."

"So you killed him."

"I had no choice. Tanner was much easier to handle. He was a solid Guild man. I told him that the ghost juice fountains were a deep, dark, Guild secret. That was fine by him. All he cared about was his next fix. I made sure he got it. He couldn't handle his Guild work anymore, though, so he was forced to resign."

"You kept him alive because you knew you might need him again someday."

"You know how it is with those damn ghost rivers. You de-rez one, and two weeks or six months later, the currents come back."

"That's just what happened this week, wasn't it? The

river came back, blocking access to the ruin. So you picked up Jake Tanner and took him back down into the jungle to get rid of it."

"He had to come out of his drug haze to do the job. He looked around and saw the other washed-up hunters we were using for labor. I realized that if he went back to the surface, he would start talking."

"So you made him one of the prisoners."

"We're always short of labor underground," Troy agreed. "In fact, I intended to pick up a few more burn-outs this week. I had plans to expand the business to the other city-states. But you've ruined all that."

"Why did you murder Jenner?"

Troy shrugged. "I didn't. Don't get me wrong, I was going to get rid of him after you fried him, but I never got the chance. He died from a stroke, just like the doctors said. I am, however, going to kill you."

"You want my job."

"Oh, yes," Troy said. "I want your job. And I'm going to get it, too. The Council will be only too happy to give it to me when I prove to them that you were running the drug lab."

"Shooting me here in your office is going to be a little messy. Bound to raise a few questions, don't you think?"

"Self-defense. You threatened me because you knew I was going to report your drug operation to the Council." Troy raised the mag-rez. "I had no choice."

Ultraviolet light flared, bathing Troy in waves of heavy psi. Shock etched his features. His hand clenched spasmodically on the grip of the mag-rez, but it was too late. The weapon's sophisticated technology died under the impact of the energy beam. Simultaneously every light in the room crackled and winked out. The computer screen went dark.

Fontana removed the ultragenerator from the pocket of his raincoat. He looked down at the unconscious man. "You were wrong. You did have a choice."

HE COMPLETED HIS SEARCH OF THE OFFICE A SHORT TIME later. There was one ultragenerator in the hidden floor safe. That made a total of five recovered. One was still missing.

Chapter 33

ELVIS WAS SITTING ON SIERRA'S DESK, ATTIRED IN HIS flower-patterned shirt, the small lei around his neck. Kay gave him an affectionate pat and then looked at Sierra.

"Time is running out for tomorrow's edition," she said. "We can't wait much longer for Fontana and Ray. We need to come up with a cover. Runtley says we should go back to basics."

Sierra eyed her warily. "Basics?"

"Sex. We need a new angle on the jungle honeymoon."

"Forget it. You've run that angle into the ground."

"Come on," Kay urged, "I'm just doing my job here while we wait for the big story. Fontana and Ray have been gone for nearly two days. Who knows when they'll get back? We need to fill space in tomorrow's edition."

"Fontana promised that he and Ray would only be gone for forty-eight hours."

"It was an estimate. You know that. Something might have come up."

Sierra shuddered. "Don't say that. I didn't sleep at all last night."

Kay made a face. "Neither did I. Kept thinking about Ray down there in the rain forest, wondering if he was okay and what he was doing."

"You're falling for him, aren't you?"

"What's not to fall for? Not only is he hot, he doesn't make a running joke out of my career as a journalist here at the *Curtain*. That makes him unique among men in my experience."

Elvis suddenly chortled and started to bounce around on the desk.

The anxiety that had kept everything inside Sierra tight and tense for the past two days metamorphosed into shattering relief. She flattened both hands on her desk and pushed herself to her feet.

"I think we've got our big story," she said.

She scooped up Elvis, plopped him on her shoulder, and headed for the door.

"What's going on?" Matt asked.

"They're back," Sierra said.

The door opened before Sierra got to it. Fontana walked in, dark hair damp and long, black raincoat swirling around the tops of his boots. He smiled a quick, triumphant smile when he saw her rushing toward him.

"Got a story for you," he said, opening his arms.

"It's about time you got back," she said.

She flung herself against his chest with such force that Elvis lost his grip. Momentum launched him forward. He landed nimbly on Fontana's shoulder and began making happy, welcoming noises.

Fontana's arms closed fiercely around Sierra. She hugged him with all of her might.

"I've been so worried," she whispered into his wet raincoat.

Ray moved through the doorway behind Fontana. He grinned at Kay.

"Hey, do I get a warm welcome, too?" he asked.

"If you want one," Kay said.

"Oh, yeah," Ray said. "I definitely want one of those."

Laughing, Kay crossed the room and went into his arms.

"Enough with the sappy greetings," Runtley bellowed from out in the hallway. "What's our exclusive?"

Fontana loosened his grip a little, but he kept Sierra tucked firmly against his side. He looked at Runtley.

"Here's your headline," he said. " 'Agents of the Crystal Guild Dismantle Underground Drug Operation.' "

"Nah," Runtley said. "Needs more punch. We'll go with 'Guild Agents Destroy Alien Drug Lab.' "

"Why didn't I think of that?" Fontana said.

"Because you're a Guild boss, not a newspaper editor," Runtley explained kindly.

Chapter 34

"DO YOU REALIZE," FONTANA SAID, TOSSING ASIDE THE wine cork he had just removed from the bottle, "that this is the first time in our married life that we've sat down to dinner together?"

"Given that the length of our marriage can be measured in days and hours, not months or years," Sierra said, "that's not terribly amazing."

She set the platter of roasted asparagus on the table next to the grilled Crystal River salmon. The highly prized salmon, available only a few weeks each year, had taken a serious bite out of her credit card, but she refused to even contemplate the expense. This was, as Fontana had just pointed out, their first dinner alone. The real question was how many more dinners they would enjoy together. But she had promised herself that, for tonight at least, she was not going to think about the future.

"Still, it's an occasion." He dropped an intimate little kiss on the back of her neck as she went past him into the kitchen. "Should I pour Elvis a glass of wine?"

"He prefers Curtain Cola. It's the caffeine."

"I saw some in the refrigerator. I'll get it."

"What's going to happen to Troy Patterson?" she asked.

Fontana's face hardened. "The doctors say that if or when he wakes up, he'll probably spend the rest of his life in a parapsych ward. But if he does recover, he'll go down for the drug operation."

"So the ghost juice was just flowing and bubbling out of some fountains inside that ruin?"

"Right. The alien drug of choice."

She thought about that. "The waters might have some therapeutic value as a painkiller or a parapsych drug."

"Maybe." Fontana set the glass of Curtain Cola on the windowsill and watched Elvis drift happily toward it. "The feds are taking charge of all research connected to the ruin."

She was amused by the cool satisfaction in his words. "More business for the Crystal Guild, hmm?"

He sat down at the table and poured the wine. "Government contracts are always lucrative. Your tax dollars at work."

She sat across from him. "I wonder how the aliens used the waters from the fountain."

"Who knows? Like everything else about them, it's a mystery."

"I'd really like to see that ruin," she said a little wistfully.

He smiled. "After all this, do you think I'd give this scoop to any paper but the *Curtain*?"

"What?"

"Ray and I are making arrangements to take you and the rest of the staff down to the fountains soon. Runtley will have his exclusive."

"He'll be thrilled. So will everyone else. Thanks, Fontana. This is wonderful."

He raised his wineglass. "To us."

The intimate heat in his eyes sent a thrill of hope, anticipation, and longing through her. She picked up her glass.

"To us," she said.

Elvis chortled from the windowsill. Fontana laughed and raised his glass a second time.

"To all three of us," he said.

Sierra used a fork to convey a piece of the grilled salmon onto Fontana's plate. "Speaking of family, I met your brother this morning."

The warm intimacy that had pervaded the atmosphere evaporated in a heartbeat. Fontana's eyes went as hard and cold as gemstones.

"Which brother?" he asked.

Okay, this was going to be a little dicey.

"Nick," she said, trying to maintain a casual, conversational tone. Just two people chatting about family matters over dinner. "He came to see me at my office today."

"What did he want from you?"

She concentrated on serving the salad. "Under the circumstances, it's perfectly natural that he would want to meet your wife, isn't it?"

"No."

"Well, I realize that this is only a Marriage of Convenience, but that doesn't mean the family isn't interested. Look at my family, for example. My grandmother will expect me to bring you to her anniversary celebration next month. If we're still married, that is."

"No."

She chilled. "Yes, I know, we probably won't be married that long. But my point is that families are curious about wives and husbands, even if the arrangements are short-term." She drew a breath. "Like ours."

"I wasn't referring to your grandparents' anniversary. I was talking about my Burns relatives. Trust me, none of us wants to get any closer. What did Nick say? And don't try to convince me that he was just curious about you."

She put down the salad tongs with great care. "Let's get something straight here, Fontana. I am your wife, not one of your hunters. You engage in conversations and discussions with me; you do not give me orders."

His brows rose. "Sounds like you're the one giving orders."

She thought about that. "I think of it as setting boundaries. Now, to return to the subject at hand, Nick told me that lately you have refused to take any calls from anyone in your family."

He stabbed a bite of salmon with his fork. "They've only been trying to call me for about a month or so. Now, if they'd been trying for a year or longer . . ."

"I get it. You would have refused to take the calls that long. Okay, you've made your position clear."

"Good. That means this conversation is over."

"Not quite," she said evenly.

"I was afraid of that." He drank some more wine and set down the glass. "Nick told you that Burns is on the verge of bankruptcy, didn't he?"

"Yes, he did. He says your other brother, Josh, can save it, but he needs an infusion of capital."

"In other words, Nick asked you to talk me into pumping money into the business."

"He sounded desperate."

Fontana shrugged. "Margaret probably sent him. She's the most desperate one in the family."

"Who's Margaret?"

"Nick's mother, my father's widow. She always believed the company was the rightful inheritance of her husband's *legitimate* children. Her worst nightmare for years was that I would somehow get my hands on Burns & Co. When that nightmare came true, I thought she'd have a stroke."

"Nick said that your father left control of the company to you, but you declined the inheritance."

"That's right. The day the will was read in the lawyer's office, I signed papers transferring my shares in Burns & Co. back to my father's *legitimate* heirs."

"Did you know the business was in trouble when you walked away from it?"

"No, neither did Margaret." His smile was cold. "Talk about life's little ironies. She was so relieved, she actually sent me a stiff little thank-you note afterward. Those well-bred, upper-class manners come through every time."

She thought about calling him on that jab and then decided she needed to stay focused.

"Okay," she said, "so when did everyone find out that Burns was in serious financial jeopardy?"

He ate some of the fish for a moment, thinking. "Josh must have realized that he had problems soon after he took over the company. Probably spent months trying to come up with some way to salvage things on his own before he approached me."

"You did take that call?"

"Yes. We talked just long enough for me to make it clear that I don't want anything to do with the business."

"Why did your father change his will at the last minute and leave Burns to you?" she asked.

"Burns was my father's passion," Fontana said. "He committed his life to the company. When he realized that his dream had become a nightmare, he couldn't face it."

She lowered her fork. "That was why he killed himself? Because he was facing financial ruin?"

"Yes."

"But that's such a dumb reason. I mean, I can see contemplating suicide because you found out that you had a fatal illness or because you'd done something dreadful and couldn't live with yourself. But to put a gun to your head just because your business was in trouble seems—"

"Weak?"

She flushed. "Forgive me. I'm very sorry. I should not have said that. Suicide is a great tragedy. Your father was undoubtedly suffering from a severe depression. It is an illness, like any other, and should be treated as such."

"Forget the politically correct spin. The truth is my father was willing to sacrifice everything for Burns & Co. Hell, he even entered a Covenant Marriage for the sake of the business. He wanted the financial connections Margaret's family could give him. The drive and ambition it took to build Burns was Dad's greatest strength." Fontana shrugged. "You know what they say about your greatest strength."

"It's also your greatest weakness," she said quietly.

"Right. The only defense anyone has is to be aware of both." He used his fork to spear another bite of salmon. "Play to one and guard against the other."

She smiled. "Words to live by."

"Thanks. Once in a while we Guild bosses actually think about stuff like that."

"Don't start," she warned.

"Sorry. Can't resist occasionally pointing out that your stereotyped image of the Guild has a few flaws." He picked up the wine bottle. "It's one of my weaknesses."

She raised her brows. "Wow. A Guild boss who actually admits to having a weakness?"

"Sure. But not in public. I'm counting on your wifely loyalty to keep that news flash out of the press."

"Hot dang, another Guild secret." She watched him refill their glasses. "All right, so your father lived his life for his business, and when it failed, he couldn't go on. I still don't understand why he left the company to you."

"That's obvious. Burns was more than just a financial empire. My father intended it to be his legacy, a monument that would live on for generations after his death. When he realized that the firm was headed straight for the catacombs, he did the only thing he could think of to preserve his reputation. He dumped the business on me."

"What was the point?"

"Don't you get it?" His mouth twisted in a humorless smile. "My father figured that when Burns & Co. eventually folded, it would look like I was the one who had destroyed it, not him. He wanted me to take the fall for his failure so that his own reputation would remain untarnished."

"Hmm."

"What?"

"Your relationship with your father was obviously pretty complicated."

"There was nothing complicated about it. I was his bastard son, a source of humiliation and embarrassment to his wife and her elite family. He met his financial obligations to me until the day I turned eighteen. Otherwise he pretended that my mother and I didn't exist."

"I've got news for you, Fontana. That description of

your relationship with him meets the definition of complicated."

"So?"

"So, here's what I think," she said. "Your father was very aware of your success within the Guild. He also knew that you had built your own financial empire."

"It's no empire. I've made some good investments, but I'm not worth anywhere near as much as he was before Burns & Co. started to crumble."

"Only because you had other priorities," she said. She was impatient with his uncharacteristic obtuseness. "You were more interested in becoming the head of the Crystal Guild than building an empire, so that's where you concentrated your energy and talent."

He gave her an odd look. "What makes you think I could have built the same kind of business enterprise that my father put together?"

"Anyone who can run a Guild can run a corporation. Same skill set."

"Is that right? I thought you were convinced that Guild bosses were only half a step away from being mob bosses."

She smiled. "Like I said, same skill set."

He looked amused. "An interesting view of the corporate world. Does your father know about this?"

"Who do you think pointed it out to me?"

That stopped him for a few seconds, although you had to know the man to notice the sudden stillness that indicated she'd caught him off guard.

"Your father told you that there wasn't much difference between a CEO and a Guild chief?" he asked, not bothering to conceal his skepticism.

"Yes. Of course, a Guild boss does have some unique options when it comes to getting rid of the competition or dealing with personnel problems. All those convenient tunnels. But aside from that . . ." She moved one hand, waving the issue aside.

Fontana slowly lowered his fork. "You're serious, aren't you? You really believe that I could have built the business empire my father built."

"Sure, if that's what you had set out to do. What's more, your father knew it, too. He would have been a fool not to realize that your rise to power within the Guild and your own personal wealth were clear evidence that you had inherited his talents." She smiled. "And that, Fontana, is why he left Burns & Co. to you."

"He left me a dying business, Sierra."

"Don't you get it? You said, yourself, Burns was more important to him than anything else. Your father knew that you were the only one who had a chance of saving it. In the end he put his reputation and the fortunes of the entire family in your hands."

Chapter 35

SOMETIME LATER HE LOUNGED AGAINST THE RAILING OF Sierra's little balcony, letting the psi-rich night envelop him. Elvis sat beside him, clutching his miniature guitar in one paw. The fog was the heaviest it had been all month.

When he looked over the edge of the railing, he could see the green glow of the sign above Simon Lugg's tavern, but it was impossible to make out the words *Green Gate*. He could hear people coming and going from the establishment, but they were no more than faint shadows in the mist.

He looked at the delicate crystal glass in his hand. It was half-filled with Amber Dew, a rare and very pricey after-dinner liqueur. Like the expensive wine, he had brought it along tonight to help celebrate the day's victory. He had planned to share the triumph with Sierra.

That was why he had not taken her out to dinner. He had wanted to be alone with her.

He had not wanted to talk about Burns & Co.

"All in all," he said to Elvis, "the plan did not go well."

Elvis made a little rumbling noise in what sounded like a commiserating tone.

"There was a plan?" Sierra said from the doorway.

He turned his head to look at her. "I'm a Guild boss. There's always a plan."

She smiled in the shadows and walked toward him. He opened his senses, unable to resist the unique, enthralling aura of feminine mystery. The sweet, hot, exciting energy aroused everything inside him, just as it had the first time she had entered his office. But the pull, the sensation of a psychic link between them, was so much stronger now than it had been that first day. He sensed that the bond was only going to grow more powerful with time. The part of him that comprehended the nuances of strategy and risk-taking was waving a red flag of warning. He had two options: cut his losses fast or stick around and hope that Sierra felt at least some of what he was feeling.

No doubt about it. The smart move would be to bail while the bailing was good. But sometimes you ignored the odds.

"What was the plan?" she asked, coming to a halt at the railing.

"I wanted to talk about some things tonight," he said. "Things that had nothing to do with Burns & Co."

"I'm sorry," she said quietly. "I realize my timing was bad. It's just that your brother seemed so anxious, and the whole situation sounded very urgent."

"I'd rather you didn't refer to Nick as my brother."

Her eyes widened. "But he is your brother."

"Technically speaking, he's my half brother. Believe me, on the rare occasions when we think of each other, it is strictly in technical terms."

She searched his face. "You have no sense of a family connection with him?"

"Why would I? I've only met him and the others twice. Once at my father's funeral and once in the lawyer's office afterward."

"I see." She turned away to look down at the Green Gate. "Well, I've said my piece. I promise you I won't mention Nick or Burns & Co. again."

She sounded truly chagrined. It was her determination to abide by the vow that made him smile.

"Right," he said.

"What's so funny?"

"The thought of you trying to keep silent about Nick and the business."

She raised her chin. "You don't think I can do it?"

"No. Sooner or later you'll bring up both subjects again."

Her brows snapped together above the dark frames of her glasses. "How do you know?"

"Because you won't be able to help yourself." He laughed. "You are what you are."

"And just what is that?"

"Goal-oriented, just like me. Just like the others in your family. You can't rest until you've achieved your objective and, at the moment, your objective is to convince me to save Burns & Co. For my own good, of course. Your fancy, high-grade intuition is probably telling you that I'll get some of what the para-shrinks like to call closure out of the whole thing."

Her mouth opened, shut, and opened again.

"What are you talking about?" she finally managed. "I'm not like you or anyone else in my family. I'm a walking definition of the word *underachiever*. Just ask anyone."

"I don't have to ask around." He rested both elbows on the railing. "You're the living, breathing definition of *achiever*. The only difference between you and the rest of us is your goals." He held up one hand to silence her. "And before you start arguing with me, remember that I'm where I am today because I'm damn good at figuring out what people want."

She folded her arms and bristled. There was no other word for it.

"What do you think I want?" she asked.

"To make the world a better place. Justice for those who can't get it for themselves. Help for people like Jake Tanner and the other hunters who disappeared. In short, you're a classic do-gooder."

"And you think do-gooders are naive, gullible, unrealistic, and downright pesky."

"I didn't say that." He paused, the glass halfway to his mouth. "Although, now that you mention it—"

"If you feel that way about me, I'm surprised you didn't file for immediate termination of our marriage this afternoon when you came out of Patterson's office. In fact, why are you even here in my apartment tonight?"

"I haven't made any move to terminate our MC because I like being married to you."

She blinked. "You do?"

"I'm hoping that the reason you didn't rush out to file for divorce yourself today is because you aren't one hundred percent opposed to the idea of being married to me."

"No." She swallowed. "No, I'm not opposed to the idea."

"Okay, that settles that. We're staying married for a while."

"In spite of the fact that I may not be able to resist urging you to try to rescue Burns & Co.?"

"In spite of that."

"Gee, Fontana, I don't know what to say. This is all so romantic. You're really sweeping me off my feet here."

"No rule says a Guild boss can't be romantic."

"My comment was intended to be taken as thinly veiled sarcasm."

He pulled her into his arms. "I'll give you a little tip."

"Yes?"

"When you use sarcasm with a Guild chief, you have to unveil it."

She smiled. "I'll remember that next time."

He kissed her before she could say another word. Her mouth was soft and warm and inviting under his. After a moment he picked her up and carried her indoors and down the hall to the shadowy bedroom.

It wasn't a full and complete victory, he thought, more like a strategic move in a delicately balanced game of chess. But it would do for now.

Chapter 36

SHE CAME AWAKE TO THE REALIZATION THAT SHE WAS alone in the bed. When she opened her eyes, she saw Fontana silhouetted against the window. He wore his briefs but nothing else. Elvis was perched beside him on the sill. They were both looking out into the solid wall of luminous fog. A couple of hunters bonding in the night.

She pushed back the covers and sat up on the side of the bed. "What's wrong?"

"Nothing." Fontana looked at her over his shoulder. "I'm just doing a little thinking."

She got to her feet and walked across the room to join him. "What about?"

"My big plan. The one I intended to talk to you about tonight."

She stilled. "I thought the plan was for us to stay married for a while."

"It was actually a little more complicated than that."

Her intuition hummed. Whatever this was about, it was important to him. She tried and failed to squelch the little spark of hope that leaped to life within her. Maybe he was beginning to understand that what they had was very, very special.

"More complicated than an MC?" she asked.

He thought about that briefly and then shook his head. "I doubt if there's anything more complicated than an MC."

"What was the rest of your plan?"

He draped an arm around her shoulders. "I'm going to offer you a job."

"Doing what, for heaven's sake?"

"Managing the Guild's charitable foundation."

So much for her intuition.

"Are you kidding?" She waved her arms. "The Foundation is a joke. Jenner used it as a private slush fund for bribing politicians and shady CEOs. Hardly any money trickled down to legitimate charities."

"I'm aware of that. The Foundation needs to be cleaned up. Who better to do it than someone who really cares about doing good with the Guild's money?"

"Huh."

"You're a natural for that job."

"Huh."

"I should warn you that it's going to be a full-time position. You would have to give up journalism."

"Huh."

"Any questions?" he asked.

"I don't know where to start. The thought of working for the Guild is, well, it's mind-boggling."

"More mind-boggling than being married to the boss?"

She contemplated the matter closely for a moment. "Guess not."

"If it doesn't work out, I'm sure you could always go back to the *Curtain*."

"Huh," she repeated. "I'll have to think about it."

"You do that." He dropped a kiss into her hair. His hand closed gently around her breast. Heat and longing rose inside her. Energy flared. So did suspicion.

"Fontana?"

"Hmm?" he nuzzled her ear.

"This isn't some sneaky scheme to stop me from pursuing my investigative reporting on the Guild, is it?"

"Absolutely not."

"You're sure? Because when I see things going on that I don't approve of, I won't keep silent just because I'm married to you and working for the Guild."

"You have my word of honor that giving you the job has nothing whatsoever to do with trying to keep you quiet." He kissed her throat. "I've got something else in mind to achieve that objective."

A shivery thrill swept through her. "Is that so?"

His hands slid down to close around her buttocks. He lifted her up against him so that she was left in no doubt about his state of arousal.

"Probably won't work," he said. "But I figure it's worth a try. A lot of tries, in fact."

"Does this strategy involve sex?"

"How did you guess?"

He carried her back to the bed, settled her down on the tumbled sheets, and lowered himself slowly on top of her. She wrapped one leg around his bare thigh, thrilling to the weight of his body on hers.

He cradled her face between his hands and kissed her long and hungrily. By the time he raised his head, she was breathless and tingling. He had come free of his briefs. She could feel him hard and rigid against her leg. She reached down and stroked him, savoring the broad length of him. The knowledge that he wanted her so fiercely sent a rush of pleasure through all of her senses.

They twisted and coiled in the shadows for a time, growing hot and damp together. Abruptly Fontana pulled free and started to work his way down her body. He left searing kisses on her breasts and belly. By the time he reached his destination, she was shivering with need; so tightly rezzed she thought she would shatter. He eased two big fingers inside her, probing gently.

"I love your scent," he said, his voice low and rough. "I can't get enough of you."

And then his mouth was on her in the most intimate of kisses. The sensation was so overwhelming she cried out and clenched her hands in his hair.

"Yes," she gasped. "Yes, please, there. *There.*"

The sweet tension that had built inside her came undone in a series of pulsing waves.

She gasped and cried out, amazed and astonished all over again that he could do this to her.

When the climax was nearly finished, he moved back up her body and thrust heavily into her. She was exquisitely sensitized. The sensual invasion was the most erotic feeling she had ever experienced. The pressure took her to the delicate point of balance that separated extreme pleasure from pain. Before she could decide which it was that she felt, Fontana's own climax struck. The muscles of his back hardened into sculpted stone beneath her hands.

She heard his harsh, muffled exclamation: satisfaction, triumph, and surrender inextricably entwined.

Together they fell into the sea of night.

Chapter 37

"HELL OF A FIRE," NICK SAID. "BURNED RIGHT DOWN TO the foundation."

"Arson," Fontana said.

"Heard that." Nick's serious expression did not alter by so much as the flicker of an eyelash. "Caused by aliens, according to your wife's paper."

"Never underestimate the investigative reporting in the *Curtain.*"

They both looked at the charred ruins of the mansion. The only thing still standing was the massive stone fireplace. It projected upward into the fog, defying the destructive force of the fire to the end. Everything else had collapsed into the basement.

The good news, Fontana decided, was that the pile of blackened rubble hid the old staircase that led down into the catacombs.

"Planning to rebuild?" Nick asked, studying the scene.

"Sure. You know what they say about the three rules of real estate."

"Location, location, location."

"There's no better location in Crystal, as far as I'm concerned."

Nick pushed the edges of his jacket out of the way and planted his hands on his hips. "Okay. I'm here. Mind telling me why you called and said you wanted to see me?"

"You told Sierra that I could save Burns."

"I told her you were the company's only chance. Didn't say it would work."

"May be a lost cause already."

"Josh thinks he can turn things around if he gets the cash he needs," Nick said. "But he doesn't want to risk going the usual venture capital route. That would start rumors, he says. The suppliers and creditors and customers would panic. He says things have got to be handled quietly."

"He's right. Even if he did convince a venture capitalist group to invest, he'd have to turn over a controlling interest in the company to the investors."

"He doesn't want to do that for obvious reasons."

Fontana said nothing.

Nick was silent for a moment. "Did you ask me to meet you here so that you could tell me to go home and instruct the rest of the family to get screwed?"

"No. You can tell Josh that I'll have the money transferred to his account tomorrow morning."

Nick exhaled slowly, stunned. "Thanks."

"There's one condition."

"Just one?"

"I want a seat on the board."

Nick winced. "Josh isn't going to be thrilled with that."

"It's the only way I can keep an eye on my money."

"Sounds fair to me," Nick said. "But then, I didn't get the flair for business that you and Josh got from Dad."

"Until recently I didn't think I got anything at all from him."

Nick studied the remains of the mansion for a while.

"Probably doesn't mean much to you," he said finally, "but as far I'm concerned, none of us got a lot from Dad. He was a lousy father and an even lousier husband. All he cared about was Burns & Co."

"I noticed that."

"You still haven't told me why you're going to help Josh save Burns."

Fontana studied the ruins of the mansion. "My wife thinks I should do it. Says it will be good psychic karma."

Disbelief flashed across Nick's face. "Uh, you believe in psychic karma?"

"No."

"So, in other words, you're doing this to please your wife?"

Fontana nodded, "That's pretty much what it comes down to, yes. I'm trying to think of it as a wedding present."

Nick whistled. "It'll be a damned expensive wedding present if you lose your investment."

"What the hell, I can afford to take the loss."

Nick gave him a quizzical look. "Thought your marriage was just an MC."

"For now."

Nick raised his brows. "It's serious?"

"Serious."

They studied the charred remains for a while longer.

"Rebuilding this place is going to be a major project," Nick said eventually.

"I know."

"Got an architect lined up?"

"No," Fontana said. "Haven't had time to think about it."

"I could fit you into my schedule."

Fontana looked at him. "You?"

"I'm an architect."

"I know."

"I've handled large residential projects like this one."

"I know," Fontana said. "Saw one of them profiled in an architectural magazine last year."

"You read architectural magazines?"

"Not usually, no. Saw your name on the cover. I was curious."

"I'll give you the family rate."

"I'll think about it," Fontana said.

Chapter 38

"ALWAYS KNEW I COULD COUNT ON ELVIS," JAKE TANNER said.

They were gathered in the Green Gate Tavern. Simon was behind the bar. Mitch, Jeff, and Andy lounged on their stools. Bottles of beer sat in front of them. Jake was drinking coffee.

Sierra stood at one end of the bar, her arms folded on the polished surface. Elvis, attired in his sparkling white cape, the new pair of tiny sunglasses that Jake had made perched on his head, sat beside her on the counter. There was a cup of coffee and a bowl of pretzels in front of him. He had already drained half the coffee.

"What made you put the coordinates behind the mirror in the miniature dressing room?" Sierra asked.

"Dunno." Jake shrugged. "Just came to me in a juice dream."

Mitch scowled. "You got the idea in a dream? How the hell does that work?"

Jake exhaled heavily. "The juice is weird crap. It takes you into another dimension. You feel so damn brilliant, like you're a god or a wizard or something. Everything seems so clear in the dreams. You think differently. It's like you're having visions."

"What happens when you wake up?" Sierra asked.

He shook his head. "That's the big downside. When you come out of a juice dream, reality and the visions get all mixed up in your head. But one day after you and Elvis visited me and brought me some cookies, I drank some juice and had this really clear vision. I saw myself getting kidnapped by aliens, just like the others who had gone missing. Somehow I knew that if that happened, it would have something to do with the ruins we had found in the jungle."

"It was probably your subconscious mind putting together some of the facts about the recent kidnappings combined with your own knowledge of the situation," Sierra said.

"No," Jake said. "After I got into the juice big-time, my subconscious brain wasn't working any better than my conscious brain. It was something you said that day, I think."

Mitch looked at him. "What did she say?"

"We had talked about the disappearances and how no one was looking for the guys who'd gone missing. She wanted to know if I had any idea why someone would want to kidnap a bunch of washed-up hunters. Then we talked about how all the juicers seemed to be ex-hunters. I guess I sort of knew all along that there had to be a connection and that they might come for me. I just hadn't wanted to think about it."

"So you wrote out the coordinates of the fountains on a piece of paper and tucked it behind the dressing room mirror," Sierra concluded. "Just in case you, yourself, went missing."

"Right," Jake said. "Knew you'd look for me."

Simon shook his head. "Great idea, but why the hell didn't you simply give Sierra those coordinates?"

Jake sighed. "Part of me didn't feel right about that. In fact, at the last minute, I almost changed my mind about putting the coordinates behind the mirror."

"For heaven's sake, why would you have had second thoughts?" Sierra demanded.

They all looked at her, saying nothing.

She raised her eyes to the ceiling. "Right. Guild secrets. I should have known."

"Patterson told me that the fountains were a classified Guild matter," Jake explained apologetically. "Hell, the man was a member of the Council. What was I supposed to do? I liked you a lot, and I trusted you, but, well, you weren't one of us at the time."

"One of you?" she repeated, going blank.

Simon grinned. "He means you weren't Guild. Now you are."

"So it's okay to tell me secrets?" She waved her hands. "What kind of crazy logic is that?"

"Guild logic," Jeff explained helpfully.

Mitch regarded Jake with a thoughtful expression. "You seem to be okay off the juice."

Jake grimaced. "Luckily the withdrawal doesn't last long. It's more mental than physical. You miss the dreamworld for a while, and you get the shakes for about a day, but then things return to normal."

Simon looked at him. "Think you'd go back on the stuff if you had a chance?"

"Not like that's going to happen now that Fontana and the government authorities have control of the source," Jeff said dryly.

"I wouldn't go back on it," Jake said. He frowned, very serious now. "I'm done with the juice."

"How do you know?" Andy asked.

"Had time to do a lot of thinking while I was filling up those bottles for the Riders," Jake said. "Something Sierra told me started to make a lot of sense."

"What was that?" Simon asked.

Jake looked at Sierra, intent and determined. "You told me I was an artist. Don't know if that's true, but I do know I get something out of making those miniatures. It's satisfying somehow."

"I understand," Sierra said.

Jeff grew thoughtful. “I’ll bet Mitch and I could sell your miniatures for you in our shop. What do you say, Mitch?”

“Sure.” Mitch said. “People love miniatures. There are collectors out there who will pay big bucks for fancy, high-end dollhouses and all the little things that go inside.”

Sierra smiled at Jake. “Congratulations. I think you’ve found yourself a new career path.”

“Thanks to you and Elvis,” Jake said.

“Don’t thank us,” Sierra said. “Thank Fontana and Ray. They’re the ones who went into the jungle to find you and the others.”

Simon chuckled. “Fontana’s First Rule: Never leave a man behind for ghost bait.”

Jake looked at Sierra. “Well, he sure as hell married the right woman. She wouldn’t leave a man behind, either.”

Chapter 39

IT WAS LATE MORNING. THE WEATHER REPORT HAD called for a slight lifting of the fog by noon, but Fontana had seen no signs of any lightening in the permanent twilight outside the windows of his office. He looked at the notes on his desk. There was a timeline and a rough sketch of the catacombs beneath what was left of his house. Ray sat in the chair on the opposite side of the desk.

"Patterson obviously knew about the hole-in-the-wall in the basement," Fontana said. "He must have also known that the closest exit was beneath the warehouse."

"In which case, it didn't take a genius to figure out that if you and Sierra went into the tunnels to escape the fire, you would head for the warehouse," Ray said. "What I find really interesting is that the Riders set their trap in the one short section of the tunnels where there was a blind curve and no intersecting corridors that you could use to evade them."

"That means that they had an accurate map of that sector of the catacombs." Fontana raised his brows. "But according to the former owner's journal, the chart he made was the only one in existence."

"Either he was wrong—"

Fontana leaned back in his chair. "Or somehow Patterson got hold of the journal and used the information in it to set up his ambush."

Ray's expression was grim. "You told me that you discovered the journal in a hidden wall safe in the art gallery. You said you never showed it to anyone else. How the hell would Patterson have known about it, let alone have a chance to study it?"

"Good question." The intercom buzzed. Fontana leaned forward and rezzed it. "What is it, Harlan?"

"I have the Foundation files that you requested, sir. Shall I bring them in now, or would you prefer to deal with them at another time?"

"Bring them in now. I want to look them over before I talk to Bonner."

"Yes, sir."

Ray's brows rose. "Why the sudden interest in the Foundation?"

The door opened. Harlan came into the room.

"I'm going to get rid of Bonner," Fontana said.

"You're going to put someone else in charge of the Foundation?" Ray asked.

"Yes. My wife."

Harlan set the files on the desk. "Here you are, sir."

"Thanks, Harlan."

Ray grinned. "Interesting choice. Sierra will clean things up in about twenty-four hours. You won't have to worry about where the money is going with her in charge."

Fontana set the file aside. "I figure my main problem will be explaining to her that I don't intend to increase her budget every time she decides to take on a new philanthropic project."

Chapter 40

"THIS PLACE IS INCREDIBLE," KAY WHISPERED, HER VOICE hushed to the point of reverence. "I've never seen anything like it."

"No one else has either," Runtley declared triumphantly. "Not unless you count the gang that was bottling and selling the juice and the guards the Guild has posted here now."

They were gathered around the amazing fountains in the glowing jungle ruin. The psi levels were so high Sierra could feel the buzz across all of her senses. She could only imagine how it affected Fontana and the other hunters in the vicinity.

The trek through the rain forest had taken less than three hours. Fontana and his team had brought Sierra and the staff of the *Curtain* into the jungle through the previously uncharted gate that Troy Patterson and the drug runners had used. It was much closer to the ruin than the official gate where Fontana and Ray had entered when they went in to rescue the missing hunters.

"As far as the general public is concerned, the very first pictures of this place will be on the cover of the *Curtain* tomorrow morning," Phil said, rezzing off a few more shots. "These pics are gonna make me famous. Man, I am gonna be up for the News Photographer of the Year award. And the cool thing is, these fountains are real. I didn't have to build them out of doughnuts and discarded Curtain Cola cans the way I did the alien Temple of Love."

"All of the slick dailies and the rest of the media are going to be begging me for permission to use the shots," Runtley said, dazzled by the prospect. "This is the scoop to end all scoops, and the *Curtain* has the story."

Fontana studied him across one of the sparkling green pools. "Just make sure the Guild comes out looking good. Remember, we have a deal here."

"Absolutely," Runtley assured him hastily. "Don't worry, what with taking down that gang of juice dealers, rescuing the hunters who were abducted by aliens, and opening this place up for the para-archaeologists, the Guild will look downright noble and heroic in tomorrow's edition. Guaranteed."

Fontana nodded, satisfied. "Noble and heroic works. My PR people like noble and heroic."

Kay walked to the nearest fountain and looked into the

effervescent green pool. "I wonder if the aliens came here to get drunk or stoned out of their weird little minds?"

"No way to know," Matt said, jotting down some notes. "The energy in those waters may have affected them a lot differently than it does humans. For all we know, this place could have been some sort of fancy, high-end health spa."

"A psychic health spa," Runtley said. "I like it."

A familiar whisper of shimmering awareness sparkled through Sierra. She left Fontana's side and circled the nearest fountain, contemplating its airy, otherworldly beauty.

"It doesn't feel like a spa," she said quietly. "And I doubt that they came here to get drunk or stoned, at least not for recreational purposes."

Fontana watched her, intrigued.

"What do you think went on here?" he asked.

She gazed down into the psi-green waters. Although the fountain pool did not appear deep, she could not see the bottom. The restless little tides, eddies, and waves sparkled and flashed and swirled in endlessly shifting patterns.

"There is an Old Earth legend," she said slowly, "about a place known to the ancients as the Oracle of Delphi. Supposedly strange vapors emanated from the ground beneath the Oracle. The fumes caused the chosen priestess to prophesy. The prophesies came in the form of strange riddles that had to be interpreted."

"You think this ruin was sacred ground to the aliens?" Fontana asked.

She looked up from the mesmerizing waters of the fountain pool. "It makes them seem more human, doesn't it?"

Chapter 41

"SOMETIMES I WONDER IF THIS FOG IS EVER GOING TO lift." Kay sat on the corner of the desk, a cup of coffee in one hand, one long leg swinging easily. "It's starting to get to me. The city always feels strange during the Big Gray."

"Think of it as atmospheric," Sierra said.

"Every year I tell myself that, but after a couple of weeks the atmospheric line doesn't work anymore."

"It won't last much longer."

"Let's hope."

"You're just feeling low because all the excitement of the Guild's big drug bust and the discovery of the Alien Oracle has died down," Sierra said.

"I know. It's been a great run. Problem is, Runtley's on a roll. He's gotten used to publishing the top-selling paper in Crystal. You heard him this morning. The ad money is pouring in, and he wants us to keep the headlines coming."

"We'll think of something," Sierra said.

"We always do," Kay agreed.

Elvis floated by in his balloon basket. The rhinestones on his white cape glittered. He chortled a greeting and munched on the bit of doughnut that someone, probably Phil, had given him.

Kay chuckled and reached out to give him a pat. "The fog doesn't bother you, does it, King?"

She gave the basket a gentle push that sent Elvis sailing regally off in the direction of Matt's desk.

"Look at it this way," Sierra said. "Coming up with new stories for Runtley won't be half as tough as explaining my Marriage of Convenience to my grandmother."

"I can see you're not looking forward to that."

The phone rang. Sierra picked it up.

"Newsroom," she said.

"I wish to speak with Sierra McIntyre."

"You've got her. What can I do for you?"

"My name is Harlan Ostendorf. I'm Mr. Fontana's executive administrative assistant."

"Yes, of course, Mr. Ostendorf. Fontana has mentioned you."

"Mr. Fontana is extremely busy today, but his schedule has opened up a bit. He asked me to call you to see if it would be possible for you to meet him for lunch at the Amber Club. He requested that I send a car to pick you up."

"Lunch at the Amber Club?" She glanced at her watch. It was almost noon. "Yes, that will be fine."

"Excellent. The car will be in front of your office building in approximately ten minutes."

The phone went dead. She put it down slowly.

"Did I just hear you say you've been invited to the Amber Club for lunch?" Kay demanded.

"Yes. I'm meeting Fontana there. That was his assistant." She frowned. "Why?"

"Oh, nothing," Kay said airily. "It's just that the Amber Club is one of the most exclusive places in town. I'll bet this is the day."

"What day?" Sierra asked.

"The day he asks you to enter a Covenant Marriage with him."

"No way," Phil said. He cranked back in his chair, twiddling a pen. "A guy might suggest an MC over lunch, but Covenant Marriage proposals are always done over fancy dinners."

Kay glowered. "How would you know? You've never asked anyone to marry you."

"It's a guy thing," Phil explained, very knowing.

Matt looked up from his computer. "He's right. Covenant Marriage proposals are evening events. Expensive dinner. Champagne. There're rules about that kind of thing. You don't do them at lunch."

"Oh, yeah?" Kay shot back.

"Yeah," Phil said.

Kay folded her arms. "So why else would a busy man

like Fontana take time out of his day for lunch at a place like the Amber Club unless he's planning to propose?"

Phil and Matt looked at each other.

Matt shrugged. "Maybe he's hoping for a nooner."

Kay yanked the flowers out of the vase on Sierra's desk and hurled them at Matt's head. The blooms struck the target, showering Matt with petals and water.

"Hey," he yelped. "I was just trying to explain a little male psychology."

Sierra ignored the uproar and got to her feet. "If you'll excuse me, I'm going to leave now."

"What about Elvis?" Phil said. "You can't take him into a fancy place like the Amber Club. Management will freak."

"I'll leave him here with you." She paused beside the balloon basket and dropped a little kiss onto the top of Elvis's head. "Be good while I'm gone, okay? I'll be back soon."

Elvis rumbled contentedly and went back to eating his doughnut. She slung the strap of her purse over her shoulder and headed for the door.

"Have fun," Kay said. "And don't forget to thank Fontana for me."

Sierra turned slightly to look over her shoulder. "Why?"

"Because he just gave me my next big scoop. 'Guild Boss Proposes Covenant Marriage to New Bride.' "

"Hey," Phil said. "Does that mean another night in the mysterious alien temple of love?"

"No," Kay said. "This is a CM. We need a new venue and some new secret rituals."

"I can help with that part of the story," Matt said.

"What would you know about secret wedding-night rituals?" Kay asked.

"It's another guy thing." Matt spread his hands. "What is it with women? You think we know nothing about this kind of stuff."

Sierra went out the door and hurried down the stairs. When she reached the lobby, she looked out through the glass doors. A long, black limo waited at the curb. A dapper-looking man attired in a uniform, black leather gloves, and a cap stood beside the big car. A tiny chill shivered through her. *It's the fog. Kay is right. It makes everything seem a little strange.*

She pushed through the heavy doors and hurried across the sidewalk. The icy sensation grew stronger. *Relax. You're still a little over-rezzed because of all the excitement lately.*

The chauffeur opened the rear door for her. She looked into the dark interior. The inexplicable rush of dread brought her to a complete stop. She could not get into the vehicle. A possibility occurred to her. Maybe this was the wrong limo.

"Is this the car that was sent for Sierra McIntyre?" she asked.

"Yes, ma'am."

The discordant hum of her intuition was rattling every nerve in her body now. "You're Harlan Ostendorf,

Fontana's assistant. I recognize your voice. You called me a short time ago to tell me that Fontana wanted to do lunch."

"Yes, ma'am. At the Amber Club." Harlan checked his watch. "If you don't mind, we're running a little late. Mr. Fontana likes people to be on time."

"But you're an executive assistant, not a chauffeur."

"Mr. Fontana likes me to drive whenever possible."

She took a step back and reached into her purse for her phone. "Just a minute. I want to give my husband a quick call and make sure he's still on for lunch."

"Get into the car," Harlan Ostendorf said. "Now."

She looked up swiftly. There was a mag-rez gun in Harlan's gloved hand.

"You have caused me a great deal of trouble, Sierra McIntyre," he said quietly. "Get into the car, or I will kill you where you stand."

Chapter 42

THE ICY, HYPERVIGILANT SENSATION WAS NOT UNLIKE the feeling he got when he encountered ghost light. But there was no dissonance energy in the room. What he was looking at, Fontana knew, was the answer to the question he had been asking ever since he and Sierra had escaped the burning mansion.

He raised his eyes to meet Ray's. He shook his head once, indicating that he wanted silence. Then he reached for a pen and wrote the name on a piece of paper. Ray glanced at it, frowning a little. His expression cleared and his face went hard. He nodded once, in agreement.

Fontana rezzed the intercom. "Harlan, would you come in here for a minute? I've got a question about the Foundation files."

"I'm sorry, sir, Mr. Ostendorf has gone to lunch," Dray Levine said. "Is there anything I can do?"

Fontana felt everything inside him turn stone cold. "Did Harlan go down to the cafeteria?"

"No, sir. He said something about going out to a restaurant."

"What restaurant?"

"He didn't say, sir."

Fontana reached for the phone and entered the number of the *Curtain*'s newsroom. Matt answered on the second ring.

"This is Fontana. I want to talk to Sierra."

"Huh?" Matt sounded bewildered. "She left a few minutes ago to have lunch with you."

"The hell she did. Who picked her up?"

"She said you were sending a limo for her. She went downstairs, and that was the last we've seen of her. To tell you the truth, we were starting to get a little worried."

Gripping the phone very tightly, he got to his feet. "What was your first clue?"

"Elvis has left the building."

"Skip the Elvis jokes."

"I'm serious. He's gone. One minute he was in his balloon basket, and the next he just disappeared. The door was open, but no one saw him leave. What's wrong?"

"I think Sierra has just been kidnapped by my executive assistant."

"Shit," Matt whispered, stunned. "I told her you weren't going to propose a Covenant Marriage over lunch."

Chapter 43

IT WAS MIDDAY, BUT THE COMBINATION OF THE DENSE fog and the heavily tinted car windows made the view so dark it might as well have been midnight. Sierra sat in the rear seat of the vehicle. The car doors had locked automatically as soon as she was inside.

She hadn't bothered with a seat belt. If she got an opportunity to make a break for it, she did not want to waste any time unbuckling.

They were headed deep into the neighborhood near the south wall of the Dead City, the most dilapidated section of the Quarter. Harlan was forced to drive slowly because of the dense mist and the narrow streets. She could see the back of his head, but there had been no conversation between them. Harlan had not lowered the window that separated the driver's seat from the passenger compartment.

He brought the limo to a halt in an alley and climbed out from behind the wheel. She heard the door to her left unlock. Harlan yanked it open.

"Get out," he ordered. He held the mag-rez steady, pointing it at her midsection. "Hurry."

"This is a Guild car," she said, sliding slowly across the seat. "Fontana probably has a way to track it."

"I'm not an idiot. This isn't from the Guild fleet. It's from a commercial limo service. Besides, Fontana has no idea that I'm here with you. As far as he's concerned, I'm his ever-faithful executive assistant, one of the few people he thinks he can trust in the organization. And he'll go on thinking that when I help him try to find you after you disappear."

Slowly she stood. "Why do I have to disappear?"

"Because you have been a great nuisance, and you are poised to become even more of a problem. I have no choice but to get rid of you. You have destroyed one of my enterprises. I will not allow you to destroy the other."

Shocked, she could only stare at him. "You were involved with the ghost juice business?"

"Yes, of course." He motioned her toward the entrance of a nearby building. "There were three of us all along. Jenner, Patterson, and myself." He motioned her forward with the nose of the gun. "But the other two were thick-headed hunters. They knew nothing about how to set up a profitable business enterprise. I was the one who was responsible for the pricing and marketing strategy. I'm the one who suggested we partner with the Riders to handle distribution and transportation. Jenner and Patterson took all the credit, but the truth is, they would have been nowhere without my genius."

"You built your business on slave labor."

"The least expensive kind." He herded her toward the entrance of a nearby building. "Jenner and Patterson needed me, but they never made me an equal partner."

"You mean they didn't give you your fair share?"

"*Exactly.*" Rage bubbled in the word. "They said that I was just their accountant. They said they were the ones taking all the risks. I only got a fraction of what I was worth, not the full one-third partnership I deserved."

"That all changed when Fontana and the other members of the Council decided to force Jenner to retire, didn't it?"

"I saw my opportunity at last. Patterson was equally happy to get rid of Jenner. We both knew that he had become a liability."

"Who murdered Jenner? You or Patterson?"

"I took care of the matter. No one took any notice of me in the hospital. Everyone assumed I was there to handle the insurance paperwork. Even Patterson believed that Jenner's death was from natural causes. I saw no reason to tell him the truth. He might have used the information against me."

"No one pays any attention to the accountant," she said quietly.

"And that is just the way I like it, Ms. McIntyre." He

motioned with the gun again. "Open the door and go inside. Hurry. I'm on my lunch hour."

"What a coincidence. So am I. Guess this means that neither of us will be dining at the Amber Club today."

"*Open the door.*"

There was a dangerous instability in Harlan's voice now. It occurred to her that he was almost as nervous as she. Sure, he had already murdered one person, but shooting a woman in cold blood was a little different from introducing a dose of poison into an IV. Harlan was an accountant, after all, not a professional hit man.

Maybe that was the good news, she thought. If he wasn't a pro, he might not be a good shot.

She took one last look around, but she knew it was futile to expect rescue. The alley was empty. She twisted the knob, pushed open the door, and moved into what looked like the back room of an old shop. No one had cleaned for years. Grime covered the windows. A dank, musty smell rolled toward her out of the darkness.

"The door to your right," Harlan said quickly. "There's a staircase that leads down to a hole-in-the-wall."

He wasn't planning to shoot her. Definitely a good news–bad news sort of day. She tightened her grip on her purse.

"You're going to abandon me in the catacombs?" she asked.

"Yes, Ms. McIntyre, you will disappear underground like so many other unfortunates. Sadly, that sort of thing happens when a person goes down below without tuned amber. A few steps into the maze, and you will be lost forever."

She opened the door of what looked like a storage closet and saw a well of darkness. The cloak of claustrophobia closed around her, threatening to choke her. *This is your only chance. If you balk, he'll shoot you right here*. Intuitively she knew that the tunnels were her best hope.

"Here, take this flashlight," Harlan said. He removed the device from his pocket and tossed it toward her.

She managed to catch it. It wasn't easy, because her hands were shaking, and she was trying to juggle her purse at the same time. She got the flashlight rezzed and aimed the narrow beam into the darkness.

The old metal staircase was a spiral design. It twisted down into endless night. She descended cautiously, one hand clutching the railing. Harlan followed.

"Hurry," he snapped. "We don't have much time."

"Yes, I know, you're on your lunch hour. Tell me, do you really believe that Fontana won't figure out that you're responsible for my disappearance?"

"As I explained a few minutes ago, he trusts me. He even turns a lot of his personal business over to me."

Understanding sliced through her.

"Oh, damn," she whispered. "Of course. You handled the purchase of the mansion for him, didn't you? That was when you discovered the journal in the gallery and found the chart for that sector of the tunnels."

"I did a very thorough inspection before I recommended to Fontana that he should go through with the deal," Harlan said. Pride reverberated in his voice. "Due diligence and all that. Yes, I found the hidden wall safe."

"How did you get it open?"

He chuckled. "That wasn't difficult. The former owner had grown quite senile. As an aid to his failing memory, he had written out the combination on a piece of paper and tucked it into a little space between the wall and the safe."

"You were already thinking about how to get rid of Fontana, weren't you? You never intended that he would be the boss for long. When you found the sector chart, you started to make your plans."

"Patterson and I knew that we couldn't afford to let Fontana remain in the executive suite. He was too smart and too set on cleaning up the organization. It was only a matter of time before he uncovered our juice operation. The plan was to wait a few months before we made our move, however. We thought we had time, you see. We assumed that it would take a while before he became suspicious of certain matters."

"Not to mention that the deaths of two Guild bosses in quick succession here in Crystal would have caught the attention of the other chiefs and the Chamber."

"Precisely."

"You must have been a trifle upset when you realized that not only did Fontana hit the ground running, he took my investigative reporting seriously."

"Upset?" Harlan's voice rose. "I was stunned. Horrified. No one ever pays any attention to the *Curtain*. When I realized he had invited you to do an interview, I notified Patterson at once. We met in the Guild parking garage. He tried to take care of you before you even got to the office that day."

"The car that almost ran me down."

"Yes. Sadly, he missed you."

"The next thing you knew, I was marrying Fontana."

"He thought he could throw the mantle of the Chamber around you and provide you with some protection. He was right. If there had been even an ounce of suspicion that you had been killed by someone in the Crystal Guild, the Chamber would have torn the organization apart."

"So when you decided to get rid of both Fontana and me, you had the Riders carry out the operation."

"The gang does have its uses."

"Because it has no obvious links to the Guild."

"This is your own fault, you know," Harlan hissed. "I didn't think it would be necessary to get rid of you at first. With Patterson removed and unable to talk, I hoped that Fontana would be satisfied. But his latest plan is simply too much. My patience is exhausted. I am forced to act."

"What are you talking about? What plan?"

"Fontana made it clear that he intends to put you in charge of the Foundation."

Sierra's intuition kicked in again. "You've been skimming money from the Foundation, haven't you?"

"I have always looked upon the Foundation's assets as my private retirement fund. So much more lucrative than the usual Guild benefits. I knew that as soon as you took over, it would be only a matter of time before you discovered that someone had been embezzling for years."

"Namely you."

"It was just too much. I felt something snap inside me. All I could think of was getting rid of you."

"Something snapped, all right. This is a really stupid plan. Fontana will figure out what you've done."

"You said it, yourself, Miss McIntyre. No one ever suspects an accountant. Or an executive assistant, for that matter."

She felt a little rush of psi. A few steps farther down she saw the faint green glow that marked one of the jagged tears in the tunnel walls. She knew very little about mag-rez guns, but the one thing she did know was that they did not function properly in the tunnels. Once she was through the hole in the quartz she would make a run for it.

When she reached the bottom of the stairwell, she stepped out on a floor of packed earth and moved toward the glowing opening.

"Stop," Harlan ordered.

She halted a couple of feet away from the entrance.

"What now?" she asked.

"The mag-rez is useless with all the psi inside the tunnels." He put the gun into his pocket.

Oh, yes, please. This was it, the chance she had been hoping for.

She took a step back, preparing to leap through the opening into the catacombs.

"From now on, I'll use this, instead," Harlan said.

There was a flash of ultraviolet ghost light. A three-foot-wide beam of energy shimmered into existence directly in front of her. It was so close that the storm of psi stirred her hair. She moved back hurriedly.

"The sixth generator," she said. "You had it all along."

"This one belonged to Jenner. Now, into the tunnels, Ms. McIntyre. I want to make sure you go so far in that you cannot possibly find your way out."

"Don't worry, I'll go into the tunnels without a fuss." She retreated toward the glowing entrance. "But I'm warning you, Fontana will find me."

"No one escapes the catacombs without tuned amber, Ms. McIntyre. You won't be able to find your way out without it, and Fontana won't be able to locate you, because you don't carry amber. You have no use for it."

She edged through the hole in the quartz. Relief, a sensation she had never expected to experience inside the catacombs, made her feel wired and jittery. Either Harlan had not seen the photo that Phil had taken on her wedding day, or else the little creep had failed to notice one very significant detail in the picture.

Feeling much more confident now, she watched him come through the opening. The ultraviolet energy beam came first. She retreated a few steps, keeping as much distance as possible between herself and the dangerous psi ray.

"Start walking, Ms. McIntyre," Harlan said.

She took a step back and then another, trying not to look too eager. After all, as far as Harlan was concerned, he was sending her to a certain death. She did not want to exhibit any actual enthusiasm.

"Go on, go on, *move*, you stupid woman." Harlan did something to the generator. The beam got stronger and larger. "Think of it as walking the plank."

She retreated more quickly. There was a vaulted tunnel entrance to her right. Spinning on her heel, she turned and dove for it.

"Wait, where's your ring?" Harlan yelled. "Where's the damn ring you were wearing in that picture on the cover of the *Curtain*?"

She heard his footsteps pounding down the adjoining corridor.

"Come back here," Harlan screamed.

"Oh, sure, like that's going to happen," she whispered.

She ran harder, clutching her purse with the ring inside like the life preserver it was. The seal ring that Fontana had given her on their wedding day was set with a large chunk of amber that simply had to be tuned. No self-respecting Guild man would carry the untuned variety. More to the point, no Guild boss would give his wife untuned amber. True, she didn't know how to use it to find her way out of the tunnels, but as long as she held on to it, Fontana would be able to find her.

A dizzying maze of vaulted corridors stretched out before her. She chose one at random and ran flat-out.

She did not want to think about the dangers of illusion traps and stray ghosts. She just kept going. Fleeing into the maze was her only chance.

But when she risked a glance back over her shoulder, she saw the bobbing beam of ultraviolet energy rounding the corner. Harlan was somehow managing to keep track of her. Panic threatened her breathing. It wasn't supposed to work like that down here. Once you lost visual contact, you were lost, period. How was he keeping up with her?

Unwittingly, Harlan answered her question.

"You can't escape me," he shouted, coming toward her with the energy ray. "Jenner made sure that every Guild man was issued one of the new locaters, even those of us who work in the accounting department."

So much for her brilliant plan to lose him. Her only hope now was to keep running. He was older than she was. Maybe he would tire sooner.

Unfortunately, Harlan appeared to be in excellent physical condition. She turned several more corners but always, *always*, the ultraviolet beam followed a short time later.

She almost missed the faint shadow in the doorway. It was barely perceptible. But it rezzed an alarm somewhere in her brain. What was it Fontana had said? *The ambient psi light in the tunnels creates no natural shadows.*

She stopped, gasping for air and stared at the doorway. The slight shift in the light could easily have been a trick of her imagination, but her intuition told her otherwise. She was looking at an illusion trap.

There was only one way to lure Harlan into the snare. She hurled her purse, the ring inside, through the entrance into the chamber beyond. She was now without amber. If she lost sight of the purse, she was doomed.

Never taking her eyes off the leather shoulder bag, she stepped back into the opening of a room directly behind her.

She heard Harlan's hard breathing and the soft thud of his shoes. Then the beam of ultraviolet appeared.

"You bitch," Harlan gasped. "You crazy, interfering, stupid bitch of a woman."

He came into view. He had the generator in one hand and a locater in the other. His attention was fixed on the locater's screen. If he looked up and to his right, he would see her standing in the doorway. But if he followed the locater, he would look to the left and see her purse on the floor just inside the chamber.

Harlan looked to the left.

She did not know what he was thinking at that moment, but it was obvious that he was winded and desperate. He was not paying attention to small details like faint shadows where there should not be any. Whatever the case, he was unable to resist the bait.

He went through the chamber doorway, triggering the trap. Sierra did not see anything; the energy released by the illusion snare was invisible to the naked eye. But

Harlan stiffened violently as though he had stumbled into a ghost.

She knew that the sound of his horrified scream would follow her into her nightmares for a long time to come. She clamped her hands over her ears and continued to stare hard at her purse.

A few seconds later the high, keening wail of anguish ended abruptly. Harlan fell, unconscious, to the floor.

She waited a few tense seconds and then stepped over him to collect the handbag. She reached inside, took out the black and amber ring, and clutched it tightly in her fingers.

Then she started to shake.

Chapter 44

A SHORT TIME LATER SHE WAS STILL ON HER FEET, WALKING tensely back and forth in front of the chamber, hugging herself and concentrating on her breathing, when Elvis appeared.

He scuttled toward her down the glowing corridor, white cape flying. She heard the faint, familiar whine of a sled engine behind him. The vehicle rounded the corner a few seconds later. Fontana was at the wheel. Ray was in the passenger seat.

"Elvis." She swept him up into her arms and buried her face in his tatty fur. "I thought you guys would never get here."

Fontana brought the sled to a stop, vaulted out, and came toward her with long, swift strides.

"Are you all right?" he demanded.

The harshness of his voice made her smile a little. She understood. This was the way it had been when they had fled into the rain forest, and he had forced himself to remain on his feet until he got her to safety. A successful Guild boss had to know how to clamp a mag-steel lid on his emotions so that he could prioritize.

"Yes." She blinked back the tears of relief that filled her eyes. "I'm fine now that you're here."

"You scared the living ghost light out of me," he said. "Promise me you won't ever do anything like that again."

"Wasn't planning to make a habit of it."

He caught her in his arms and pulled her hard against him. Elvis, squashed between the two of them, squeaked in protest, wriggled free, and scurried up to sit on Sierra's shoulder. Satisfied that all was well, he preened his ruffled fur.

"I was so damned afraid," Fontana said into her hair.

"How did you find Elvis?"

"He found us down here in the tunnels. We were all headed in the same direction. He must have some kind of psychic link with you."

Ray prodded Harlan's body. "What happened to Ostendorf?"

She turned in the circle of Fontana's arm and looked down at Harlan. "I was running from him. He was using a locater to track me. I saw a shadow in a doorway and remembered what Fontana had told me about illusion traps. I had the ring in my purse."

Fontana's hand tightened on her shoulder. "You threw your purse into that chamber to lure him inside, didn't you?"

"Yes."

His jaw tensed. "You tossed away your only amber? Damn it, Sierra, if you had lost sight of it—"

"Take it easy," Ray said to Fontana. "It's an old hunter trick, and you know it. Sure, it's risky, but it wasn't like she had another option, now, was it?"

Fontana pulled Sierra more snugly against his side. "No, it's not."

Ray grinned. "Looks like the Crystal Guild has a brand-new legend, and the *Curtain* has another scoop."

Chapter 45

"HOW DID YOU HANDLE IT?" FONTANA ASKED QUIETLY.

She knew what he meant. "The claustrophobia?"

"Must have been bad."

They were on her apartment balcony overlooking the Green Gate Tavern, glasses of wine in hand. Elvis perched on the railing, munching on the remains of the pizza they had all shared earlier. He still wore his white cape and dark glasses.

Sierra drank some of her wine, thinking back to the sensations she had experienced that afternoon. "Running from Harlan's ultragenerator was certainly a distraction. But later, after he triggered the illusion trap, I couldn't seem to stop shaking. So I just kept walking up and down that hall past the chamber. I knew it wouldn't be long before you came for me. That's what I kept telling myself." She paused. "That's how I got through it."

"It was my fault. Should have figured out sooner that Ostendorf was involved."

She rounded on him, outraged. "That's ridiculous. You moved amazingly fast as it was, taking down the drug operation and cornering Patterson within days of getting into the executive suite. Harlan Ostendorf covered his tracks well. It's amazing that you figured out what he was up to at all, let alone realized that he had kidnapped me today. I think you must have a pretty strong streak of intuition, yourself."

"I should have understood immediately that he was the only one who could have known about the sector chart in the journal."

"Listen up, Mr. Guild Boss. If you intend to make it in the business, you're going to have to learn when to beat yourself up over a perceived failure and when not to beat yourself up over one. What happened today was not your fault. Get over it."

He went still for a moment. Then his mouth twitched.

"Maybe you've got a future as an executive career coach," he said.

She wrinkled her nose. "No, that wouldn't be any fun. I've met a few executives, and let me tell you, none of them take direction well. You're a perfect example."

"You're probably right. Stick to the do-gooder gig." He rested both forearms on the railing, wineglass cradled between his hands. "It's definitely your forte."

"What about the six ultragenerators that you recovered?"

"They are going straight into the vault at the research lab."

The old, familiar irritation spiked within her. "In other words, they have become official, classified Guild secrets."

"Damn straight. What's more, if I see so much as a word about those generators on the front page of the *Curtain*, I am going to be one very pissed-off Guild boss."

"I've got four words for you. Freedom. Of. The. Press."

"Trust me, you do not want news of those weapons getting out to the general public," he said quietly.

"Is that right? And just what, exactly, are the lab people going to do with them?"

"Deactivate them."

She blinked. "Really?"

"It's already been done. I oversaw the process this afternoon."

That stopped her cold. "Good heavens. *How?*"

"Turns out dissonance energy is still dissonance energy, no matter where it comes from on the spectrum or how it's generated. The old rule still applies."

"What old rule?"

"Takes a ghost to kill a ghost."

"I don't understand."

"Remember how I was able to punch a hole through that beam when we ran the Rider ambush?"

"Of course."

"It gave me the idea that maybe an ultragenerator could be burned out if it was confronted with too much ghost light. So I called in all of the Council members as witnesses. We put the generators into a quartz-walled chamber underground and arranged them so that the beams would collide with each other. Then we activated them and ran like hell."

"Oh, my gosh."

"There was an impressive explosion." Fontana smiled. "But afterward we were left with half-a-dozen burned-out generators. As far as the lab techs can determine, the mechanisms were thoroughly and permanently fried. Useless."

She thought about that. "You know, since the story has a happy ending, it really would make a terrific scoop for the *Curtain*."

"No."

"Fontana, if you intend to move the Crystal Guild into the mainstream, you're going to have to get past this obsession with secrecy."

"No," he repeated.

"You do realize," she said coolly, "that there will be more dangerous artifacts coming out of the rain forest as time goes on?"

"We'll worry about it when it happens."

"The Guilds won't be able to keep all of them secret."

"We'll see."

"Fontana—"

"You know, it's been a long day. Would you mind very

much if we put off arguing about Guild secrets until some future date?"

"Oh, all right. But don't think I'm going to just up and forget about this."

"Never crossed my mind."

For a time they did not speak. The silence between them grew, but it was not tense or awkward, Sierra thought. It felt good to stand here with Fontana, sharing the night with him. They drank their wine. Elvis got down off the railing and helped himself to another slice of pizza.

After a while, Fontana stirred a little.

"This afternoon Kay told me that Ostendorf got you to go out to the limo by telling you that I had invited you to meet me at the Amber Club," he said.

"Mmm-hmm."

"She said she was sure that I was going to propose a Covenant Marriage over lunch."

"Kay's a bit of a romantic."

"She was wrong about me planning to propose over lunch."

Sierra looked at the Green Gate sign. "I know."

"Nobody proposes a Covenant Marriage on his lunch hour."

"That's what Matt said."

"You're supposed to propose CMs over dinner," Fontana explained very seriously. "Every guy knows that."

"Right. Dinner."

"So," Fontana said, "since we just finished dinner, will you consider entering into a Covenant Marriage with me?"

She felt as if she had just fallen off the balcony. Weightless. Dazed. Disoriented.

"What?" she yelped.

"Not exactly the response I was hoping for."

"Are you serious?" she demanded.

"Maybe I should tell you another little secret. Men never joke about Covenant Marriage."

"Neither do women. What is going on here? We've only known each other a few days, and it was a business arrangement from the start."

"Not quite."

She drew a breath, thinking of the passion they had shared. "Okay, not quite."

"I knew I wanted you forever the day you walked into my office. I've been waiting for you all of my life."

"Oh, Fontana," she said softly.

"If you need more time, I'll understand. Traditionally, there's a long engagement before a Covenant Marriage. We can have one of those if you like. But it won't change anything for me."

The strange, off-balance sensation evaporated. A wonderful sense of certainty took its place.

"I felt the same way about you the day I walked into your office," she said. "The moment I saw you, my intuition kicked in. I knew you were the one."

He set the glass aside and cradled her face in his powerful hands. "I love you, Sierra."

She smiled, gloriously sure. "I love you."

"Guess this means I'll be going to your grandparents' anniversary party."

"It looks that way, yes. Think you can handle it?"

"I'm a Guild boss."

"You can handle anything."

He laughed. "As long as I've got you."

He kissed her then, sealing the promise. After a while they went into the apartment and down the hall to the bedroom.

The energy of love flashed and flared and sparked in the night.

OUT ON THE BALCONY ELVIS TOOK UP A POSITION ON the table beside the empty pizza box. His white cape glittered in the angled beam of light that shone from the living room behind him. He waited.

It didn't take long for his audience to appear. The dust bunnies materialized out of the fog by the dozens, lining the balcony railing and crowding the prime front row seats, the chairs and the lounger.

Elvis picked up his guitar. Time to rock 'n rez.

TURN THE PAGE FOR A LOOK AT

RUNNING HOT

An Arcane Society Novel
by Jayne Ann Krentz

Available December 2008 from G. P. Putnam's Sons.

MARTIN WAS GOING TO KILL HER.

She stepped off the gangway and onto the sleek, twin-engine cabin cruiser, wondering why the cold despair was hitting her so hard. If there was one thing you learned fast when you were raised by the state, it was that ultimately you could depend only on yourself. The foster home system and the streets were the ultimate universities, awarding harsh degrees in the most basic kind of entrepreneurship. When you were on your own in the world, the laws of survival were simple. She had learned them well.

She thought her past had prepared her for any eventuality, including the possibility that the only man she had ever trusted might someday turn on her. She had been mistaken. Nothing could blunt the pain of this betrayal.

Martin emerged from the cabin. The dazzling Caribbean sunlight glinted off his mirrored glasses. He saw her and gave her his familiar charismatic smile.

"There you are," he said, coming forward to take the computer case from her. "You're late." He glanced at the man in the white shirt and dark blue trousers coming up the gangway with her suitcase. "Weather problems?"

"No, sir." Eric Schafer set down the small suitcase. "We landed on time. But there's some kind of local holiday going on. The streets were jammed. You know how it is here on the island. Only one road from the airport, and it goes straight through town. No way to avoid the traffic."

Eric straightened and wiped the sweat off his forehead with the back of his hand. His shirt, embroidered with the discreet logo of Crocker World, had been military-crisp this morning when he had climbed into the cockpit of the small corporate jet in Miami. It was now badly wilted from the island heat.

"The Night and Day Festival," Martin said. "I forgot about it. Big event down here. A combination of Mardi Gras and Halloween."

He was lying, she thought. She watched the strange dark energy flash in his aura. It was all part of the plan to kill her. The festival would provide excellent cover for a murder. With so many strangers on the island, the local authorities would be too busy to notice if Mr. Crocker returned from his private island alone.

"Will there be anything else, sir?" Eric asked.

"Where's Banner?"

"Left him back at the airport. He's keeping an eye on the plane."

"You two can take the jet back to Miami. No point both of you cooling your heels on this rock for an entire week. You've got wives and kids who will probably be very happy to see you. I've been keeping you guys busy these past few months."

"Yes, sir. Thanks."

Eric's gratitude was real. Martin knew how to bind his people to him with a combination of generous salaries and benefits and his own natural charisma. She had often thought that he could have been a very successful cult leader. Instead, he had chosen a different career path.

He went up the short flight of teak steps to take the helm.

"Get the lines for me," he called down to Eric.

"Sure thing, Mr. Crocker." Eric crouched to uncoil the ropes that secured the powerful boat to the dock.

She wondered what he and the others on the staff would think when she disappeared. Martin had probably already prepared a convincing story for them. Something to do with falling overboard, perhaps. The currents around the island were notoriously tricky.

She felt the vibration beneath her feet as the boat's engines started to churn. Eric gave her a friendly wave and dashed more sweat off his forehead.

There was no veiled look of masculine speculation in

his expression, no sly wink or grin. When he got back to the airport, he and his copilot, John Banner, would not make any comments about the boss going off with one of his girlfriends. No one on Martin's staff had ever mistaken her for one of Martin's many lovers. His women tended to be tall, willowy, and blonde. She was none of those things. She was just the hired help.

Officially she was Martin's butler, the one person who traveled with him everywhere. She kept his life organized and oversaw the operation of his many residences. Most important, she supervised the entertaining of his friends and business associates, and the occasional visiting politician, lobbyist, or head of state.

She raised her hand in farewell to Eric and squeezed back tears. Regardless of what happened today, she knew that she would never see him again.

The boat slipped gracefully away from the dock, headed toward the entrance to the small harbor.

Like many who moved in the stratospheric circles inhabited by those of great wealth, Martin owned several houses and kept a number of apartments in various locales around the world. The Miami mansion was his main residence but the place he considered home was the small island he had purchased a few years ago. The only way to get to it was by boat. There was no landing strip, just a single dock.

Unlike his other residences, which were always maintained in a state of readiness, Martin kept no staff on the island. The house was much smaller and far more modest than his other dwellings. He considered the place his private retreat.

Once past the stone pillars that marked the harbor entrance, Martin revved the engines. The boat picked up speed, slicing eagerly through the turquoise water. He was busy at the wheel, not paying any attention to her as he concentrated on piloting the craft. She heightened her other senses and took another look at his aura. The dark energy was stronger now. He was getting jacked up.

The boat felt very small around her. There was nowhere to hide, nowhere to run.

She had known for days—weeks, if she was brutally honest with herself—that Martin was planning to get rid of her. She was even sure she knew why. Nevertheless, some small part of her had clung to the slender thread of denial, even as it unraveled. Maybe there was some logical explanation for the disturbing changes in his aura. Maybe the new darkness was the result of mental illness. As dreadful as that possibility would be, at least it would allow her the comfort of knowing that he was no longer in his right mind; that the real Martin would never plot her death.

But her own finely honed survival instincts had refused to let her deceive herself any longer. Martin might have had some affection for her at one time, but deep down she had always known that their relationship had been rooted in her usefulness to him. Now he had concluded that she had become a liability so he was going to get rid of her. In his mind the situation was not complicated.

She stood at the stern and watched the harbor and the small town grow smaller and smaller. When they became tiny, indistinct blobs, she turned around. Martin's private island was very close now. She could make out the house perched on the hillside.

Martin slowed the boat and brought it neatly alongside the wooden dock.

"Get the lines," Martin said sharply, his attention on maneuvering the boat.

That did it. For some inexplicable reason the simple, routine order flipped the last switch somewhere in her head. The unholy brew of pain, sadness, disbelief, and mind-numbing fear that had been swirling through her in alternating currents for days was suddenly swept away by icy cold rage. Her other senses leaped violently in reaction to the adrenaline rush.

The son-of-a-bitch was planning to murder her. Now. Today.

"Sure thing, Martin," she said, amazed by how cool and controlled she sounded. But, then, she'd had a lot of practice concealing her emotions and reactions behind a gracious, exquisitely polite facade. She could have given a geisha lessons. But she was no geisha.

She grabbed the stern line, then stepped lightly out of the boat and onto the narrow dock. It didn't take long to tie up. She had done it countless times in the past.

Martin left the wheel and came back down the steps.

"Here, take this," he said, handing her the computer. "I'll get your suitcase and the supplies."

She took the computer from him and waited while he swung the suitcase and the two bags of groceries up onto the dock. He glanced around, making sure he had everything he wanted out of the boat. Then he stepped onto the dock.

"Ready?" he said.

Not waiting for a reply, he scooped up the bags of groceries with an easy motion and tucked one into the crook of each arm. His aura flashed with impatience and a really scary excitement. The pulses of dark energy were becoming increasingly agitated. This wasn't just business, she realized. He was actually looking forward to murdering her. Her own fury flared higher.

"Of course." She gave him her best professional smile, the one she used to greet his guests and business associates. She thought of it as her stage smile. "But just out of curiosity, when do you plan to do it?"

"Do what?" he said. He was already turning away from her, heading toward the small SUV parked at the end of the dock.

"Kill me."

He froze in midstride. She watched the torrent of shock crash through his aura. The indescribable colors flashed across the spectrum. She really had taken him by surprise, she realized. Had he actually believed that he could plot her death without her sensing it? Evidently the answer to that question was a resounding yes. Then again, she had never told him all of her secrets.

When he turned to face her, his expression was a mix of anger and impatience.

"What the hell are you talking about?" he said. "Is this is your idea of a bad joke?"

She folded her arms, hugging herself a little.

"We both know it isn't a joke," she said quietly. "You brought me here with the intention of murdering me."

"I haven't got time for this. I've got work to do."

"I assume I'm going to be the victim of a tragic drowning accident?" She smiled bleakly. "So sad. The butler went swimming and went under. Happens all the time."

He searched her face as though wondering if she had a high fever and then shook his head. "I don't believe this."

"I didn't, either. But in hindsight I saw it coming weeks ago."

"All right, let's play this out," he said with the air of a man who has begun to suspect that he is dealing with a crazy person. "You and I have been a team for a long time. Twelve years. Why would I want to kill you now?"

"I think there are a couple of reasons. The first, of course, is that I recently discovered that for the past few months you've been allowing some very nasty people to use the resources of Crocker World as a cover for illegal arms dealing. All that agricultural equipment you so generously donated to various developing countries? Turns out those tractors and plows fire real bullets. Imagine my surprise."

For an instant she thought he was going to continue the charade a little longer. But this was Martin. He could get to the bottom line faster than anyone else she had ever met. That was part of his talent.

He smiled with just the right touch of genuine regret. "I knew you would have problems with my little sideline. That's why I didn't bring you on board at the start of the project."

"It isn't just what you're dealing, although that's bad enough. It's the people you're working for."

Fury sparked in his eyes and in his aura.

"I don't work for anyone else," he said through his teeth. "Crocker World is mine. I built the company, damn it. I am Crocker World."

"You *were* Crocker World. But you've handed the company you built, that I *helped* you build, to some sort of criminal organization."

"You had nothing to do with my success. You should be down on your knees thanking me for what I did for you. If I hadn't come along, you'd still be working in that low-rent flower shop, living all by yourself with a couple of cats because you scare off every man you meet. Hell, sometimes you even scare me."

That shook her. "What?"

"The way you take one look at a person and figure out what makes him tick. What he'd kill for. What scares the shit out of him. His strengths and weaknesses. It's damned spooky. Why do you think I'm getting rid of you?"

"You're forgetting something, Martin. If you hadn't offered me a job twelve years ago you'd still be operating a cheap, way-off-the-strip casino in Binge, Nevada. I'm the one who identified the cheats who were robbing you blind. I'm the one who helped you pay off that mob boss. If it hadn't been for me, you'd have been buried in some shallow grave out in the desert by now."

"That's a lie."

"And I'm the one who identified those first investors for you, the venture capitalists who backed you when you decided to sell the casino and start building condo towers."

Martin's aura was an inferno now.

"I would have found the investors on my own," he shouted.

"That's not true. You're a midrange strategy talent, Martin. You can sense opportunities and put together a plan with a skill few can match because you're psychic in that way. But you're no good when it comes to reading people."

"Shut up, you stupid woman."

"Without that talent, all the business insight in the world is useless. Building a financial empire isn't just about numbers and the bottom line. It's about identifying and exploiting your opponent's strengths and weaknesses."

He gave her a sharklike smile. "You think I need a lecture on the art of the deal from you?"

"For twelve years I've been your personal profiler. I'm the one who tells you when a business associate is in trouble, either financially or in his personal life. I warn you when someone is trying to con you. I identify the strengths and weaknesses of your opponents and your partners. I tell you exactly what you need to offer someone in order to close the deal, and I'm the one who tells you when your best option is to walk away from the table."

"You had your uses, I'll grant you that. But I don't need you anymore. Before we finish this, though, I'd really like to know how you stumbled onto my little arms dealing sideline."

"As far as your guests and business associates are concerned, I'm just a trusted member of the staff. No one looks twice at me. No one notices me. But I take a good look at them. That's what you pay me to do, after all. Sometimes I see things and sometimes I hear things. And I am very, very good when it comes to research, remember?"

"How much do you know?"

"About the people you're involved with?" She raised one shoulder slightly. "Not a lot. Just that it's some sort of cartel run by very powerful sensitives and that they've seduced you into doing their dirty work."

Martin's aura flared higher. "No one has seduced me."

"Until recently I would never have believed that anyone could buy you," she said. "I mean, what could a bunch of gangsters offer one of the most successful men on the planet that would make it worth his while to risk his freedom, his reputation, and his life?"

Martin's rage showed in his eyes now. "You don't know what the hell you're talking about. The organization isn't some mob."

"Yes, it is, Martin. The first time you brought those two men to the Miami residence I told you that they were very, very dangerous."

"So am I," Martin hissed. He reached up and slowly removed his mirrored glasses. "More dangerous than you can imagine, thanks to my new business associates. And thanks to them, I no longer need you."

"What are you talking about?"

"The organization those two men represent is about much more than money." Martin's eyes were unnaturally brilliant. The dark energy in his aura had a feverish aspect. "It's all about power, real power; the kind that world leaders and war lords and billionaires can only dream about."

Suddenly she understood. She had not thought that she could be any more appalled than she already was, but she had been wrong.

"I guess this explains the changes in your aura in the past couple of months," she said.

Martin looked startled.

"What changes?" he demanded.

"I thought perhaps you had become the victim of some kind of mental illness that affected your para-senses."

"I am not sick, damn you."

"Yes, you are, but not because of some natural disease process. You did this to yourself. With a little help from your new friends, of course."

Martin took a step closer. He didn't look horrified. He looked eager. Excited. So did his aura.

"You can see the effects of the drug in my aura?"

"A drug," she repeated. "Yes, that's the only logical explanation. Those two men supplied you with some sort of drug that affects your para-senses."

"There's an excellent likelihood that it will also increase my natural life span, as well, maybe by as much as a couple of decades. What's more, they'll be good decades. I won't be weak and frail. I'll maintain my powers."

"I can't believe I'm hearing this. Martin, you're a brilliant businessman. Don't you know when you've been sold a bill of goods? The promise of longevity is the oldest scam in the world."

"The reason the researchers aren't certain about the extended life span is because the new drug hasn't been around long enough to test the theory. Those at the top have been using the stuff for only a few years. But the lab data look very promising."

"You're a fool, Martin."

"It's true," he insisted. "Even if they're wrong about the drug's ability to lengthen my life, that doesn't alter the fact that the formula *works*. It can kick a Level Seven strategy talent like mine all the way up to Nine or a Ten."

"You're not a Nine or a Ten. I'd know. Something has changed in your aura, though. Whatever it is, it isn't—" She broke off, groping for the right word. "It isn't wholesome."

"Wholesome?" He laughed. "Now there's a silly, old-fashioned word. Do you think I care how *wholesome* I am? For your information, you're right, though. The drug they gave me didn't elevate the level of my strat talent. It wasn't intended to have that effect."

"I don't understand."

"The drug can be genetically altered in a variety of ways to suit an individual's psychic profile. The version I'm taking has provided me with an entirely new talent."

"If you believe that, you really have gone off the deep end."

"I am not insane," Martin shouted.

The words seemed to echo around them. A few seconds of terrifying stillness followed. Then Martin's aura flared with a sickening heat.

She knew then, that the moment had come. He was going to try to kill her now. The only question was whether he intended to use a gun or his bare hands. One thing was certain: standing here at the end of the dock left her nowhere to run.

The mind-searing blast of energy came out of nowhere. It roared over her, bringing with it disorienting pain and the promise of an endless plunge into the abyss.

Not a gun. She fell to her knees under the force of the lightning that slashed at her senses. *Not his bare hands, either.* A slight miscalculation on her part.

Martin stared down at her, enthralled with his own power.

"They were right," he breathed. "They told me the truth about the drug. Congratulations. You are about to become the first person to witness what I can do with my new talent."

"Don't touch me."

"I'm not going to touch you. It isn't necessary. I'm going to incinerate your para-senses. You will go into a coma and then you will die."

"Martin, no, don't do this." Her voice was steadier now. So were her senses. She had recovered somewhat from the initial traumatizing shock. She was getting a handle on the pain, which meant that she was pushing back the invading waves of energy. "Maybe it's not too late. Maybe some of the experts in the Society can help you."

"You're pleading with me. I like that."

"I'm not going to beg for my life. But there is one thing you should know before you do this."

"What?"

"If you hadn't come along, I would have owned that florist shop by now, a whole chain of flower shops."

"That was always your greatest flaw," Martin said.

"Your dreams and ambitions were so much smaller than mine."

He heightened the psychic heat of the dark energy he was generating, his face tightening with effort. She pushed back harder, pulling energy from her own aura. The pain lessened some more.

"Die, damn you," he hissed. He took another step closer. "Why won't you *die*?"

Her strength was coming back. She was able to focus clearly on maintaining the energy shield that her aura had become.

Martin staggered but he did not seem to notice that she was fighting him. Instead, he appeared disoriented.

Angrily, he pulled himself together and took another step toward her, almost touching her. He forced more energy through the murky bands of dark lightning he was generating.

"You're supposed to die," he shouted.

He reached down to seize her by the throat. She raised her arms in a reflexive, defensive gesture. He grabbed her hands. She gripped his wrists.

Her palms burned. The world exploded, sending jolt after jolt of shockwaves through her senses.

Martin Crocker convulsed once. He looked at her with the eyes of a man who is peering into hell.

"No," he screamed.

He reeled, lost his balance, and went over the side of the dock into the water. His aura winked out with terrifying suddenness.

She rose, heart pounding. For the second time in her life she had killed a man. Not just any man this time; a very powerful, influential multibillionaire who just happened to be involved in a dangerous criminal enterprise.

And her hands still burned.

New from

Jayne Ann Krentz

Now Available

M217JV0408

ALSO BY *NEW YORK TIMES* BESTSELLING AUTHOR
JAYNE ANN KRENTZ WRITING AS

Jayne Castle

SILVER MASTER

Cadence City matchmaker and para-resonator Celinda Ingram meets her match in security specialist Davis Oakes. On the hunt for the powerful relic that Celinda supposedly bought as a toy for her pet dust bunny, Davis must use all of his unique psychic abilities to try and wrest the ruby red object from the suspicious duo. But he'll also have to keep his desire for Celinda in check, and keep them all safe from those who will do anything to possess the relic.

M280T0408